B.

Lying on the ground, right beside my motorcycle, was a body. Blood pooled around him and beneath my tires. Blank eyes stared at the sky above our heads. His throat had been opened from ear to ear and a silver cross lay smoldering in his forehead. He was quite clearly dead.

I didn't have time to see much else. A growl came from behind me and I spun around to find half the bar's patrons had spilled out onto the lot. Feral yellow eyes were looking past me to the body on the ground, at the blood that had ceased pumping. The wolf's nostrils flared as he took in the scent.

It pushed him over the edge.

He started to shift. . . .

Books by E.S. Moore

TO WALK THE NIGHT

TAINTED BLOOD, TAINTED NIGHT

BLESSED BY A DEMON'S MARK

BLOOD FROM A SILVER CROSS

Published by Kensington Publishing Corporation

Blood From A Silver Cross

E.S. MOORE

KENSINGTON BOOKS
KENSINGTON PUBLISHING CORP.
www.kensingtonbooks.com

KENSINGTON BOOKS are published by

Kensington Publishing Corp.
119 West 40th Street
New York, NY 10018

First Electronic Edition: February 2014
eISBN-13: 978-1-60183-242-9
eISBN-10: 1-60183-242-7

First Print Edition: February 2014
ISBN-13: 978-1-60183-245-0
ISBN-10: 1-60183-245-1

Printed in the United States of America

This one is for all of my friends and family. Without you, I wouldn't have gotten this far.

1

Ethan drummed his fingers on the table in a steady staccato. He eyed me warily, doing his best to watch me without actually looking directly at me. He was chewing his lower lip. Every few seconds he would glance down at the glass sitting between us.

I looked at it and grimaced. The concoction was a deep blue easing into purple. It smelled like something he might have fished out of a sewer after a flood. The glass itself was turning a light blue as if it were absorbing the liquid it contained.

Yeah, I was so not drinking that.

"Come on, Kat," Ethan urged. "I'm sure it doesn't taste as bad as it smells."

I glared at him. At least he had the decency to look away before grinning.

I reached out and gently touched the glass with my fingertips. It felt oddly warm. I knew for a fact Ethan hadn't heated it up. The outside of the glass felt slick, almost as if I were actually touching the ooze inside.

I withdrew my hand without picking up the glass. I had a sudden vision of being a little kid again, sick with a cold. My mom would shove a tiny cup of vile blue cold medicine into my hand. I would steadfastly refuse to drink it even though I knew it would make me feel better. That taste . . . it just wasn't worth it.

I closed my eyes and took a deep, calming breath. Thinking of the old days always brought on a twinge of pain and loss. Everyone who'd been a part of my life when I was a kid was dead. My brother, Thomas, was the last to go. He was buried in the backyard, like a family pet.

I glanced out of the glass back door and sighed. I couldn't see the tree he was buried under from where I sat in the dining room, but I knew it was there. The world was in full bloom outside. The leafy trees surrounding my property hid the view from me. Winter was long past and life had gone on after the nightmare of the last few months.

My gaze traveled to the worn path that led to the forested slope. I'd walked to and from Thomas's grave so many times, I was starting to wonder if I should just pave it and get it over with. He deserved that at least.

Ethan cleared his throat and I turned back to him. He had a concerned look on his face that had nothing to do with the glass between us. He knew what I'd been thinking.

"I'm fine," I said, reaching for the glass as if to prove it. This time when my fingers touched the slick surface, I didn't pull away.

I didn't bring it to my lips, either.

"I could add some cinnamon or mint or something," Ethan said. "I'm not sure how it would react with some of the, uh, other ingredients in there." He made a strange laughing sound that only served to make me more nervous. "It would at least make it smell better."

"What exactly *is* in here?"

"This and that. It's probably better if you didn't know."

Like that was going to make me want to drink it.

But I'd promised him I'd try. This was his third attempt at finding a blood substitute for me since I'd told him he could. He'd been working long hours over the last few weeks, trying to come up with something that worked.

So far, his efforts had been in vain. The first two attempts hadn't tasted too bad, but they'd done nothing to curb my hunger. This—I didn't even want to consider what this stuff might do to me.

I pulled the glass a little closer. It moved easily over the wooden table. A sudden urge to keep pulling until the glass toppled to the floor almost overtook me. I managed to keep from doing it, but it was close.

I groaned as the cloying smell of the blue liquid intensified. Someone behind me chuckled.

I glanced back to see Jeremy Lincoln leaning against the wall at the bottom of the stairs. He was wearing a T-shirt and jeans with no shoes or socks. His hair was mussed with sleep, but it didn't dim the glimmer of amusement in his eyes.

He gestured to me with his one remaining arm and grinned. "Go ahead. I *have* to see this."

I glowered at him and turned away. Jeremy had lost his arm the night we'd captured Thomas in a doomed attempt to save my brother from his own blood. I felt guilty about his lost appendage, but if he kept it up, I was going to make him eat his remaining one.

I sighed as dramatically as I could and picked up the glass. The liquid sloshed around in a sort of jiggly, ponderous motion. It was so thick, chances were good I'd have to chew it to make it go down.

It was looking less and less appetizing by the moment.

"Kat," Ethan said, "if this works, you won't have to feed ever again."

"I know that," I snapped. Why was I being such a baby about this? I've stood in puddles of blood and gore before and had barely batted an eyelash.

"It's perfectly safe," he went on. "I didn't taste it or anything, but I was assured you'll suffer no long-term ill effects from it."

The glass went back to the table. "No long-term effects?" I glared at him. "What's going to happen in the short term?"

Ethan reddened. "There might not be any."

"Ethan . . ."

"Seriously," he said with a shaky laugh. "You might have a bad taste in your mouth for a few weeks and your tongue might turn blue, but if it works, it would be worth it, don't you think?"

"A few weeks?"

He looked away.

I groaned and clenched my hand tightly over the glass. I couldn't believe I was actually going to go through with this.

I raised the glass to my lips and tipped it so that some of the thick goop rolled down. I closed my eyes against the tears that immediately filled them. The smell was so bad, it was stinging my eyes. I'd have an easier time drinking from a public toilet.

The gunk pooled against my lips, but I couldn't bring myself to open my mouth and actually drink it. I mean, I could drink blood from people who hadn't bathed in their lives, yet I couldn't bring myself to drink this? My priorities were seriously screwed up.

Jeremy grunted another laugh and the steps creaked as he turned and walked back up them. I gave him a one-finger salute with my free hand, though I knew he'd already gone.

"You have to drink it all for it to work," Ethan urged, leaning forward as if to get a better view.

I parted my lips and the sludge oozed into my mouth.

The taste was instantaneous. It was like dumping raw sewage in my mouth, yet I somehow managed to choke down the first swallow. It burned all the way down.

I gagged and slammed the glass down. I'd only managed a quarter of the contents and knew chances were good I wouldn't be able to finish the rest.

I tried to breathe normally, but could still smell the stuff. It permeated everything. I burped and something thick and slimy bubbled up with it.

"Oh God."

Ethan recoiled as I leapt to my feet. My chair crashed against the wall behind me and I nearly tripped over it as it bounced into my path on the way to the stairs.

I'm not going to make it! I'm not going to make it! The thought repeated over and over in my head like a mantra.

A thick, wet burp filled my mouth and I started making gagging, choking sounds. I hit the stairs at a near run and slipped on the bottom step. My shins cracked hard on the stairs, but I didn't let it stop me. I crawled the rest of the way up on all fours.

"Kat?" Ethan called from the bottom of the stairs.

I ignored him. If I stopped now, he was cleaning up the mess.

I somehow reached the top of the stairs without puking all over myself. I used the bathroom doorknob to pull myself to my feet and then tried to turn it.

It was locked.

"Occupied," came Jeremy's voice from the other side. It sounded like he was laughing.

"Glurg." Thick gunk filled my mouth and I spun toward my bedroom. My eyes were watering so badly now, I could hardly see. I bounced off the doorframe as I bolted into the bedroom. I staggered against my bed and then scrambled toward my private bathroom.

Made it just in time.

I buried my face in the bowl as everything I'd eaten in what felt like the last year came up. Ethan's concoction stuck to my teeth and no matter how many times I spit and gagged, I couldn't get it out of my mouth and throat.

"Kat?" Ethan said from the doorway.

I looked up, saw the concern in his eye, and growled. I scooted away from the toilet enough so that I could reach the door with my foot, and slammed it closed in his face.

I crawled back to the toilet and leaned over it as another bout of retching overwhelmed me.

"I'm so sorry," Ethan said, his voice muffled by the door. There was a heavy thump as he apparently slammed his forehead against the wood. "I didn't mean for it to . . . I should have . . . ugh . . ."

My stomach emptied for a third time. I leaned there for a good minute, panting while trying not to smell or taste anything. I reached up with a shaky hand and flushed down the bluish mess.

"Kat, I'm so, so sorry." Ethan was babbling apologies nearly nonstop now. "I think I know what went wrong this time. I'm sure I can fix it. I just need more time. I can do this. Oh man, I'm so sorry."

"It's fine," I said, standing. I wobbled over to the sink, grabbed the mouthwash, and gulped down two swallows, hoping it would quell some of the vile burps I knew would haunt me for the rest of the night.

Weeks? Did he say weeks?

I spat out my third mouthful and leaned over the sink. My throat was raw and I could still taste the bluish goop. No amount of mouthwash was going to mask that taste.

Ethan fell silent on the other side of the door. I knew he was still there because I could hear him breathing. I was just happy he'd quit apologizing.

I gave it another five minutes to be sure I wasn't going to throw up again before I left the bathroom. I opened the door and found Ethan sitting on my bed. I walked over and plopped down beside him. My legs were shaky and my stomach kept doing flips, but I thought the worst was over.

"I'm sorry," he said again.

"I said it was fine."

"I'll do better the next time."

I looked at him. Skepticism must have been all over my face because he looked away, face reddening in embarrassment.

"I can do this," he said. "I mean, I'm trying to do something here that no one else has managed to do. If I can just figure this out, then maybe it'll help others, not just you." He picked at his fingernails.

I looked away. What could I tell him? So far, the only thing that had ever helped curb my hunger was the blood bags Levi had given me, and really, they weren't much of an improvement over hunting. They might sate my hunger for a little while, but they tasted like shit and didn't last nearly as long as fresh blood.

Besides, you had to have someone willing to donate enough blood to keep the fridge full. I didn't have that luxury and I wasn't about to ask anyone to volunteer.

"You'll figure it out," I said. As much as I hated to admit it, I'd go through just about anything if Ethan could find a way to keep me from having to feed. I was tired of having to kill just so I didn't go on a hunger-induced rampage. I was struggling enough with the rage that my vampire caused. Taking away the hunger would make dealing with it much, much easier.

Ethan sagged next to me. "Thank you," he said, sounding immensely relieved.

"For what?"

"For understanding."

I looked over at him and he gave me a small smile.

A short burst of music came from down the hall. It cut off almost immediately and I realized it must have been Jeremy's cell phone. The werewolf was the only person in the house to own one.

I frowned, knowing who had to be calling. It was the only person to ever call him, as far as I knew.

"So, it might be a few weeks before I'll have something else ready for you to try," Ethan went on. "I've got to find the right balance, I think." He paused and cocked a brow at me. "Aside from the taste, can you tell me anything else about the experience? Are you hungry?"

I gave him a *What in the hell do you think?* look.

"Right," he said. "I'll see what I can do."

He started to stand, but just then, the bathroom door down the hall crashed open. Jeremy ran toward us, trying to button his pants with his one hand without tripping all over himself. His cell was sticking out of his pocket in a way that said he hadn't been too careful when he'd shoved it in.

I rose, tense. Something had happened.

He entered the bedroom just as his button snapped. He looked wildly around for a moment, like he fully expected there to be someone else in the room, before his eyes settled on me.

"We have to go," he said. He started to turn away.

"Why?" I planted myself firmly in the middle of the room.

Jeremy turned back and frowned. "It's important." He said it like he thought it was all I needed to know.

I clenched my jaw and crossed my arms. "What did he want?" I already knew the Luna Cult Denmaster, Jonathan Alucard, had been the caller. While I appreciated what he'd done for me, I wasn't about to take off running just because he said to—not without an explanation.

Jeremy's hand went to his cell. He pushed it deeper into his pocket instead of drawing it out as I thought he originally intended. "Something has happened."

"I figured that much out on my own. At the Den?"

He nodded.

My mind raced. What could have happened that would have Jonathan calling me?

"Did he tell you what?"

Jeremy's eyes flickered to Ethan and he swallowed. "Sort of."

I tapped my foot.

Jeremy sighed and his face tightened. "A Cult werewolf was killed," he said. "We have to go."

Ethan sucked in his breath next to me.

"Let me get my things." My words were clipped because I didn't want to let anyone else know how much the thought of someone dying at the Den bothered me. I'd finally given in and allowed myself to care about the people there—werewolves included—and now something had happened to one of them.

"You need to get ready too," Jeremy said, turning to Ethan. "He wants you to come along."

"Me?" Ethan's eyes widened. "Uh . . ."

I grabbed my leather clothes, knowing I might need them. Chances were good Jonathan wanted me to find and kill whoever killed his wolf.

"He's staying here," I said as I tossed the bundle on the bed.

"But Jonathan said . . ."

"I don't give a fuck what he said." I stripped off my shirt and both men looked away. "Ethan stays here. I can take care of this on my own without putting him in harm's way."

Jeremy hesitated a moment before turning and walking out the bedroom, back stiff. He was pissed, but I wasn't going to drag Ethan out of the safety of the house for something like this.

"Thanks," Ethan said. He was pale and trembling. He might have managed to leave the house to save Jonathan's life, but it didn't mean he was going to keep doing it. His fear of the outside world wasn't something he could turn off and on at will. It was a part of him and I respected that. I wasn't about to make him do something so fully against his nature.

He glanced my way just as my pants hit the floor. The blood returned to his face as he looked away. "I'll, uh, go get your weapons."

He nearly tripped over his own feet in his haste to get away.

I got dressed as quickly as I could manage and headed downstairs. Ethan had my gear laid out for me. I strapped on my belt and shoulder holster, complete with sword, gun, and knives. I threw my long leather coat over that and checked my pockets for the silver packets I kept there but rarely used.

"I'll be back," I told him as I headed for the stairs. Ethan stayed behind.

I found Jeremy waiting for me in the garage.

"I'll take my bike," I said. "You lead." I started for the motorcycle, but instead of getting on, I turned back to Jeremy. "How did he die?"

"The body was found in front of the Den." He swallowed, looking paler and paler by the minute. Whatever had happened had really shaken him up.

"He wasn't just killed," he went on. "He was crucified."

2

Jeremy pulled into the Luna Cult garage ahead of me. I followed him down as a feeling of dread crept into my gut. I kept thinking about what he'd said. No matter how I looked at it, I kept coming to the same conclusion.

The werewolf had been crucified.

The Left Hand had to be responsible.

I didn't have any actual proof that they were involved, but it was too much of a coincidence *not* to be them. While I'd never heard of the Left Hand crucifying anyone, I wouldn't put it past them either. They wanted to show the world what they were capable of. They didn't hide the bodies. It just wasn't their style.

I knew they'd been working their way into Columbus ever since I'd killed the woman who'd nearly killed me. She'd been near insane as far as I could tell and I seriously hoped they all weren't that way.

But despite the certainty that they were involved, I kept hope alive that someone else was responsible. I hadn't heard about any bodies popping up lately bearing the Left Hand's mark, but that meant little if they'd just arrived.

Jeremy parked on a lower level, deep down where anyone who managed to wander into the garage was unlikely to go. I pulled into a space next to him and shut off the engine. He got out of the car looking pale and shaky.

"You okay?" I asked. There was still a tightness to his eyes that told me he was just barely holding on.

"Yeah," he said as he started walking. "I'm just a little shaken up by the call is all. I'll get over it."

I could relate. You didn't simply get over stuff like this, especially if you knew the victim.

The night was clear and bright as we exited the garage. If it had been any other night, I might have chosen to ride the streets for a few hours, content to breathe in the fresh air. I'd found that doing something as simple as going for a ride helped me relax, helped me control the monster that lurked beneath the surface. Some nights, I needed it more than others.

"Did Jonathan tell you anything else about what happened?" I asked.

Jeremy glanced at me, looking worried and maybe a little scared. I remembered that look. I'd seen it when I'd held him down and threatened to drip blood into his mouth. He was young enough back then that he hadn't known it would have taken a lot more blood than that to taint him any more than he already was.

He'd come a long way since then. It was almost like looking at an entirely different person now. He'd grown a little harder, a little more cynical, but I often saw the scared kid he once was beneath the tough-guy persona he was trying to use as a shield against all of the cruelties he faced on a nightly basis.

"All he said was that one of our newest recruits was crucified outside the Den. He wanted me to get both you and Ethan here as soon as possible. I think he wanted you both to stay until he figured out what to do."

I bristled a bit at that. I knew why Jonathan wanted us there. He thought he could protect us even though I'd done a good enough job of keeping us safe for years without him. Sure, I'd been screwing up pretty badly recently, but I was better now. I could do this.

I bit my lip and forced away the anger. Jonathan was only trying to do what he thought was best. I couldn't blame him for that. It was my fault I was in the mess I was in. If I hadn't done so many stupid things recently, then perhaps my life wouldn't be so damn fucked up that he felt I needed protection.

"Did you know the wolf?" I asked.

Jeremy slowed his pace. It was as if he wasn't looking forward to reaching the Den. And really, I didn't blame him.

"Not well," he said. "Philip came to us scared out of his mind. He didn't know what was happening to him. He wasn't attacked or anything as far as he can remember. He just woke up one night with blood in his mouth and . . ." He shrugged. "You know."

Damn, this was going to be hard. It sounded like this guy was new in more ways than one. He might not have even known much about werewolves outside what he'd seen on the news. The media tended to portray them solely as violent killers, so he probably had a pretty terrifying view of himself by the time he got to the Den.

I felt an odd pang in my chest thinking of the dead wolf. I never knew him, yet a part of me wished I had. I'd just started to learn that not every werewolf was a bad guy. I'd always been so closed off, so stubborn about accepting anything but my own personal view of things, I'd missed out on a lot of would-be friendships. I wasn't going to let that happen again.

We fell silent as we approached the Den. The old library looked abandoned from the outside, though I knew it was anything but. Jonathan wasn't just a werewolf and the leader of the Luna Cult; he was also a sorcerer. He claimed he could only cast glamours, and he used his ability to hide not only the look of the building, but his own damaged face. From the outside, you'd never know there were lights blazing inside.

We ascended the large concrete steps with Jeremy in the lead. I glanced around, hoping to catch a glimpse of the scene of the crime, but wherever the wolf had been crucified, they'd either removed the evidence or I wasn't looking in the right spot. I scanned the trees and upper reaches of the building in the hopes of spotting one of the many hidden cameras, but I couldn't find them. I was hopeful they'd caught the culprit in the act.

Jeremy hesitated just outside the doors and I nearly ran into him. He gave me a nervous look before taking a deep breath and holding it. He opened the doors to the Luna Cult Den.

I closed my eyes to the light I knew was coming. I could still see it through my eyelids as I crossed over the threshold, but the effect was dampened enough that I only had to blink a few times to clear my vision. When it did, I was met with more people than I'd ever seen in the Den at one time.

There were Cultists everywhere, many I'd never seen before in my life. Groups were huddled together, talking in loud voices so they could be heard over the next group. There was hardly an inch of floor space that wasn't occupied, and I realized that the buzz of what had happened was still fresh.

Jeremy reached a hand back and touched my own. I recoiled out of pure reflex as his fingers touched mine. He turned wild eyes on me and held out his hand as if my grip was the only thing that would help him get through this.

I grimaced and took his hand. He looked so frightened, I would have felt horrible if I hadn't done something to ease his mind. There was something about his posture that told me he was just barely holding on. I often forgot how young he really was.

He led me through the crowd, though it wasn't easy. There were just too many people crammed into the room. One guy in particular refused to move. He stood in our way, clearly defiant, as if challenging us. I wasn't sure if he knew what Jeremy was because most Cultists wouldn't do anything disrespectful to one of the creatures they worshipped, yet here he was, muscled body blocking our path.

If things had been different, I would have jammed an elbow into his ribs, or worse, broken a few of them for him. I didn't have patience for idiots who thought they were better than everyone else.

But I held back. Tonight was not the night to start a fight.

The stairs leading up to Jonathan's sitting room weren't as packed as the floor below. We were able to go up without having to push our way through. The only time we stopped was when a girl stopped Jeremy, leaned in close, and whispered something to him. She was pretty in a way, though the bald head detracted from her beauty and the tattoo on her forehead looked as if she'd spent some time scratching at it when it was new.

Jeremy's hand tightened on mine as he gave her a quick nod. She glanced at me and her jaw tightened before she looked away. It was clear she wasn't happy to see me.

I wanted to pull my hand free of Jeremy's grip in the worst way. I knew he needed the comfort, but I was far from the best person to give it. I could tell that quite a few of the Cultists weren't comfortable with me being there. Not everyone thought of me as their savior.

We reached the top of the stairs and Jeremy led me through the gilded doors to Jonathan's rooms. Two large men I didn't know stood outside them, arms crossed. Neither had a tattoo, which meant they were both more than likely werewolves.

I pulled my hand from Jeremy's own as the two wolves stepped aside and opened the doors for us. Jeremy entered first and I followed quickly behind, not really liking the idea of being alone with the two unfamiliar werewolves. As soon as I was through, they closed the heavy doors, remaining outside to stand watch.

The loud voices from the main room were cut down to a faint murmur. My ears were ringing with the sound of it as I glanced around the room, quickly taking in those present.

As soon as we entered, Jonathan rose from where he'd been sitting on his couch. A woman I didn't recognize remained seated next to where he'd been.

She was tall, even while sitting. Her hair was cut short and gelled so that it stood out in spikes all around her head. Her eyes were a deep, chocolate brown, as was her skin. Both her left eyebrow and upper lip were pierced in a way that told me the jewelry would stay in if she shifted into wolf form. At one look, I knew she was a werewolf.

And I instantly didn't like her.

"Where's Ethan?" Jonathan asked, crossing the room.

I glanced behind me and frowned. Nathan was nowhere in sight, which I found odd.

"At home," I said, turning back to Jonathan. "Where he belongs."

"You should have brought him."

I narrowed my eyes. "He'll be fine where he's at."

Jeremy walked past me and went to stand awkwardly by a chair. It was obvious he didn't know what to do with himself. He'd been living with me for so long, I don't think any of us knew what his place in the Den hierarchy was anymore. He'd done his job in bringing me here, but now he wasn't sure if he should sit or stand or go wait outside.

The tall woman stood and walked over to stand beside Jonathan. She was wearing black, knee-high boots with heels that made her even taller. She towered over everyone in the room, including Jonathan.

I paid her a quick glance and felt my insides boil. I turned back to the Denmaster, angrier than I should have been.

"Who's she?" I asked, a little sharper than I intended.

Jonathan looked startled, as if he'd forgotten the woman was even there. He glanced at her and a small smile lit the corners of his mouth, which only irritated me more.

"This is Keira Emery," he said, gently touching her wrist. "She came to us last week."

I clenched my jaw and stared her down. I really, really didn't like her and she had yet to say a word. I gave her the hairy eye for a good couple of seconds before turning back to Jonathan. "Another wolf?" I asked to be sure.

He nodded. "Keira and three other weres came to us after the fall of one of the Minor Houses. They were able to escape before what would have become their new master could establish control." He gave her a smile so sickly sweet, I just about puked.

"So, you're Kat?" She made it a question. Her voice was deep, warm, and reassuring. It was the sort of voice that would be right at home in a room lit only by candlelight.

I pointedly ignored her.

"Why am I here?" I asked, crossing my arms.

Jonathan gave me a strange look before gesturing toward the couch. "Please, sit," he said. "We might as well get comfortable."

I kept my arms crossed as I stormed past him to sit in the chair farthest from the couch. I knew I was being sulky and knew it had to do with Keira. I just wasn't sure *why* she bothered me so much.

Jonathan nodded to Jeremy who took the other chair, looking relieved. I think he'd expected Jonathan to ask him to leave.

Keira and Jonathan resumed their seat on the couch next to each other. Her hand immediately went to his wrist.

Jonathan spoke as soon as we were all seated, clearly unaware of how uncomfortable they were making me.

"The Left Hand has struck close to home."

"Are you sure it's them?"

"As sure as I can be."

"How?" I asked, frowning. "You still have security cameras, don't you? Couldn't you have stopped them before they finished the job?"

He sighed. "We do. Whoever did this managed to disable the cameras without anyone noticing."

My eyebrows rose at that. "All of them?"

He nodded.

My gaze flickered to Keira and she stiffened. She knew as well as I did that the newest members of the Cult would be the most likely suspects. To disable all of the cameras, someone would have to know where they were all placed around the campus, or at least, how to remotely shut them down. To me, that screamed inside job.

I turned back to Jonathan. "Why are there so many people here? Are you asking questions?"

"We're calling in all of our members, even the ones who have never been inside the Den before. Over the last few days, five Cultists have turned up dead. I don't believe all five were killed by the Left Hand, but I don't want to take any more chances. We're being hunted."

I shuddered as I thought about the cross I'd picked up off the last Left Hand victim I'd seen. His throat had been cut and he'd bled to death without much of a fight. I'd even felt the pinch of a Left Hand syringe, the helplessness as the concoction went to work, paralyzing me and thinning my blood so that it wouldn't clot.

"I didn't think they went after Purebloods," I said. "Not even those that worship wolves."

"Neither did I."

I really didn't like where this was heading. Were the Left Hand expanding their reach, killing anyone and everyone who had any sort of contact with supes? That would leave everyone I knew as a potential target.

"How can you be sure it was the Left Hand?" I asked, hoping it had to be someone else. "Crucifixion doesn't seem to be their style. And if they're killing pureblooded humans . . ."

Jonathan spread his hands. "I can't be sure of anything, but it's the most likely scenario. Philip was crucified, and a cross was burned into his forehead, and he . . ." Sudden pain lit up his eyes and he looked down at his hands. Keira squeezed his wrist.

"He was branded?" I asked, trying my best to pretend I didn't see her touching him.

"No." Jonathan shook his head. "The metal was heated and

pressed into his forehead where it burned away the flesh. It was fused with his skull when we found him."

I felt sick. Since Philip was a werewolf, chances were good he'd been conscious throughout the entire process. I was pretty sure that anyone who went to the trouble to burn a cross into his forehead would have done it while he was alive and aware. It would have hurt like hell and more than likely would have driven him insane.

I found my gaze once more traveling to Keira. I wondered how well Jonathan actually knew her and if he'd shown her where the cameras were.

"Where's Nathan?" I asked, never taking my eyes off her. It seemed awfully convenient that a new wolf showed up just about the same time as people started dying. And now Jonathan's second wasn't around while we were talking about the murders? It didn't make sense. He wouldn't have missed something like this.

Jonathan was silent long enough that I turned my gaze back to him.

A sudden fear gripped me. "Is he . . . ?"

"He's fine," Jonathan said with a heavy sigh. "In a manner of speaking."

"What's that supposed to mean?"

Jonathan shook his head, telling me he wasn't going to get into it. I turned to Jeremy who shifted uncomfortably in his chair under my scrutiny. I wasn't sure if that meant he knew something or if he was as concerned as I was. If I thought about it later, I'd have to ask him. He wasn't going to talk about it now.

"Fine. So why am I here exactly?" I asked, forcing myself to stare at Jonathan and not the girl hanging on to him.

He flipped a hand over and took Keira's in his own, which only served to make me steam even more.

"I wanted to know that you were safe," he said. "I wanted to make sure the Left Hand could not get to you or Ethan."

I laughed. It was a bitter, angry sound. "And this place is supposed to be safe? I don't recall anyone getting crucified outside my front door."

It was cruel and I regretted it the moment I said it. It was obvious I wasn't in complete control of my anger. As much as I wanted to say and do the right thing, I sometimes couldn't help myself.

Jonathan winced and pulled his hand free from Keira's grip. She glowered at me, and rightfully so. I was being a bitch. Her presence was rubbing me the wrong way and with everything else that was happening, having her there was only making it harder to control my vampire-induced anger.

"Now that we know the Left Hand is here and that they know where we are, we can watch for them," Jonathan said, adopting a businesslike tone to his voice.

"But how did they find you?"

Jonathan shrugged. "I do not know. But this is still the safest place I know, especially now that we know to be watchful."

"I'm not staying here." I wanted to say it before he asked.

Jonathan actually smiled a little. "I knew it was unlikely you would, but I had to at least try. I had hoped if Ethan was here, he might have been able to convince you to stay."

"If I may?"

My fists tightened as Keira spoke. I really didn't want to hear anything she had to say.

Jonathan nodded for her to go on, however. He seemed oblivious to my silent protests.

"I know very little about you," she said. "And I understand from what Jon has told me, you value your privacy."

Jon? She called him *Jon*?

"What of it?" I asked. She'd barely said a word, hadn't even said anything expressly bad, yet I wanted to punch her in the mouth.

"I am hopeful you may help in this as you have helped him before," she said. She touched his elbow before withdrawing her hand. "I haven't been here for long, but I know how much the Cult means to him . . . to all of us."

I stared at her for a really long time, saying nothing. She didn't know me. She had no right to ask for my help.

But deep down, I knew she was right. The Cult meant everything to Jonathan. I couldn't turn my back on that.

Jonathan's sigh drew my eye. "I just want you to stay safe," he said. "I'm not sure what we can do against the Left Hand since we know so little about them. If we still had Davin, I could see what else he might know. But since he's no longer here . . ." He trailed off.

I flinched a little inside. I knew where Davin was, but wasn't about to tell anyone. There were things the insane vampire knew that I wasn't ready to explain to anyone. He wouldn't keep silent if I led the Cult to him.

"So I guess there's little we can do but watch out for crazy people carrying syringes," I said, frustrated.

Jonathan shrugged, looking miserable.

"And you called me all the way out here to tell me this?"

Keira frowned, but I ignored her. I didn't care what she thought of me.

I stood. I wasn't going to waste my time there any longer than I had to. My time would be better spent searching the streets for signs of the Left Hand. It wouldn't be easy—they looked like regular people and I doubted they'd all be carrying those big metal cases—but I wasn't just going to sit around talking about it. I had to do something.

I started to walk away, but stopped when another thought hit me. There was still one more thing I could do at the Den that might help me.

"I want to see the body," I said.

Jonathan looked at me with surprise. "There isn't much to see."

"That's fine," I said. "But I want to see it anyway."

Jonathan didn't look as if he approved. I was pretty sure he was blaming himself as being responsible for the wolf's death. To show me the body would be admitting he couldn't protect those under him.

It was Keira who broke the tense silence that had fallen.

"I think we should let her."

I looked at her in mild surprise. With the way I was treating her, I would have figured she'd have wanted me gone more than anyone. Yet here she was, taking my side.

Jonathan glanced at her and sighed. He rubbed at his face and then stood. "All right," he said, still clearly reluctant. "The body is down in the basement."

I very nearly grunted. Where else would it be?

I nodded once and stepped aside. "Okay, then," I said. "Lead the way."

3

The crowd of Cultists parted more readily for Jonathan than they had for Jeremy, which wasn't much of a surprise. Jeremy hadn't been to the Den too much over the last few months, so I was pretty sure quite a few of the newer residents had no idea who he was.

I still got glares here and there, though. That was something I'd never fully escape here. I mean, these people might worship werewolves as gods, but the same didn't go for vampires. In fact, vamps were viewed as the enemy. It was a wonder I hadn't been attacked by now.

Keira walked at my side, though not by my choice. I would have much preferred her to walk in front of me where I could keep an eye on her, but at least she wasn't at my back. I was positive she distrusted me as much as I did her, no matter what she'd said. I hadn't given her a reason to trust me, let alone like me, so I didn't hold it against her.

What I *did* hold against her, however, was how quickly she'd attached herself to Jonathan. That was something I was going to find very hard to forgive.

Jeremy followed at the rear, but before we reached the office door, the girl he'd talked to before stopped him. She grabbed his arm and held tight when he tried to break away. With a sigh, he motioned us on and moved to a corner where he could talk with her.

I wasn't quite sure what was going on there, but I did like the fact he was talking to someone that wasn't me, Ethan, or Jonathan. Ever since he'd moved in with me, Jeremy had been cut off from so many things. It would do him some good to spend time with someone else, especially a girl.

I was very nearly smiling as we walked through the office doors. Jonathan let Keira and me through before closing the door. He walked across the room, briefly touching Keira's arm as he passed, and then pressed the button beneath the lip of his desk. The secret door opened with a click.

"This way," he said needlessly. I'd been down in the secret basement before. It had yet to be a pleasant experience and I doubted this time would be any different.

Jonathan led the way down the stairs. He walked with his back stiff and moved as if each step was a struggle. He wasn't looking forward to this, that much was obvious.

I motioned for Keira to walk ahead of me. She hesitated a moment before giving me a slight smile and a dip of her head. She put her back to me without flinching, telling me that she wasn't worried about me stabbing her in the back. I vaguely wondered how much Jonathan had told her about me.

I brought up the rear and followed the two werewolves down. Damp air wafted up the stairs, bringing with it the smell of blood and death. I had to pause a moment to take a few deep breaths before I could continue down into the depths of the Den. Thankfully, I wasn't the only one. Keira had to stop twice, her head bowed, her breathing ragged.

Jonathan turned on the lights the moment he reached the bottom even though all three of us could see in the dark. It would be far easier to pick out details with the lights on. Night vision was nice and all, but there was just no substitute for good lighting.

Keira reached the bottom and moved to stand next to Jonathan. Without realizing I was doing it, I put my hand on the hilt of my sword and took the last few steps down.

The body was lying on a metal table in the middle of the room. A sheet lay across him, hiding his features. There were a few bloodstains, but they were small, telling me he'd stopped bleeding long before they covered him up, but not entirely.

Empty cells lined the walls of the basement. My eyes lingered on a certain three that had become synonymous with the Den in my mind.

Davin had spent time in the cell in the far corner before he'd escaped with the help of Adrian and his wolves. It was kind of odd to be down here without his mad laughter and taunts. If I squinted just right, I could almost see his gap-toothed grin peering at me from out of the shadows.

My gaze traveled down the line to the cell where Jonathan had kept the Left Hand woman whose throat I'd torn out. There were still bloodstains on the floor. It was unlikely they'd ever come out. I wondered if her death was what had precipitated the attack on the Den's wolf or if it would have happened anyway.

I didn't want to, but I couldn't help but look at the cell in the middle. Thomas had been kept there. There was no blood inside, but I could still see the scrapes in the stone where he'd tried to claw his way out.

I looked away, feeling sick.

I found myself looking at a broken cross on the floor beside the table. It was wooden, held together by what looked to be railroad spikes. The crossbar was snapped off the main post and broken into two pieces. The entire thing was covered in blood.

"Nathan tore it down," Jonathan said. "Once we took Philip down, Nathan threw it against the wall. It took three of us to calm him down or else he would have destroyed the entire thing."

"Oh," I said. I'd seen Nathan mad before. It was a wonder he hadn't killed someone in his rage.

I approached the table, stepping carefully around the remains of the cross. There were splinters of wood on the floor, some as long as my forearm. I doubted they'd puncture my boots, but I didn't want to disturb them. Stepping on them seemed somehow indecent, as if I was disrespecting more than just the man who'd died upon this particular cross.

I reached for the top of the sheet covering Philip, but hesitated before pulling it down. I glanced toward Jonathan to make sure it was okay to uncover him. It felt right to get his permission first.

Jonathan nodded from where he stood a few feet away. Keira had moved to stand a little behind him. Her eyes glowed a faint yellow.

"Is she going to be okay?" I asked, keeping the sheet firmly in place. I didn't like the idea of sharing a room with a werewolf who was about to lose control around a dead body. I might have the weapons, but if she was as quick as she looked, she might get to me before I could draw them.

Jonathan glanced back and frowned. "Keira?"

"I'm fine," she said, but it was clear she was just barely holding on. Hair was starting to sprout around her cheeks. She kept flexing her fingers as if anxious to tear someone apart.

"Go upstairs," Jonathan said. "Clear the main floor and find a place for everyone to sleep. Anyone who doesn't plan on staying should wait until first light before leaving. It's unlikely they will be attacked then."

Her upper lip rose in a snarl, but she nodded anyway. With a stiff stride, Keira went up the stairs.

"She needs to work on that," I said as soon as she was gone. "I'm not going to stick around long if you let her stay, especially if she goes wolfy every time she smells blood."

Jonathan's frown deepened, but he didn't say anything. He just nodded toward the body, clearly wanting to get this over with as soon as possible.

I took a shallow breath, painfully aware of my own hunger. It wouldn't do to point out Keira's deficiencies in her control, only to have my own fangs sprout while I looked over the body.

I pulled the sheet off the corpse.

Philip was lying faceup on the table. His eyes were closed, which was a good thing because something pink had leaked from his eyelids and had dried on his cheeks. I had a pretty good feeling that it was what was left of his eyes.

A silver cross was embedded into his forehead. The skin around it was blackened and had peeled away, exposing the skull beneath. The silver was indeed fused to the bone.

I swallowed with some difficulty and looked down the rest of his body.

His throat had been cut ear to ear, which was typical of the Left Hand. His neck and chest were painted red with dried blood. His left hand was torn nearly in two and a gaping hole was in his right. There were two more holes in his wrists.

"We think they tried to crucify him by his hands first," Jonathan said, following my gaze. "He tore free of that."

I nodded. Religious nuts who didn't know how to crucify someone properly? Great. The hands can't support the weight of a body, especially if the body in question is thrashing around, trying to get free.

"Why didn't he shift?" I asked, as I took in the rest of him. His feet had holes in them from where the spikes had held him in place, but the rest of his body appeared untouched. I covered up his nakedness with the sheet, leaving his face and throat exposed.

"They could have injected him with their serum," Jonathan said. "We couldn't find a puncture wound, but that could have been lost when his throat was cut."

I studied Philip's face, my disquiet growing. "If they'd burned the cross into his head first, he would have been paralyzed by the silver. He wouldn't have been able to fight them." I leaned in closer. "Unless . . ." I started to reach for the cross.

"It's real silver," Jonathan said, hastily. "Nathan touched it, thinking he might rip it free. It burned him."

I pulled back. If I'd touched the cross with Jonathan knowing it was real silver, I'd have some big questions to answer. I often forgot I was now immune to silver, thanks to something Adrian had done to me when he'd forced me into the Oath. No one else knew about it. I wanted to keep it that way.

"It doesn't make sense."

I walked around the table as if seeing the body from another angle might tell me something. If he'd been paralyzed by the silver, he couldn't have fought, meaning he wouldn't have ripped his hands from the spikes. But if he hadn't been paralyzed, it was likely he would have shifted to fight back.

Then again, Philip was a big man. He had to weigh at least two fifty, most of it muscle. Perhaps his own limp weight had torn his hands free.

I turned away from the corpse. Blood was starting to trickle into my mouth where my fangs were starting to push through. As much as I was disgusted by the body, at the brutality, I was still hungry. My inner beast needed to be sated every now and again, and I'd been putting it off. Ethan's concoction had done nothing to ease the hunger.

I closed my eyes and focused on breathing slowly. I'd done this before. Hell, I'd been in rooms with dozens of dead bodies and had held it together. Why was I having such a hard time now?

"Are you okay?"

I jumped at the closeness of Jonathan's voice. He was standing right behind me, close enough to touch. If I simply leaned back, our bodies would be pressed together. I felt myself start to move, but caught myself just in time.

"I'm fine," I said, suddenly aware of my breath. I'd almost forgotten about the stuff Ethan had me drink.

Still, Jonathan didn't step away. I didn't move either.

"I don't mean about this," he said, gesturing toward the body.

I glanced over my shoulder at him. His face was whole, completely void of the damage I'd done to him all those years ago, back before we got to know each other. I longed to reach up and touch the spot where I knew his skull had been cleaved by my sword, but to do so would be to give in to something I'd been fighting hard to ignore.

"I said I was fine," I said, taking a step away from him.

"We haven't talked since Baset—"

I cut him off with a quick slashing motion of my hand. I didn't want to think about Countess Baset, especially not now.

His lips tightened and he waited all of two seconds before starting in again. "What happened to you that night?" he asked. "You came in looking pale and scared. We didn't know where you'd been and I . . . I was afraid something had happened to you. I still am."

He didn't know about Adrian or what the big wolf had done to me. I wasn't even sure he suspected.

I had no intention of telling him.

I clenched my jaw and just glared at him. It was none of his business where I'd been. I knew if he found out I was bound to Adrian, he might try to kill the rogue werewolf himself to free me.

While I wouldn't mind Adrian's death so much, I knew it was unlikely Jonathan could pull it off. He had maybe six or seven wolves at his disposal. Adrian had dozens. A fight between them wouldn't even be close. I wasn't so sure I could handle it if Jonathan died because of me.

"Kat . . ." He started to move a little closer, but caught himself. Instead, he put his hands behind his back, respecting my need for space. "I want to help you. If something has happened, please let me know."

"I don't want to talk about it." I felt my lower lip begin to tremble and I bit the inside of my mouth to keep from crying. I couldn't believe I was about to break down over this.

Jonathan's face fell and he nodded. I don't think he heard the pain in my voice, but he understood. There were just some things I couldn't talk about, not yet anyway. Maybe somewhere down the line I'd be able to tell him without worrying so much about how it would affect him.

But it wouldn't come easy. He'd already been tortured once because of me. I didn't plan on ever letting it happen again.

"I want to talk about Nathan," I said, changing the subject so I wouldn't be tempted to tell him everything just so he wouldn't worry.

"What about him?"

"He's not here. How sure are you that he isn't somehow involved in this?"

Jonathan's eyes flashed an angry yellow. "He is not." Terse.

"And are you positive of this?"

"Yes."

"Then someone else," I pressed. "There's no way the Left Hand could have gotten on your property and disabled the cameras without help. You would have seen them coming."

"I've thought of that."

"But you don't want to believe that it could have been anyone close to you who did it, is that it?"

"It couldn't have been Nathan," Jonathan said through clenched teeth. "Or any of my weres for that matter. Have you forgotten the Left Hand kills those of our kind? They would not work with them knowingly, even if it furthered their goals."

"Exactly," I said, causing him to give me an odd look. "Just because we know who is and isn't a werewolf, doesn't mean the Left Hand always knows. They could be receiving anonymous information, for all we know. They might not have met the person they're working with."

Jonathan shook his head in stubborn denial.

"Or perhaps one of the Pureblood Cultists is involved. Just because they bear your mark and wear your robes, doesn't mean they're loyal to you. Are there any new Cultists, someone who's been snooping around a little more than usual, that might be responsible?"

Jonathan turned angrily away. He didn't like this line of thought any more than I did. He'd been betrayed by one of his own before. I didn't want to know what he'd do to the person who betrayed him now.

A twinge of guilt sifted through me as I thought about what I wasn't telling him. He really did deserve to know about Adrian and his wolves being immune to silver. It was also his right to know that I was bound to Adrian. And then there was all of the other shit I've been hiding from him over the last few months, things that he would desperately want to know . . .

God, I wasn't any better than the rest of the monsters. Lying by omission was still lying.

And a betrayal.

"Someone is keeping an eye on the Cultists," he said. "But it's unlikely any of them would have had an opportunity to take down the systems. Only a few would know how to do it and I trust them."

"There aren't very many more options," I said with a sigh. "I hope there is some other explanation, I really do, but usually the most obvious answer is the right one. You need to consider the fact that someone from the inside might have tipped off the Left Hand and could be plotting against you even now."

He nodded, though it was clear he didn't want to listen. He'd fought so hard to make sure his wolves stayed safe from vampire control, that those who worshipped his kind did so safely, that it would probably kill him to find out someone he was close to was trying to ruin it all.

"I'll see what I can find out," I said. "But there is only so much I can do with so little to go on. I doubt I'll just stumble across wherever the Left Hand is hiding. Nor do I have any idea how I'm going to tell them apart from anyone else."

I thought about the upcoming Monday and worried that Baset would have a name for me. It would just make my week complete to have *that* to worry about on top of everything else.

I hated my life sometimes.

Jonathan looked over at the body of his wolf and his shoulders slumped. He looked downright miserable. He nodded with a sigh that looked like it was seconds from becoming a frustrated sob.

"It isn't your fault he died," I said. "You can't protect everyone."

He glanced at me, a faint smile on his face. "That sounds like something I might tell you."

I laughed. It wouldn't surprise me in the slightest if he had. "Maybe there are a few things we can still learn from each other after all."

Jonathan's smile slid away. "I wish you would reconsider staying here," he said. "You may be able to do something here. I could use your input."

I shook my head. "I can't. I have Ethan to worry about."

He looked like he might protest, but instead, turned toward the stairs. "Shall we?"

We headed back up into his office. I waited while he took a moment to compose himself. It was clear he wanted to appear strong in front of the Cultists. Seeing the body again had shaken him up pretty badly. It took only a few seconds, but in that brief instant, I saw something in him that made me want to stick around longer. He was willing to show vulnerability in front of me. Could I really turn my back on that?

Before I could think to say anything, he walked across the room and opened the door. We stepped out into the main hall where Jeremy was waiting for us. He rose from his seat on the stairs and joined us. The room was empty of everyone else.

"I'm leaving," I said. "I'll let you know if I learn anything." I headed for the door.

"Are you going home?" Jonathan asked in a way that told me he was still trying to watch out for me. I wasn't sure if I should be flattered or pissed.

"No," I said. "I have something else I need to do."

I stepped outside, leaving both Jonathan and Jeremy behind. I stood on the steps for a good long minute, wondering if I were doing the right thing by leaving now. If I were to go back in, my life would change. I could send Jeremy for Ethan and we could work on the Left Hand problem together.

I think I might have stayed if Jonathan had followed me out. He wouldn't even have to ask. I'd simply turn around and go back inside with him.

But the doors remained firmly closed behind me.

He wasn't coming.

A combination of frustration and irritation washed over me. In the stories, the man would always come rushing out after the woman and everything would work out in the end. Why couldn't I have that? Why did I always have to be so damn stubborn just so I could appear strong?

God, I really needed a drink.

And you know what? That's exactly what I was going to do.

4

The Bloody Stake parking lot was surprisingly empty at this hour. There were a couple of cars, but not the usual heavy traffic I normally would expect. Even the sign above the bar looked tired. The woman appeared as if she was no longer interested in repeatedly staking the overdressed vampire. In fact, it all seemed sort of depressing.

Or maybe I was just projecting.

I hesitated just outside the doors, not sure if I'd be welcome after the last time I was there. I'd been jumped by a trio of Adrian's wolves and we'd fought, though I'd actually tried hard to avoid it. Bart had ended the lives of two of the wolves. I was thankful he'd decided to let me go.

I firmed my resolve and pushed through the doors. Bart might be unhappy with me, but since he'd let me go, I had to believe he wouldn't object to my return. I figured if he wanted me to stay away, he would have told me so.

Or shot me and been done with me for good.

Mikael Engelbrecht was sitting at his usual booth. A girl was fast asleep against his shoulder. He gave me a slimy smile and a nod before closing his own eyes.

The rest of the bar was practically empty. An older man who smelled of whiskey sat on a stool at the bar and a young couple huddled close together across the room, but that was about it. The music had been turned down to accommodate the smaller crowd. I wondered if there had been a fight recently that had scared off—or killed off—most of Bart's usual clientele.

Then again, a fight would have probably brought in a larger crowd. People did love their violence . . . as long as it was happening to someone else.

I hurried across the room and slid into what had once been my favorite booth. It gave me a good look at the room and put my back at a wall so no one could get at me. I used to come in and sit here all the time, but somewhere along the way, the only time I ever came to the bar was to get information.

The thump of footsteps approached. I stared down at the table, trying to look as innocent as possible. I could tell by the way one leg dragged a little behind the other that it was Bart. He'd gotten his limp, as well as a scar across his face, from fights in and around the Bloody Stake. Thankfully, I had yet to be involved in the sort of fight that would cause him to become injured. If I had, I doubted I'd be alive.

Bart wasn't known for his forgiving ways, so I was tense. He'd killed other vamps for less than what I'd done. The fight might not have been my fault, but in his mind, I could have done something to stop it. I couldn't help it that Adrian was an idiot who'd send his wolves after me in some of the worst places imaginable. Maybe he thought I'd come along quietly if he came at me where others could see.

Obviously he didn't know me as well as he thought.

Bart stopped by my table and I tried to push thoughts of Adrian out of my head. I could still feel him out there, thanks to us being bound together by the Oath. I couldn't tell exactly where he was or what he was doing, but I was pretty sure I could walk right up to him if I'd wanted.

There was a thump as Bart set an open bottle of beer on the table in front of me. He sat down on the other side of the table, sighing heavily as he took his weight off of his legs.

"I'm surprised to see you back," he said. He looked tired, like he hadn't been sleeping well lately. It was a wonder he could ever sleep at all with all of the monsters he dealt with on any given day. You'd think someone would have come after him by now, yet here he was, day after day, serving the creatures of the night beer after beer like they were any other persons.

"Do you want me to leave?" I looked up at him. While I didn't want to beg, I was sure he saw the pleading look I couldn't keep out of my eyes.

"Nah," he said. "Not many people here for you to antagonize tonight."

I smiled and picked up my beer. I took a swig and closed my eyes as it slid smoothly down my throat. After everything I'd seen that night, I really needed this.

"Slow night tonight," I said, after I'd basked in the warmth blossoming in my gut for a few minutes. I took another drink and glanced around the bar. "Something happen?"

Bart frowned and followed my gaze. "It depends on what you mean by happened. Since the day you scuffled in my lot, there've been no fights within or around my property."

"Then why is it so empty? Have a rough singles night?"

He grunted and very nearly smiled before it bled away into his more natural troubled frown. "I think people are scared. I'm not sure of what, but they aren't coming in like they used to. Half the time, they only stay long enough for a drink or two before shuffling off to their homes to hide. It's as if they're waiting for something to blow over." He sighed. "I just hope it happens quick so I can get back down to business."

It wasn't too much of a mental workout to figure out what a lot of people were afraid of. If the Left Hand was in town killing people, I was sure word of it had spread. Going out alone was dangerous normally, but with these psychos running around, slashing throats, things were getting more dangerous than even the most fearless of predators could stand.

I chugged a good half of my beer and slammed it down. I was tired of things always popping up, seemingly every other month. I could use a year off where everything didn't go to shit the moment someone new breezed into town.

"Rough night?" Bart asked. I was surprised to see a little concern in his gaze. "That's life, isn't it?"

I grunted noncommittally and finished off my beer.

"Look," I said, setting down the empty bottle. "I'm sorry about . . ."

I trailed off as Bart shook his head. "Don't apologize to me. I got something out of the whole affair, so I can't complain."

He shifted and I glanced down at his now extended foot. My silver knife was strapped to his boot, hilt *and* blade exposed to anyone who deigned to look.

I raised my eyebrows at him. "Isn't it dangerous to show off silver like that?"

He shrugged. "Who's going to give me shit about it?"

He had a point there.

The door opened and closed, drawing Bart's eye. I turned my gaze back to my empty bottle, wishing I had a fresh beer. I wouldn't get drunk, but I definitely could use a few more to help wash away some of the bad thoughts that had invaded over the last few hours.

"I'll leave you two be," Bart said, rising.

I looked up and was surprised to find Jeremy standing beside my table. He looked ten kinds of embarrassed.

Bart slid out of the booth and gathered my empty bottle. "I'll get you another," he said, walking off.

"May I sit down?" Jeremy asked. He wouldn't meet my eye.

"Sure," I said with a sigh. I wasn't sure I was in the mood for company, especially if he decided he wanted to talk to me about Philip.

"Jonathan said you'd probably be here."

"Glad he knows me so well."

"He's worried."

I shrugged.

Bart returned. He set two bottles on the table and limped away without a word.

"He wanted me to tell you that he regrets asking you to stay. He keeps forgetting how goddamn stubborn you are."

My head snapped up and I found Jeremy smiling at me.

"His words, not mine."

I couldn't help but laugh. "Good thing he sent you instead of coming himself."

Jeremy chuckled and picked up his beer.

We sat in silence, simply drinking and sharing each other's company. I tried hard to focus on anything but the Left Hand, but couldn't help it. They scared me more than any Pureblood group should. They'd gotten onto Luna Cult property and crucified one of their werewolves before he could shift. It was pretty damn hard to sneak up on a werewolf, though I knew it could be done.

The Cult had to be compromised. It was the only way they could have pulled it off. It also meant that whoever was involved might very well know where I lived. How long would it be before someone ended up dead in my front yard?

It was hard not to jump up and go rushing back home to make sure Ethan was safe. My fingers tightened on the bottle and I had to work hard to keep from squeezing it until it exploded in my hand.

"I'm not staying at the Den," Jeremy said. "I'm coming home with you."

"Is that what Jonathan told you to do?"

"No. It was my decision."

I looked at him. I mean, I really looked.

Jeremy lost his arm because of me. When I'd first met him, he was overconfident and raw. I scared the crap out of him and then a few months later, nearly got him killed.

And now here he was, acting all grown up, sharing beers with the woman who nearly killed him. It was kind of nice to think that despite all the damage I'd done to him physically, he appeared to be stronger mentally. I wasn't about to take the credit for it, but it gave me hope that things would eventually work out. And hey, if he was stronger because of what I'd done to him, then it proved that despite how horrible I could be, I could still do some good every now and again.

"I'll leave you be." He started to climb out of the booth.

"No. Stay." The words came hard, but I meant them.

Jeremy hesitated. He looked around like maybe it was some sort of trick before sliding back into place. His beer was still mostly full and he reached for it with his one good hand. He toyed with the bottle without taking a drink.

"I could use the company," I added.

He smiled and took a large drink. He sighed contentedly.

"So, who was the girl you talked to tonight?" I asked, taking a drink of my own. "Girlfriend?"

Jeremy's eyes widened and he nearly choked on his beer. "Her? No. I don't know her."

"She seemed to know you."

He shrugged. "I've seen her around, but don't know her name." His brow furrowed. "In fact, she didn't even tell me tonight."

I laughed. "I'm not surprised," I said. "Most guys aren't really interested in learning a pretty girl's name before they take her to bed."

Jeremy actually looked appalled. He sputtered for a moment before shaking his head and looking away.

I chuckled and sat back. Why had I never done this with him before?

"You do know he only wants to help, right?" Jeremy said after a few moments.

I groaned inwardly, knowing he was trying to get me back for those comments about the girl. I was pretty sure he knew I still struggled to sort out the tangled emotions I had for the Denmaster. Everyone had seemed to key in on the fact long before I did.

"I know that," I said. "But he needs to remember that I've helped myself for a long time now. Letting someone else help doesn't come naturally to me."

"But is it really so hard to let him try?"

"Yes," I said. "It is."

Jeremy smiled. "Somehow, I knew you'd say that."

I shook my head and took another drink.

There was a long stretch of silence when we both just drank quietly. I could feel Bart's eyes on us and wondered if he knew who Jeremy was or if he thought the young were was my boyfriend or something. I smiled at the thought.

Then again, what did Mikael think? He might have his eyes closed, but I was positive he knew everything that was going on in the room. Did he know who Jeremy was? Did he know where he'd been? It was one of those things I wished I knew for sure. I didn't like the idea of Mikael storing any sort of information on my friends.

"Thank you," Jeremy said suddenly, startling me out of my thoughts.

"For what?"

"For taking me in." He took a deep breath and let it out slowly. "I don't think I would have made it through those first few months after this"—he motioned toward his missing arm—"without you and Ethan."

"Ethan took you in first. You should thank him."

"But it was because of you that I was there. Sure, you might not have been in the house at the time, but I felt your presence there anyway. It was as if a part of you had never left."

I gave him a funny look. I might have been the reason he'd moved in, but I was also the reason he'd lost his arm. I didn't deserve thanks for that.

Jeremy's bottle was empty. He spun it slowly on the table, not looking up as he spoke.

"Those first few days were hard. After Lei couldn't . . . when she couldn't put my arm back . . ." He took another deep breath and I thought I saw tears in his eyes.

"You don't have to do this," I said. Something in my chest hitched and I had to clear my throat lest I start bawling myself.

"I was stupid," Jeremy said, going on as if he hadn't heard me. "I thought I was tougher than I really was. And when those Tainted came through the door and tore me apart like I was just some rag doll, I realized I had no business living this sort of life."

My beer was empty. I held on to the bottle, afraid that if I let it go, I'd give in to the emotions suddenly throbbing behind my eyes. I couldn't imagine losing a part of myself like that.

"It's hard to slit your wrists when you only have one arm."

My hand tightened on the bottle. I refused to look up at him now. I knew if I saw tears trailing down his cheeks, I'd lose it and break down too.

"So I tried to chew my way through them instead." He gave a bitter laugh. "How that would help, I have no idea. I healed long before I ever bled out."

The couple across the room stood and walked out together. As they left, a trio of men came in, looking as much like vampires as anyone could without showing fang. They scoped the room and then wandered to a table, seemingly disappointed there weren't more people there they could target.

"I think I might have starved myself or tried again if it wasn't for Jonathan. He told me to watch over Ethan, giving me something to do. At first, I thought he was trying to get rid of me, but soon started to realize he was giving me a reason to go on. He showed me I was still useful."

The sound of his voice finally caused me to look at him. He was staring at me with an intensity that was almost scary.

"But even while I knew I was getting better inside, I was still torn up. When Ethan was asleep, I'd sometimes watch him and think about everything I could no longer do. It was hard to simply get through the day sometimes."

I nodded in a way that I hoped told him that I understood. I'd been to my own dark places.

"But I got over it. I learned that even though I couldn't do something as simple as clap anymore, I could still be important to someone. I refuse to shirk my duty out of fear of failure. Just because I'm missing a part of myself, doesn't mean the rest of me is useless."

Jeremy sighed and forced a smile. "So anyway, thank you for not kicking me out when you came back. Thank you for giving me a reason to live." He raised his bottle toward the bar.

I didn't trust myself to speak. Bart brought over a pair of beers, clearing away the empties as he did.

I waited until he was gone before I forced a smirk to my face and said, "No problem." I wanted to sound cocky, but my voice broke on the second word.

Jeremy seemed to get it, though. He broke out into a wide grin, picked up his beer and tipped it my way. "To staying alive."

I raised my own bottle. "To staying alive."

Our bottles made a faint clink as we tapped them together.

5

It was late when we finally decided to call it a night. Thanks to our higher metabolisms, neither of us were drunk, but Jeremy looked like he was ready for a good long nap. I told him I'd meet him at home and waved him off when he offered to follow me home. I had things I wanted to do and didn't want an audience while I did them.

Jeremy gave me a friendly smile and wave as he slipped into the black car Jonathan had given him after I'd pretty much destroyed his old clunker. He started it up, waved once more, and took off out of the parking lot.

Besides my Honda, there were only two other vehicles in the lot. The bar had remained dead all night, though at one point it had started to pick up when a group of eight Purebloods came in for about ten minutes. Otherwise, not much had happened.

As soon as Jeremy was out of sight, I got on my motorcycle. I was in a strange mood after spending the night drinking with Jeremy. I felt like there were things I should do before diving headfirst into the Left Hand problem. If I didn't, then these things would nag at me, distracting me from what I really needed to focus on. If I left now, I was pretty sure I could get them all done before first light.

I drove toward Delai, wishing I could forget about the place. There was nothing I could do to help the people trapped inside the mystical town. Di'leviathan—Levi to me—was an angel who dedicated his life to "curing" supes, though his cure was more of a mental wipe that turned the people into mindless shells he apparently could control through his will.

He'd planned on doing the same to me. If it hadn't been for Beligral's Sight, I'd probably be staring blankly at a wall right now. Levi had a calming influence, something I should have picked up on long before it was pointed out to me. Only through the demon's help was I able to avoid succumbing to Levi's mental touch long enough to see what he really was.

But now, the town was gone, as were its inhabitants. I knew they were out there somewhere, but I couldn't get to them. When Levi discovered I'd learned what he was, he kicked me out. The road, the town, and everyone who lived there, vanished as if they'd never existed.

Still, I found myself drawn to where I'd last seen the town. Sienna, Levi's adopted daughter, was there. I'd promised to save her.

I drove fast and hard, just wanting to get this over with. If I saw that the town hadn't magically reappeared, I could put it behind me for a few days. I knew deep down that it wouldn't be there, that I'd more than likely never see Delai or Levi again, but damn it, I had to try.

The empty field came into view and I walked my Honda off the road a way before staring off into the distance. There was nothing out there. I wasn't sure if Levi could see me when I came here or if he'd completely forgotten me by now. I'd come here a few times and screamed at the sky, challenging the angel to fight.

It was probably a good thing he never answered. I had a feeling a fight between me and a creature that was akin to a demon wouldn't end up in my favor.

I sat there for a few minutes before walking the motorcycle back onto the road. I didn't have time to go wandering the empty field in the hope I would see something promising. Nothing had been there before, and I figured it would be the same now.

I took off toward home. There was a moment when I very nearly changed course and headed toward Adrian's place. I could feel him out there. I was pretty sure Davin would be with him and I really wanted to talk to the vampire about the Left Hand. I wasn't sure if his insanity would allow him to tell me anything of use, but it was worth a try.

But not yet. I had one more thing to do.

I arrived home with a little over an hour to spare before night. I pulled into the garage, shut off the engine, and made for the side door. I used the fingerprint reader Ethan had installed at every outside door. The door unlocked with a click and I stepped inside my sanctuary.

The smell of bacon nearly overwhelmed me as I entered the kitchen. I wasn't sure when I'd actually eaten anything of substance. My mouth watered and I glanced at the stove. It was cold and the bacon grease had long ago congealed in the skillet. My stomach grumbled and I mentally promised myself I'd eat something later.

Ethan was sitting on the couch, an empty plate beside him. The TV was on, but I don't think he was watching it.

"Hey," he said, rising as I came in.

"Hey." I hesitated and then took off my coat, followed by my shoulder holster and belt. I wouldn't need weapons where I was going.

"I take it you didn't get into a fight?" he asked as he walked past me, into the kitchen. He rinsed off his plate and set it in the sink.

"Not tonight. I'll try harder tomorrow."

He laughed and returned to lean against the wall between the dining room and living room.

"Where's Jeremy?" I asked. I rolled my shoulders, causing my neck and back to both pop. It sounded like someone balling up a sheet of bubble wrap. I hadn't fought anyone, but my body was stiff and tired.

"Asleep," Ethan said. "I think. Apparently, he had a few too many to drink tonight. I guess his wolf couldn't keep up with it."

I smiled. I still couldn't believe I'd sat there drinking with him. I couldn't remember the last time I relaxed in a bar with someone.

"So, how did it go?" Ethan was nervous and was trying to hide it. He fiddled with the bottom of his shirt, rubbing at a stain that wasn't there.

I shrugged. "As good as it could, I guess."

"Any idea what happened?"

I sighed. "The Left Hand. They crucified the werewolf and left him in front of the Den."

Ethan's eyes widened. "Are you serious?"

"Serious as can be."

He licked his lips and gave a little shudder. "What are you going to do about it?"

"Same as always," I said. "I'll go out, find them, and then take care of the problem."

"Maybe Beligral could help?"

He said it like he didn't want to. I had a feeling he'd promised the demon he'd bring it up. I wasn't sure how much Beligral knew of our world and I didn't want to add to his knowledge by recruiting his help.

"No fucking way," I growled. I took a deep breath, closed my eyes, and then forced an apologetic smile. "Sorry," I said. "I just don't want to deal with him on top of everything else right now."

I glanced toward the back door. Time was wasting and I wanted to get this done.

"I'll be back in a minute," I said.

Ethan nodded and went back into the living room. I turned and unlocked the back door. I had to mentally ready myself before sliding it open and stepping outside. When I closed the door, it automatically locked. I'd have to use the fingerprint reader to get back inside.

I walked the worn grass toward the woods where Thomas's grave lay. This was going to be hard, like always, but a sense of serenity washed over me when I saw the unmarked stone beneath the tree. Thomas might be dead, but it felt like his spirit was still around, watching over me.

I knelt by the stone and placed a hand on it. "Hey, Thomas."

There was no answer, of course.

"I just wanted to come out here to let you know that I'm still trying." The wind rustled my hair and even though I knew it wasn't him, I took it as a response. "I still fuck up every once in a while, but I haven't been nearly as bad as before."

I ran my fingers over the stone. I'd have to get his name carved into it sometime. While the plain marking would suit him and would also prevent others from messing with the grave, he deserved more.

"I . . ." I felt my throat close up and coughed. I refused to cry. "I'm sorry things turned out the way they did. Maybe someday I'll find a way to fix this."

I instantly thought of Baset and how she'd been brought back from the dead. Could the same be done for Thomas? Could her necromancer, Henri, somehow bring him back to life without the gruesome consequences?

No. I refused to do that to my brother. Even if he could avoid coming back as a rotten half-corpse, there's no telling in what state his mind might be. There'd been so little left when he'd been tainted. It was impossible to believe that things would magically get better after rising from his grave. In fact, I could only see them getting worse.

"I've got to head back in now," I said, hand still on the stone. "It's going to be light soon."

I stood. "Sleep tight, Thomas."

I turned and went back into the house.

Ethan was sitting at the table, head bowed when I came in. The TV was off and the house, except for a single lamp in the living room, was dark.

"You okay?" he asked when I entered.

"Yeah." I didn't sound it.

"Did something else happen while you were out tonight?"

I almost laughed. Ethan was so good at reading me. The only time I ever went to see Thomas's grave was when I had something on my mind. It calmed me in a way. He knew that. Ethan could often tell when I wasn't telling him the whole story.

I took a seat across from him. "Nathan wasn't at the Den when I got there. Jonathan wouldn't tell me where he went."

Ethan frowned. "And you think he might have had something to do with this?"

I shook my head and shrugged. "I have no idea. It strikes me as odd that when something this big happens, he's nowhere in sight."

"Maybe something else drew him away."

"Yeah, but why wouldn't Jonathan tell me?"

"It might not have been Cult business."

I just gave him a look. The Luna Cult was Nathan's life as far as I knew. He'd want to be there when Jonathan and I talked strategy. I don't think he trusted me with him. He wasn't my biggest fan and would much rather be there whenever I was alone with his Denmaster.

Of course, we hadn't been alone this time. Keira had been there nearly every step of the way. A frown crept onto my face.

"So what else is bothering you?" Ethan asked. "I can tell there's something else going on."

"Nathan wasn't there. It's a big deal."

"And?"

"And what?" I refused to look at him.

"And there is more to it than that. Come on, spill it."

I sighed. "And there was another werewolf at Jonathan's side instead."

"I see." Ethan sat back. "So, um, you don't like this wolf?"

I chewed over that for a long moment. "I don't know. I barely know her."

"Ah." I could hear the smile in Ethan's voice.

I looked up and glared at him. "What's that supposed to mean?"

His grin widened. "Her."

"What about her?"

"Exactly."

I narrowed my eyes and he laughed.

"Competition," he said with a wink.

"Competition for what?" I felt my face growing hot.

Ethan just shook his head as he stood. He picked up my bundle of weapons and tucked them under his arm. "I'll go ahead and take these down tonight. I'll work on them tomorrow sometime. Maybe by then, you'll figure it out." He walked away chuckling.

I grumbled something decidedly unfriendly, but couldn't stop the smile from crossing my face as I headed for the stairs. I felt a little woozy from too much to drink and decided it was time I soaked it out of me. A bath sounded really good by then.

I paused outside Jeremy's bedroom door. He was snoring loudly inside. I smiled, marveling once more at how I was coming to accept the werewolf as a part of my family. A few months ago, I was ready to kick him out, and now I was sharing drinks with him.

I rested my hand on the door a moment before heading to my room. It wouldn't do to have Ethan come back upstairs and see me like that. He'd never let me hear the end of it.

I entered my bedroom and closed the door behind me. My head was far clearer than it had been earlier. Sure, the Left Hand were going to be a problem and I still had Baset and Adrian thinking they could control me, but I was starting to feel like I could deal with them. If I took everything one step at a time, I'd find a way out from beneath their thumbs.

I started to strip down, but stopped about halfway through.

I was humming.

I had to really think about that.

My life had been such a mess over the last few years, I couldn't remember when I last sang, let alone hummed. Normally, when I'd come to my room at the end of a night, I'd be a mess inside, too busy trying to figure out what disaster I'd have to deal with next.

But things had changed. *I* had changed.

Smiling and naked, I walked into my bathroom and started the bath. The windows in here were covered so that no sunlight would penetrate the room. I could bathe for as long as I wanted without worrying about the sun's rays.

I looked into the mirror as the bath filled. My back was still scarred, my body hard with muscle, yet I didn't think of myself as ugly anymore. The scars weren't my best feature, but they proved that I'd survived some pretty tough situations. No matter what life threw at me, I could handle it.

The tub filled and I turned off the water. I sank down and closed my eyes. I wouldn't sleep. I didn't need to. But I could enjoy these quiet few moments alone.

6

I felt beyond relaxed when I headed downstairs the following night. For once, I was going to head out, do something dangerous, and wasn't going to torture myself over it. Last night had done me some serious good. It was as if all the stresses of my entire life had bled away into a small little ball tucked in my gut. I could feel it there, but refused to let it expand and overwhelm me.

Ethan was sitting at the table sipping coffee when I came down. His hair was mussed and he looked as if he'd just gotten up a few minutes ago.

"Sleep well?" I asked, surprised at how chipper I sounded.

Ethan grumbled something into his coffee.

I laughed and stretched. My body creaked nearly as much as my leather. I was feeling a little stiff and there was a headache lurking, but I had a feeling that had more to do with what I drank the night before than anything major.

I grabbed my coat off the back of a chair and folded it over my arm. "I'm going to head out. I've got a few things to take care of tonight."

"Where?" Ethan managed through a yawn.

"Not sure. I'm hoping once I get going, I'll figure it out."

He frowned slightly into his mug.

"I'm not holding out on you," I said. "I really don't know where

I'm going tonight. I want to take care of the Left Hand, but don't know where to look. I'll drive around a bit, see what I can find."

"K." Ethan sighed and gulped down his steaming mug of coffee. I had no idea how he didn't scald himself. "I'm going to have a shower."

He lumbered past me as if his clothes were weighing him down. I wondered how long he'd stayed up after I'd gone to soak in the tub. I hadn't paid much attention to whether he'd even gone to bed at all.

I watched him ascend the stairs and stagger into the bathroom. As soon as the door was closed, I headed downstairs for my gear.

Ethan had checked over some of the stuff the night before, telling me he'd stayed up later than he should have. The gun and weapons were resting on top of the table, looking fresh and ready. I checked the Glock to make sure it was fully loaded, and slipped it into the shoulder holster he'd set aside. I was in the process of putting it on when Jeremy came down the stairs.

"Do you want me to come?"

I glanced at him as I finished settling the holster in place. "Not tonight. You should stay here and keep an eye on Ethan."

"I could call Jonathan and he could send someone else to sit with him."

I paused with my belt halfway around my waist. It wouldn't be such a bad idea to have someone watching my back. The Left Hand had snuck up on me before. They'd done the same to countless vampires and werewolves. As much as I wanted to believe I could handle myself, I knew it would be safer to have someone else there with me.

But could I really risk getting Jeremy hurt again?

"I'm just looking tonight," I said. "I don't plan on doing much else."

"And what if you come across the Left Hand?" he asked. "I'm pretty sure you wouldn't simply walk away."

I sighed and finished putting on my belt. I grabbed my knives and sword and sheathed them. My coat came next. It settled around me, hiding the weapons.

"I can take care of myself," I said. "I need to do this alone."

Jeremy looked like he wanted to protest some more. He took a breath like he was going to speak, but it came out as a sigh. He bowed his head and stepped aside.

"I'll be home tonight," I said. "If I'm not back by sunup, call Jonathan; not before."

He nodded.

I started to walk past him, but hesitated. I couldn't leave it at that. "I'll see you tonight. And . . . thank you."

I went up the stairs without waiting for a response.

The garage was stifling as I mounted my Honda and opened the garage doors. Cool air poured over me and I closed my eyes to it. I could feel rain in the air, but it did nothing to dampen my spirits. In fact, I almost welcomed it.

I took my time as I headed for the city. While I was out looking for the Left Hand, I wasn't going to go at it with the fierce tenacity I typically did things. If I did that, I'd make a mistake. I couldn't jump into something before I was ready to deal with the consequences of my actions. I needed to stop, evaluate, and do things the right way. I'm not sure when I got away from doing it that way.

As I headed for the main part of the city, I considered what I knew.

The Left Hand was in Columbus, that much was obvious. They hunted supes and if what Jonathan said was true, they were also going after Purebloods who spent time with supes. They'd somehow managed to get onto Cult property to set up a crucified werewolf.

But where had they taken him? Had he already been near the Den when they took him? Had he been out on a hunt of some sort? He was new and inexperienced, so I doubted he was out alone.

So how did they take him?

I knew within moments that I needed to go to the abandoned portion of the old college campus. There might be clues that would help me understand what had happened and how they'd managed to do so much, so fast, without anyone else noticing.

Since I was already heading that way, all I had to do was speed up. I could peek around the campus for a little while, maybe investigate the part of the college still in use, then head to the Den to ask Jonathan more questions. It was looking more and more like someone on the inside was responsible for this and I had a pretty good idea who to blame.

Keira. Her appearance was just too convenient. She might not have done the actual deed, but I had a feeling she was the one who'd disabled the cameras and distracted Jonathan long enough so that the wolf could be set up without the perpetrators being discovered.

I reached Cult property and slowed. The roads here were dangerous. Many were blocked off by debris intentionally placed so that anyone who might wander onto the property would be forced down a path the Cult could monitor. Someone on foot was okay, but no one would be getting around this part of the old campus with a vehicle.

Still, I did as good a job as I could, exploring. I'd hoped to find someplace where a broken-down car had been moved or a fallen tree had been shoved aside, but everything looked as if it hadn't been touched. It would have been hard for the Left Hand to get a crucified wolf, unconscious or not, all the way in front of the Den. Either they had someone really strong carrying him, or they'd worked well together. I was sure they'd moved him at least part of the way in a vehicle of some sort.

That meant the garage. While the Cult were the only ones to use it, if there was someone working from the inside, helping the Left Hand, chances were good they would have told them about the garage. It would allow the Left Hand to park somewhere that wasn't out in the open, that was relatively close to the Den itself, and still get Philip on his cross there.

I headed for the garage, not quite sure I bought it. They could have come at the Den from another angle. Maybe they'd come from the other part of the campus. As far as I knew, the Left Hand had set up headquarters among the college kids. Someone there could be housing them, someone who'd discovered the Luna Cult hideout by accident one night after a party.

I neared the garage, but didn't pull in. Instead, I shut off the engine and sat there, looking at the opening. I tried to picture someone carrying a cross out of there.

I just couldn't do it. It would have been too easy for someone from the Den to happen by them.

So where?

Before I could restart the motorcycle's engine, someone appeared. He was walking briskly from the direction of the Den. He was big and kept his head down so I didn't get a good look at his face.

Still, I would know that build anywhere.

He vanished into the garage. I walked my Honda back into the deeper shadows where he might not see me. A few minutes later, a car drifted out of the garage and turned down the road. I caught a quick glimpse of the face through the window and my heart started racing.

Nathan.

I waited until he turned a corner, started up the engine, and took off after him.

My first inclination was to race to catch up with him. I wanted to pull him right out of the car and demand to know what he was doing. Maybe Keira wasn't the one who'd betrayed Jonathan this time. Nathan hadn't been around when the Denmaster had needed him most.

Of course, if I were to try to catch him, he'd see me coming. In which case, I'd never learn where he was going.

I kept my lights off until we were out on the main roads. I made sure to stay well back, knowing that if he even thought I was following him, he would change direction. I tried to come up with reasons for why he'd leave alone, especially with everything that was going on, but I kept coming back to the fact that when I was at the Den, discussing the murder, Nathan wasn't there.

He drove a good twenty minutes before turning off onto a residential street. I had to wait for him to go a long way down the road before I could follow. There was no one else on the road. I shut off my lights, knowing it would do little good against a werewolf's sight, but hoped for the best anyway.

"Where are you going?" I muttered as I followed.

Just as I started to pull onto the road, I saw the red glow of brake lights reflect off a house. I quickly shut off the engine and walked the Honda off the road, behind a shed where he wouldn't see it if he were to suddenly come back. I hopped off and hurried down the road, hoping I'd catch sight of him before he was gone.

The brake lights glowed for a few moments before winking out. I didn't hear a car engine, so I assumed he'd shut it off instead of driving off.

I came around a slight bend in the road just as Nathan stepped out of the car, which was parked just off the road. He sniffed the air and looked around. I managed to slip behind the corner of a wooden fence before he looked my way. I watched him through the crack.

A light mist started up. He looked to the sky, almost as if irritated by the extremely light rain. It would make it harder to sniff anyone out and would also force anyone inside who might be out.

Was he hunting? It was like a stab to my gut. Jonathan had assured me his wolves didn't go out and hunt like this. I wasn't sure exactly how they got their meat and blood, but from what I could tell, he hadn't been lying.

So did that mean Nathan was going against orders? Was he responsible for some of the bodies that might have been attributed to the Left Hand?

As much as Nathan and I didn't get along, I didn't want to believe he could be capable of something like that. Jonathan had been betrayed more than once, the last being Gregory Hillis, a werewolf who'd joined with Adrian Davis. It had been a mess that had really done a number on Jonathan. If Nathan were to go against his Denmaster's wishes, I didn't want to know how it would affect him.

Nathan, seemingly satisfied no one was watching him, started suddenly forward. I slipped out from around the corner of the fence and gave chase, keeping myself low to the ground, using his car for cover.

While there were quite a few empty houses here, there were also some where the lights were still blazing inside. It was still early enough so that some of the more daring Purebloods had yet to shut down for the night. Perhaps some were planning on a night out, even now. There was a reason High Street and places like that were so popular.

Nathan darted in and out of yards, avoiding some entirely. One of the ones he skipped had a light above the back door. I knew without having to test it myself that it was a motion detector light. It appeared the big wolf had done this before.

Unease grew the farther we went. Why had he parked so far away? Was he meeting someone out here? It seemed the only reasonable explanation.

I followed Nathan's path as near as I dared. If he'd done this more than once, he would know where the alarms were. Just because some of the Purebloods here kept lights on, didn't mean they were stupid. The moment an alarm went off, they could vanish into a bolt hole, perhaps a panic room built to withstand a werewolf or vampire until help arrived.

Something howled in the distance and Nathan froze. He sniffed the air again and I cringed back, thankful the rain was starting to pick up. Vampires didn't put out much of a scent and the rain only helped to obliterate it, though my leather would be obvious if he got a good whiff of it.

I cringed back, knowing that if he turned around, he'd have me. There wasn't anywhere to hide here.

Thankfully, he started forward again. He went about six paces more before veering off into a yard surrounded by a low hedge that looked as if no one had cared for it for years. He shifted his weight and slid along sideways until he was facing the house across the street. He remained crouched there as if waiting for something.

I moved as close as I dared before stepping off Nathan's chosen path. I went the long way around the yard to where a rusted metal shed stood. I crept along the side and then peeked around the corner.

A light was on in the house across the street. A large glass back door gave a good look into the house. An old woman sat at a dining room table, sipping from a teacup. She was in a wheelchair and was clearly having trouble lifting the cup to her lips. Her hands were shaking so badly, it was a wonder she didn't dump it into her lap.

A moment later, a younger woman came into view. She looked like she might be in her forties, but it was hard to tell at this distance. She patiently took the cup from the older woman's hand and held it to her lips for her.

And that's when the older woman started to cry.

Nathan started to lift from his crouch and I reached for my gun. I didn't know what he was thinking, but I would *not* let him harm either of those two women. I didn't care that he might be only killing the elderly and sick, putting them out of their misery while sating his own hunger. I'd kill him before I let him hurt someone else.

The woman wiped at her eyes and smiled at the younger woman. Nathan eased back down as if the smile had changed his mind. He was breathing fast and hard, but wasn't shifting.

Yet.

The young woman walked out of view again as the other woman started flipping through a book. I couldn't be sure, but I thought it might be some sort of photo album. She sighed heavily and then looked toward the back door.

Nathan stiffened and ducked down, but before anything else could happen, the younger woman returned and closed a curtain over the back door.

My hand was still on my gun as Nathan rose from his crouch. He was facing the house and I could tell he was considering approaching. The light inside snapped off, leaving the home dark except for a single, upstairs light that looked as if it might be a candle.

A low growl was my only warning.

The wolf came out of nowhere. I managed to turn and raise an arm just as the were leapt at me from the other yard. She was fully shifted and, like all weres, was naked. She was tall, her fur dark.

The wolf was on me before I could pull my gun. She hit me hard in the chest, knocking my hand away from my Glock before I could draw. We slammed hard into the metal shed, causing it to clang loudly. Teeth snapped at my face and it was all I could do to keep an arm up so her fangs didn't close on my flesh.

I reached down in an attempt to get at my sword or one of my knives, but my coat was trapped closed. The werewolf was strong and no matter how hard I pushed, I couldn't get her to back off. She snapped and snarled in my face, splattering me with warm saliva.

She had me pinned to the side of the shed, one hand completely useless. The other I had jammed at her throat and I pressed with all my might in an effort to keep her from biting my face off and to choke off her air supply. I was beginning to tremble and knew that if something didn't give soon, my arm would give out.

I opened my mouth to call out for Nathan, knowing he would be pissed at me for following him, but at that moment, I didn't care. I needed help.

Before I could yell for him, another snarl brought both our heads around. A new were, this one smaller than the one holding me, crashed into the female wolf. Her grip on me loosened and both wolves went rolling out into the open.

I drew both my gun and sword as soon as I was able and took aim at the fighting wolves. Neither was familiar, though it was hard to tell in their wolf forms. I only was sure that neither was Nathan.

The fight was quick and I didn't have to shoot, which meant I still might avoid Nathan's detection. I wasn't sure if he'd stuck around to watch the fight or if he'd taken off at the first howl. I wasn't about to look either. I kept my gaze locked on the snarling wolves.

Werewolves are violent naturally, but something about this fight went far beyond the normal. The little one wasn't as strong as the bigger female, but he fought with a tenacity the other couldn't match.

With a yelp, the female rolled away from the male and took off running. The smaller let her go.

He turned to me and I raised my gun. "Don't try it," I said, ready to pull the trigger at the first aggressive move. He might have saved my skin, but that didn't mean he would let me walk away. He might have simply wanted me all to himself.

The werewolf studied me a moment and then started shifting. He cried out as the change overtook him and I was forced to look away. It was an extremely painful process that wasn't pleasant to witness. I was thankful as a vampire I didn't have to go through that.

A moment later, a man stood before me, nude as the day he was born. Sweat and rain glistened on his body. He turned his face up to the sky and took deep, gasping breaths, before locking eyes with me.

He didn't say anything. He stared at me for a good five seconds before turning and walking away.

Surprisingly, I let him go.

I lowered my gun, but kept it in hand, waiting for him to vanish completely from sight before risking a look around the corner. I doubted he would have stuck around, but I needed to know for sure.

The hedge was empty.

Nathan was gone.

7

My first instinct was to drive straight to the Den and confront Jonathan about Nathan's activities. I didn't care whether the Cult's second was there or not. I'd accuse him just like I would anyone else. If he was up to something, Jonathan deserved to know about it.

Then again, hadn't Jonathan acted as if he knew what Nathan was doing when I'd asked about him the other night? Did that mean he was allowing his weres to hunt again? Was that even what Nathan had been doing?

I wasn't sure what I would do if Jonathan were letting the Cult werewolves feed. I don't think I could kill him, but it would put a pretty quick halt on us working together. Werewolves weren't like vampires, who could simply drink a little blood and leave their victims alive if they chose. They needed the meat too. Hard to keep someone alive when you're eating their flesh.

I went as far as to start in the direction of the Den, but turned for home instead. I wasn't positive Nathan was up to anything sinister and if I were to go to Jonathan without thinking about what I planned on saying, chances were good I'd fuck things up.

And that's not to mention the fact that Keira might be there. I had a sinking feeling she'd been the female wolf who'd attacked me. Going to the Den now might end up in a bloodbath.

It was a surprising moment of clarity for me. The old me would have gone straight to the Den to demand answers. I would have alienated the people who might actually be my friends, all because I didn't know what was going on. Cooling down seemed like a far safer course of action for everyone.

Still, it wasn't easy to turn away from the confrontation. The beast inside demanded blood and it was hard not to give in. I'd have to feed soon or I wouldn't be able to control myself at all. I'd probably end up hurting someone I cared about, all in a hunger-induced frenzy.

The rain was really falling by the time I pulled up the driveway. It just added another reason to get somewhere cozy and warm while I sorted through things. If I'd gone to the Den, I would have had a longer drive to get back home and would have been soaked even worse. I had a feeling this was going to be one of those night-long rains.

There wasn't a dry bone in my body as I parked in the garage. I shivered and shut off the engine. I sat there for a long moment, calming myself down. I was angry. I couldn't go inside pissed at the world. This was the sort of thing I was trying to avoid.

It took me a few minutes before I felt like I could face Ethan and Jeremy without finding something to nitpick. I entered through the side door and peeled off my coat. Despite the leather, it felt as if my underclothes were just as soaked as the rest of me. It felt like I might never get dry again.

I sludged my way into the dining room and deposited my coat on the table to dry. I should have asked Jeremy if I could take his car since I knew it was going to rain. There'd been no reason for me to go driving around in the downpour on my Honda when I could have kept myself nice and dry in the car.

Then again, I might not have been able to follow Nathan if I'd been in the car. He would have spotted the black car almost immediately.

I sat down to peel off my boots. They came away with a plop. My socks were soaked through.

"Wet night," Jeremy said from the couch. I hadn't even seen him there when I'd come in.

"Very."

"Find anything out?"

I shook my head and set my boots under the table. I'd have to take them down and light a fire later so they could fully dry. Otherwise, I'd be walking in wet boots tomorrow night. The same went for my coat and leathers.

Jeremy hesitated like he saw something in my face that said I wasn't telling him something, which of course, I wasn't. I didn't want to accuse Nathan or Keira of anything until I had some proof.

"Where's Ethan?" I asked, rising. My socks made wet squelching sounds as I walked across the linoleum. I paused long enough to pull them off so I wouldn't track water through the house.

"Downstairs." Jeremy turned back to the TV.

I studied the werewolf for a moment, wondering if he was mad at me. While he'd been the one to initiate conversation, I hadn't actually given him much in the way of answers. I definitely needed to work harder at including him, though it wasn't going to happen tonight.

"Thanks," I said, heading for the stairs. I wanted out of my wet clothes in the worst way. I could deal with Jeremy in a bit.

I closed my bedroom door and went about the slow process of peeling out of my leather. Wet leather doesn't like coming off. At times, it almost felt as if it wasn't worth it and I should simply lay down in front of a fire for a few hours before trying again.

Thankfully, the leather wasn't exactly tight. I preferred motorcycle leathers, the loose kind that are strong enough to save you from scraping yourself too badly if you hit the pavement, but not so tight as to restrict movement, so I was able to get them off before growing too frustrated. I hung them on the edge of the hamper, figuring I'd go down and put them in front of the fire once I was dry and changed.

I shivered again and decided it would be a good idea to get a warm shower before doing anything else. I wouldn't get sick from the chill, but it was uncomfortable. The hot water would serve as a quick fix in warming me up through and through.

I jacked the heat up and stepped inside the cascading water. I closed my eyes and simply let it wash over me. It melted all of the stress away, warming my chilled bones. It felt so good, it took me a moment to realize something was wrong.

I slammed my hand against the wall before I could fall. Everything was spinning and there was a churning in my gut that made my knees weak.

I slid down to my knees and fought the urge to retch. I was breathing fast and hard, unable to catch my breath. My body was covered with goose bumps despite the fact the water was almost as hot as it would go.

Steam blurred my vision and I closed my eyes against a world that refused to sit still. I hitched in a breath and held it, knowing that if I were to try to breathe normally, I'd end up puking all over myself.

And that's when the pain hit.

It came from right behind my ear, where Beligral's mark was raised. I screamed and collapsed to all fours where I vomited non-stop for at least ten agonizing seconds. The water washed it away almost immediately, but the smell filled my nose and wouldn't go away. It smelled worse than the stuff Ethan had given me to drink the night before.

I threw up again.

I jerked my head back as another wave of pain hit. My skull cracked hard against the side of the tub and my knees bent back the wrong way, but I was past the point of caring. Stars were flashing in my vision and the world did another slow loop that just about had me flat on my back.

The bathroom door burst open, but I kept my eyes closed. Wave after wave of pure agony shot through my head, blinding me to anything but the pain. I was gagging and shaking so badly, it was like having a seizure.

The shower curtain was jerked back and I was pretty sure I heard it tear. Someone spoke, but the pain not only blinded me, it had struck me mostly deaf. I doubted I'd have made sense of the words even if I could've heard them over the ocean of sound going on within my head.

A hand took me by the shoulders and gently shook.

And just like that, the pain was gone.

My eyes snapped open to find Jeremy leaning into the shower. His hair was soaked. Water ran into his eyes, yet he didn't seem to care. His one good hand was holding me down, as if he feared I might leap up and rip out his throat.

"Kat?" he asked. He sounded terrified. "What's happening?"

I swallowed back the rush of bile that was still assaulting me. The pain might be gone, but I still felt woozy. "Let me up," I said. My voice came out gravelly. I probably looked as bad as I sounded.

Jeremy leaned back, but kept his hand on me. I used his arm to lift myself into a sitting position. My head was still swimming horribly and I was forced to lean back against the tile to steady myself. Standing was completely out of the question.

I blindly reached out and turned off the shower. The water was still hot, meaning my attack hadn't lasted long, though it felt as if it had taken a lifetime.

"Here."

I opened one eye. Jeremy was holding a towel out to me. He was looking the other way.

"Thanks," I said, taking the towel from him. I draped it across my legs and chest and crossed my arms over it to keep it in place.

Jeremy glanced at me and, noting that I was covered, turned to face me once again. "I heard you scream," he said. I was surprised to hear how much worry was in his voice.

"I'm okay," I said, though I was far from it. I knew what had happened. It pissed me off to no end. I wasn't sure how much Jeremy knew of Ethan's demon, so I wasn't about to explain things to him. I didn't want to scare him away.

Jeremy licked his lips and sat back on his heel. He wiped his hand down his face to sluice away most of the water. Droplets dripped from his hair onto his shirt, which clung appealingly against his chest.

God, I must have hit my head harder than I thought.

"I thought someone had gotten in somehow," he said. "Christ." He laughed shakily. "I thought you were dying."

"I'm fine." I took hold of the faucet and used it to leverage my way to my feet. I swayed a moment before steadying. "But I have to talk to Ethan. Now."

Jeremy rose with me. He kept looking at me and then looking away. It took me a moment to realize I'd loosened my grip on my towel. It had been hanging down around my waist and the poor were had no idea where to look.

"Help me out," I said, reaching out a hand. I wasn't going to be embarrassed by my nudity. He was a werewolf; he should be used to that sort of thing by now.

Jeremy hesitated a moment before taking my hand. He kept his eyes averted, which was actually sort of endearing. The poor kid was embarrassed and trying damn hard not to let it show.

My legs were weak and shaky, but I was able to step over the lip of the tub and out onto the floor without falling. Now that the pain had passed and I was able to move again, anger was starting to creep in. I could have cracked my skull in there. I could have drowned. The fucking demon had probably planned it that way.

"Do you need me to stay?" Jeremy asked. "I can wait outside if you need me to help you downstairs."

"I'll be okay," I said. "I just need a few minutes to get changed and I'll be down."

Jeremy nodded, but didn't leave right away. He looked into my face, studied me as if trying to decide if I were really okay. I forced a smile and that seemed to do it for him. He turned and walked out of the bathroom, though I did notice him glance back over his shoulder once before he was gone. I wasn't sure if that last gaze was to check on me or to check me out. I was flattered either way.

The bedroom door closed a moment later, leaving me alone in the privacy of my room. My entire body ached as I dried off. The mark behind my ear was throbbing now and the scar on my back had flared up during the attack. My fingers were tingling oddly and I had a sudden fear that something worse had happened while I'd been suffering, something permanent.

I shook off the thought. There was no use dwelling on it. If I didn't get better by the time I was done with Beligral, I'd break the demon's goddamned neck.

Once dry, I grabbed clean underwear, a pair of jeans, and a T-shirt and pulled them on. My boots were downstairs and still wet, so I snatched a dirty pair of tennis shoes out of the closet and slipped them on. I took a few deep breaths to calm myself before leaving my room.

Jeremy was waiting for me in the dining room. He watched me, face full of concern, but didn't rush over to help when I swayed on the bottom step. If I'd asked, I was sure he'd be there in an instant. He realized I wanted to do this on my own. It was built into the both of us.

I was still having a hard time putting one foot in front of the other without stumbling, so I leaned against the wall before heading all the way downstairs. It wouldn't do to show weakness in front of the demon. He'd take too much pleasure in it.

It was then I noticed Jeremy was holding his phone. By the way he was squeezing it, I could tell he had yet to make a call.

"Don't call him," I said. "I'll take care of this. There's nothing he can do."

Jeremy nodded and slid his phone into his back pocket like he'd known that from the get-go.

I gave him a thankful nod and then headed down the next flight of stairs.

The fireplace was cold in the sitting room. I wanted a warm fire more than ever, but it would have to wait. I couldn't put this off any longer. If I waited, chances were good Beligral would send more pain to remind me of my mark. The next time he did, I might not be standing in a shower. I could be riding my motorcycle. If that happened, I'd probably break my neck.

I took the stairs into the basement slowly, trying hard to manage my anger. I really didn't want to do this. I was afraid of what I might say to the demon once we were face to face.

As soon as I was in the basement, I resolutely made my way to the door that led down into Ethan's lab and pressed the intercom button.

"Ethan," I said, sounding far angrier than I wanted. I needed to calm down fast. I really didn't need Beligral pissed off at me any more than he already was.

It took him only a moment to answer, as if he knew I'd be coming. "I'm here." He paused. "What's up?"

I took a deep breath and grimaced. It tasted horrible, like bile and raw sewage. My hair was still wet and I think I'd puked in it, which only added to the stench. I felt like hell, yet there was no turning back now.

I glanced at the table with my weapons. What I wouldn't give to take them down with me, but knew that would only irritate Beligral. What came out of my mouth was probably already going to be bad enough.

"Open the door," I said. "I need to talk to your demon."

There was a pause, followed by a faint, "Oh."

A moment later, the door clunked open.

8

The lab was cool and demon-free as I descended the stairs. I looked around, noted that everything looked pretty much the same as the last time I'd seen it, including the cage at the far end of the room, and then turned to face Ethan.

He was watching me, red-faced. There were no half-finished weapons on the table, nor were there used weapons in need of cleaning. There was no hint that he'd summoned Beligral that night at all, or had had any intention of doing so until I'd arrived. I briefly wondered what he'd been doing down here by himself, but decided I probably didn't want to know.

"I need to speak to your demon," I said, glancing around the room again. The circle was still there, clear of debris and dust like always. The chair remained in the center, though I thought it looked as if it might have been turned a little so it faced the doorway more fully. I wasn't sure if that meant anything or not.

Ethan bit his lower lip when my eyes fell on him again. "You sure?"

I gave him a flat look.

"Right," he said with a shaky laugh. He turned and gathered his supplies.

I'd seen Ethan do this a few times, yet each time, it surprised me that someone like him could do something like this. He didn't seem the type. He'd been doing it since he was a kid and I wondered how he ever got himself into a situation where he felt the need to summon a demon. I mean, people didn't just suddenly decide to start summoning demons because their life wasn't going the way they'd hoped. Something had to have happened.

I'm not sure if I'd ever ask him. It felt too invasive.

Ethan set up his flesh candles and drew a chalk outline around the silver circle set in the concrete. He glanced up every few moments to check on me and I caught a hint of pity in his eyes.

I looked away. It was my fault I was marked. I kept calling it *his* demon, but really, I was just as involved as he was. Every time I came down here, I was making deals with Beligral when common sense should keep me from doing something so mind-numbingly stupid. Yet somehow, he always knew what to say to hook me. It's what made him so dangerous.

Not this time, I promised myself. *He won't get me this time.*

If only it were that easy. What he usually offered was a way for me to help someone I cared about. He'd allowed me to see Levi for what he really was. He'd checked my brother, Thomas, to see if his mind could be saved. Each time I took on a mark, I did so out of my own free will to help someone else.

Still, I didn't feel any better about what I was doing.

I sulked in the corner as Ethan finished setting up the circle. No matter what happened here, I was determined to walk away mark free. Maybe someday, once I was clear of the demon's influence, and clear of some of my other troubles, I'd find a way to set Ethan free.

He started his low chant, something he told me wasn't entirely necessary, but somehow helped him focus. He was already starting to sweat, though the heat had yet to build in the room. I straightened and braced myself for what was to come.

The dark speck appeared in the middle of the circle. It was little more than a black, button-sized hole in the fabric of reality. Heat poured from it. It blasted into me and knocked me back a step, though I thought I'd been prepared for it. I was forced to shield my eyes from the heat, causing me to miss the demon's emergence.

I felt, more than heard, the tear between realms. I tried to see past the waves of heat, but it was impossible. I caught a glimpse of red skin and black wings, and perhaps a horn or two, through my parted fingers before his glamour took hold and he was just another man, dressed in a suit and tie. This time, he was wearing a bowler hat. He tipped it my way as the portal closed behind him.

"It's so lovely to see you, my dear," he said with a smile. His teeth were yellow and sharp.

"You didn't leave me much choice." I wiped sweat from my brow and lowered my hand. It felt like I was standing in an oven.

Beligral leaned on a cane that suddenly appeared in his hand. "Enough time had passed," he said, glancing casually around the room. His gaze passed right over Ethan as if he weren't even there. "I thought it was a good time to remind you of what you owe me."

"Oh, I haven't forgotten." I stared into the circle, but refused to look directly into the demon's eyes. It was far too easy to get trapped in his gaze.

Ethan edged his way to his workbench where he sat down and started chewing his nails. He was watching us, almost as if he knew something was coming and was simply waiting for it to happen.

"So what do you want?" I demanded. I tried to sound tough, but damn it, Beligral scared the hell out of me. Even trapped within the circle, he was dangerous. One mistake and something very, very bad could happen. Yet even though I knew that, I kept coming back for more.

What exactly did that say about me?

"I'm simply interested in your paying off your mark, is all," Beligral said. "There is no reason for you to be angry."

Yeah, right, I thought, but wisely kept my mouth shut. Somehow I knew he'd get too much pleasure out of me voicing my doubts.

About a thousand questions shot through me right then. I'd sworn to myself that I wouldn't ask anything of the demon, yet now that he was there, I couldn't help but think about everything he might be able to help me with. There was Delai, of course, but what about the Left Hand? Could he do something that would allow me to find them without having to search the entire damn city?

I groaned inwardly. There was no way I could simply walk away from the demon. He knew too much that could help me. The bastard had me and he knew it.

"What can you tell me of the Left Hand?" I asked, chancing a glance up toward Beligral's face.

His smile was knowing as he turned and strode over to his chair. He took off his hat, twirled it on his finger a few times before sitting. He slung a leg over the armrest and sat back, looking as comfortable as could be. The hat was gone, as was the cane.

"The Left Hand," he said, acting as if he was mulling it over. "What do I know of the Left Hand?"

I shifted uncomfortably from foot to foot. I knew he was drawing this out on purpose. He would do anything to keep a hold on me and I bet he was trying to find something he could use to coax me into a mark without actually telling me anything. It was the way he worked. I'd only gain something if I took on another mark.

But I refused to let that happen. I would find a way to get the information from him without getting marked. There had to be a way, right? All I had to do was push him the right way and he might let something slip.

I knew I was fooling myself. If demons were that easy to manipulate, then everyone would be doing it.

I clenched my jaw and stared hard at Beligral's knees while he continued to hem and haw.

Finally, he shrugged and swung his leg to the floor. "They are of no importance," he said. The cane reappeared and he gently tapped it on the floor. "They are but pureblooded nuisances, are they not? Hardly worth your effort."

"So you can't tell me anything about them?"

"I didn't say that," he said with a smile.

I growled deep in my throat. "Can you tell me anything meaningful about the Left Hand?"

He seemed to consider it before shrugging. "Nothing that would help you do what you wish." He stood and began pacing. The cane was gone again.

"Then we have nothing to talk about," I said, turning away. I wasn't going to stand there and let him toy with me any longer. If I got out now, I might avoid another mark for good.

"I wouldn't be so sure about that."

Something in his voice made my breath catch in my throat. The room seemed suddenly hotter, which I knew was something he could do at will. My legs felt weak and my head started swimming again, as if I was having a relapse of my attack in the shower.

I staggered to the side and had to brace myself on the wall, lest I fall. My mark felt scalding hot. I wondered why it wasn't gone yet. Usually, his marks vanished as soon as we started talking.

"There are things we should discuss," Beligral said. "I've put it off because there hasn't been a reason for me to bring it up in anything more than passing. I am starting to wonder if now might be the time."

I turned back to him. The demon was standing right at the edge of the circle, so close, his foot was nearly touching the silver. Ethan was standing by his workbench, looking nervous as hell. I don't think he was positive Beligral couldn't escape.

"I've let our friend here continue on with this farce for long enough," the demon said. "I could let him keep trying, but I know he will never find the answer. He doesn't have the knowledge for it, the resources."

"What are you talking about?" I cleared my throat, hating how my voice had come out sounding weak. I was shaking all over. Whatever he was doing to me, I was at the demon's mercy. It was either hear him out or pass out and I sure as hell wasn't going to do the latter. There's no telling what he'd do with me while I was unconscious.

"In time, in time." Beligral grinned and stretched. He actually yawned before walking slowly around the circle, eyes on the room as if he was investigating it for the very first time.

"It is interesting what you have done with the place," he said after a few moments. "A cage is something meant to hold things inside, yet I have never seen anyone or anything contained within." He took a deep breath, and let it out with a sigh. "But I can smell the wolf. He comes for a few nights and then leaves again. Who is this wolf?"

I glanced at Ethan. He shook his head with the slightest of motions. He hadn't told the demon about Jeremy.

"A friend," I said. "Is that what you want to talk to me about? Because if it is, I'm done."

"No, but it interests me."

The stairs were right there. All I had to do was turn around and walk away. The mark still might be there, but I had a feeling that once things ended here, it would go away. He normally just asks that I come back to see him, which is exactly what I'd done. I didn't have to hang around any longer than I had to.

But I knew I'd always wonder. I couldn't walk away if there was a chance he could tell me something that would help me.

"This wolf," the demon said. "He is more than a friend, is he not? He is someone important to you?"

I shrugged. "As much as a werewolf can be, I guess."

He glanced at me as he continued his circuit around the inside of the circle. "But he isn't the one, is he? He is just the beginning."

I frowned. I had no idea what he meant. "If you don't get to the point soon, I'm leaving."

Beligral chuckled. "I feel that the day is coming when my services will no longer be required. You are gaining power of your own, power that you hardly know what to do with."

"That doesn't sound like a bad thing," I said.

He laughed again, this time a full-throated laugh that shook the walls, before turning his burning gaze on me. "But with that power, you will lose something you so desperately want."

"Yeah," I said, swallowing hard. It was a struggle not to meet his eye. "What's that?"

"Your humanity."

I couldn't help it. My eyes rose to meet his own. Our gazes locked and he had me. I couldn't look away. I could feel him rooting around inside my head and there was nothing I could do to stop it. I felt paralyzed, weaker than I'd ever felt before.

"Stop," Ethan said. I could feel him next to me, but couldn't look away from the demon long enough to reassure myself he wasn't going to do something stupid. "Stop now or I'll send you back."

Beligral held my gaze a moment longer before turning away.

My entire body sagged as if his stare had been the only thing holding me up. I leaned against the wall, breath coming fast and hard. I felt like I'd just gone twenty rounds with a dozen very pissed-off werewolves. My chest burned and my head thumped so hard, it felt like my skull might explode.

"Are you okay?" Ethan whispered, resting a hand on my wrist.

I nodded and forced myself to stand erect. "I'm leaving," I said. "We're done. Don't *ever* bother me again." I turned away, this time fully intent on leaving for good. I could no longer feel the mark behind my ear. Apparently, it had vanished sometime during our little staring contest. I was free.

My foot hit the first step just as the demon spoke.

"I can make you human again."

I froze.

I could feel his eyes on my back, could almost feel the knowing smile he was directing my way.

He had me and he knew it.

I turned slowly around. My hands were balled into fists. I felt like I might shake apart from the inside.

"What?" I managed. My lips didn't want to move.

He laughed. "I see I finally have your attention."

"What did you say?" I took a step toward him, legs wobbly.

"No, Kat," Ethan grabbed at my arm, but I shook him off. "Don't listen to him."

"I can purify your blood so that the taint, as you call it, will no longer be present," Beligral said. "You won't need to feed ever again. This isn't a temporary cure. You will be a pureblooded human."

I swallowed. Was he serious?

"But this is something I will not give freely," he added.

I stopped about a foot away from the circle and stared at him. I was looking at his face, yet he didn't try to capture me within his gaze this time. He just stood there, smiling as if he knew exactly what I was going to do.

"What do you need?" I asked, hating myself for even thinking of going through with this. I knew he was just trying to trap me again, that it was some sort of trick, but I couldn't help myself. To be human again . . .

Beligral sighed. "For now? Nothing. There are a few . . . problems standing in our way. Until they are taken care of, I can do nothing for you. But I assure you, this thing can be done."

"How?"

He walked over to the chair and sat down, seemingly bored. "There is no need to discuss this further now. I've made my point. You know I can do this, though you might not like the methods when I tell them to you. As it stands now, you are not ready. There is too much you have to do and far too much to lose." He smiled.

Right then, I hated him beyond anything I thought possible. He tempted me with my humanity, with the purification of my blood, and then he was going to shut down and not tell me how it could be done. It was almost too cruel, even for a demon.

"I'll show myself out," he said, standing.

Rage blurred my vision and I very nearly leapt forward, into the circle, intent on strangling him.

Somehow, I held back.

"Tell me," I said through clenched teeth. "You can't walk away now."

Beligral watched me with glee in his eyes. I think he wanted me to attack him. If I broke the circle, he'd be free to do as he pleased.

After a few moments, he sighed. "Pity," he said, waving a hand. The tear between worlds ripped open, spilling heat out over me. "I'll be waiting for the moment when you are ready." He turned and stepped through the portal.

"No!" I shouted, lunging forward, but it was already too late.

The heat vanished and I sagged to the floor, half in, half out of the circle. Tears were on my face, but I couldn't bring myself to wipe them away.

"Don't listen to him," Ethan said, kneeling beside me. "I'll find a blood substitute. You don't ever have to deal with him again."

I looked at him numbly. "No more blood," I whimpered. I sounded like a scolded child. "I could be free of it."

Ethan took me by both arms and stared hard into my eyes. "No," he said. "You don't want this." He gave me a gentle shake when my eyes drifted back to the circle. "He lies. Please, Kat—I know him. He won't cure you. He'll do something that will destroy you."

He's never lied to me before.

I looked down at my hands and took a few deep breaths. "I'm okay," I said. "I just let him get to me."

"You're free," Ethan said. "You don't have to come back here ever again. You're not marked." He sounded both relieved and jealous at the same time.

I nodded and let Ethan help me to my feet.

"Don't let him trick you," he said.

I nodded again, unable to speak. I walked slowly toward the stairs, leaving Ethan alone in his lab.

Ethan was wrong. Beligral hadn't marked me physically. He didn't need to.

No, this time the mark wasn't physical.

It was mental.

And it was going to be far harder to rid myself of it.

9

By the next night, I was officially a mess. I couldn't get what Beligral said out of my head. Could I really be human again? Did I even want to be? It had been so long since I'd seen the sun, it seemed like it had happened to someone else. To see it again would be a blessing, but at what cost?

And that was the rub. I couldn't quite see myself stepping away from my current life, no matter how much I might want to. There was too much at stake, too many people who could get hurt if I wasn't around. Just because I might no longer be a vampire, doesn't mean my enemies would just walk away. In fact, they'd be *more* likely to come after me and those I cared about.

Still, I had to admit it was appealing. It was a struggle not to demand Ethan to summon his demon again so I could force him to tell me everything he knew about the process. He said I wouldn't like how it was done, which meant there was no way I was going to walk into it blindly.

But as much as I wanted to hold Beligral down and beat the information out of him, I couldn't do that; there was too much to do. Life wouldn't wait while I sorted things out.

The Left Hand wouldn't wait.

I didn't relish the thought of searching for them, but it didn't stop me from getting dressed, grabbing my weapons, and heading out with a quick good-bye to both Jeremy and Ethan. I could tell Jeremy wanted to come. After one look at me, he decided to step back and let me do what I had to do.

My first thought was to head to the Den to get the mess with Nathan and Keira sorted out. If either one of them were responsible for the Left Hand knowing where the Den was located, I could use them for information. The problem would be, of course, getting that information out of them. Werewolves aren't exactly the easiest of beings to intimidate. Violence wasn't always motivation for them to talk, either.

I decided it might be better, especially in my current mental state, to ride around for a bit. I headed for High Street, thinking that it would be a good place to start in my search for the Left Hand. I'd been attacked in one of the alleyways here. I figured other Left Hand members might find the sleazy street ideal for hunting as well.

The lights were bright, as always, as I coasted down the packed road. Screaming neon and strobing lights came from nearly every building. Windows in the motels that had taken over a large stretch of the road were curtainless. I could see more than my fair share of young girls pressed against the glass while things were done to them, not all of them bloodless.

It seemed busier than usual and I wondered if it had anything to do with the recent murders. Coming to a place like High Street was always dangerous, unlike the Bloody Stake. Here, death could be around the corner, though it rarely happened out in the open. There was a sense of nearly averted disaster with every visit.

I'd like to think most people would be smarter than to head into a private room or down a dark alley with someone they didn't know, but I knew better. The Left Hand could find dozens, if not hundreds of victims here and a good portion of them wouldn't be missed. Why would one death in a dark alley matter when the bloodstains of a hundred others marked the pavement?

I pulled into the gloom of the parking garage and began winding my way around, looking for a place to park. I had no idea how many of these cars were abandoned, left by owners who hadn't come back to retrieve them after a fatal visit with some vamp or wolf.

It wasn't a pleasant thought, but it was reality. Why would I want to become a frail human again?

I found a spot near the top of the garage. I parked and headed back to High Street on foot. While driving around would allow me to cover ground faster, I wouldn't be close enough to the action to get a good look at what was going on.

I squinted into the neon as I stepped out onto the street, amid both men and women wearing tight leather, and began my search.

It didn't take long for my mind to start wandering from my goal. As much I wanted to forget about it, I kept coming back to what Beligral had said. And then there was the whole thing with Nathan. It was bad enough that Monday was approaching and I knew—*knew*—Baset would have a name for me. I was afraid everyone was going to start pulling me in a dozen different directions.

And, of course, there was Adrian. I could feel him ahead of me somewhere. He wasn't home, that was for sure. I vaguely wondered what he was doing and if it would end up getting someone killed.

I was so distracted by my thoughts, I didn't see the sudden movement beside me until it was too late.

I didn't have time to think, let alone react. A huge arm clamped around my arms, trapping them, and another hand covered my mouth so I couldn't scream. I was yanked off my feet and dragged into the shadows of the alley where the noise and light was dimmed to almost nothing.

My fangs instantly dropped, spraying blood into my mouth and onto the hand that held me. I tried to pull away so I could open my mouth enough to bite down, but was held so tightly I could barely move my head. Whoever had me sure as hell wasn't a Pureblood.

I growled deep in my throat and tensed. Tonight was not a night to fuck with me.

"Quiet," Adrian's breath was hot on my ear. "Don't scream. I'm going to let you go. I want to show you something."

Anger flared through me, but I nodded anyway. Screaming wouldn't help. No one would bother checking on me here. I was on my own and there wasn't a damn thing I could do because of the Oath.

Adrian waited a moment longer before releasing me. I immediately spun, hands going for my weapons, but I didn't draw. It would do no good.

"Look," Adrian said, pointing past me. "Watch."

I glanced over my shoulder, but saw nothing. People were walking the streets in groups, and cars coasted down the street, but otherwise, I had no idea what I was supposed to be looking at. I was too pissed to even care—pissed at Adrian for jumping me and pissed at myself for not realizing how close he'd been when I'd felt him through the Oath.

I turned back to him, anger bubbling over. I'd promised myself I'd stop verbally abusing my friends, but Adrian sure as hell wasn't a friend.

"What the fuck is wrong with you?" I didn't quite scream the words, but it was close.

He glanced at me, face blank as ever, and then looked past me again. I honestly think he didn't understand why I was so pissed.

"You must watch if you want to see what I have to show you."

"You were following me, weren't you?"

He didn't respond. He simply continued to stare.

I cursed under my breath and turned the way he was facing. We were deep enough into the alley that no one would notice us. Our view was likewise limited so that all I could see was a short stretch of road, a sidewalk, and the building across the street. I tried to catch faces as they passed, thinking there was someone in particular whom he wanted me to see, but if there was, I didn't. Everyone looked the same to me.

I was about to turn on him again when the door to the building across the street opened. A woman stepped out, looking harried. She wiped at her mouth and I noticed her lips were a little redder than they should be. She checked to make sure no one was watching and then headed for the street where she waited for traffic to ease enough for her to cross.

"Who is that?"

"Wait," Adrian said. Anticipation was heavy in his voice.

A moment later, the door opened again and someone else walked out. The man was wearing a long, brown trench coat and carrying a brown briefcase. He looked quickly around until his eyes fell on the woman. He started toward her, but just then, there was a break in the traffic and she started crossing. He hurried after her.

My breath caught in my throat. Had Adrian actually led me to a member of the Left Hand? If so, how had he known I was looking for them?

I didn't have time to ask. The woman reached our side of the street with the man hot behind her. They both passed our alley without a second glance.

"Let's go."

Adrian moved forward before I could protest. I was left with little choice but to follow. I couldn't let this opportunity pass.

It wasn't hard to follow the two. Adrian kept a good couple of yards between us, which he really didn't need to do. He could have come up right behind the man and no one would have noticed. The streets were so crowded, it was impossible to tell if someone was following you or just heading in the same direction.

I stuck close behind Adrian, not wanting to walk next to him. He might take it as an invitation to talk and I was still pissed at him. Besides, I could watch him better this way. He must have known I was looking for members of the Left Hand. He also had known I would end up here on High Street. I wasn't sure if it was the Oath that was helping him or if someone was tipping him off.

The woman suddenly turned down an alley. The man followed and Adrian was quick on his heels. I dropped my hand to my waist, ready to draw my sword the moment the fighting started. I turned the corner.

Eyes looked up and stared at me through a haze of sweet-smelling smoke. There were a few couples making out against the wall, and at least one was doing it with blood mingled between them. I couldn't tell if they were vampires, werewolves, or just two Purebloods who got off on blood. In the end, it didn't really matter.

Adrian had already passed the group. I could no longer see the woman or her tail, which meant they were moving pretty fast now.

I started after them, but before I took more than three steps, one of the men by the wall stepped in front of me.

"Hey there," he said. He blew smoke out of his nose and looked me up and down with bloodshot eyes. "You lookin' for a little action tonight, baby?"

I slowed long enough to rear back. I didn't have time for this. I punched him right in the mouth and he dropped with a cry of pain.

I stepped over the man, eyes focused on Adrian's retreating back. I figured I'd made my point, but the guy grabbed my foot before I could get past him. Two of his friends stepped away from the wall, blocking off the alley. Two more moved behind to keep anyone else from getting in.

"You stupid bitch," the guy holding my foot said. He jerked hard as if he thought he could take me down. Instead, I spun and kicked him in the teeth, causing his already bloody mouth to spurt.

His grip on my foot loosened as his eyes rolled up into the back of his head. His skull hit the pavement with a crack and I winced, hoping I hadn't accidentally killed him. I wanted them to leave me alone, but didn't want to kill anyone. These were just stupid kids; they didn't deserve to die.

I turned to face his two friends who were keeping me from following after Adrian.

"I'd move if I were you."

They glanced at each other and for a moment. I thought they were going to comply.

Instead, they both smiled and drew long knives from within their coats. They weren't silver, but could do a whole hell of a lot of damage to me if they knew how to use them. The edges looked sharp enough to cut flesh.

I really didn't want to have to fight these guys. From what I could tell, they were simple Purebloods out looking for a good time. They were also high as kites, which meant they weren't thinking too clearly. The couples were still making out against the wall as if nothing was going on.

"I don't want to have to hurt you," I said, which only served to earn me a pair of grins.

That's when Adrian chose to return.

He came out of the shadows like a ghost. He was surprisingly silent for such a big man. He grabbed one of my attackers by the hair and jerked his head back so hard, it was a wonder the guy's neck didn't snap. Adrian spun him around and threw him face-first into the wall. The knife clattered to the littered pavement as the guy collapsed, unconscious.

The second man spun and struck out with his knife. Adrian easily caught his hand well before the blade could come anywhere close to him. He twisted. With a horrendous crack, the man's forearm snapped. With his other hand, Adrian grabbed the guy's hair, jerked his head to the side, and then opened his mouth as if he was going to rip out the man's throat with his teeth.

"No!" I shouted, reaching out and grabbing his hand. It wasn't like I could stop him if he really wanted to strike. I hated to admit it, but Adrian was stronger than I and because of the Oath, I wouldn't be able to hurt him. "Don't kill them. They're just idiots."

Adrian's eyes flashed in anger, but quickly returned to their normal emotionless state. He let go of the man's hair and instead of breaking his neck or ripping out his throat, he reached down and broke the man's other arm before dropping him, screaming, to the ground.

"This way," he said, giving me a look that said more than words that he thought this was somehow my fault. He spun away and hurried down the alley, nose raised, sniffing the air.

The others were watching me now, including the kissing couples. There was fear in their eyes, as well as a sense of excitement. The guy with the broken arms was screaming for someone to take him to the hospital. There was no blood, which was a relief; the bones hadn't broken the skin.

I stepped over the wailing man, wishing I could do something. Just because he was a moron, didn't mean he deserved to suffer.

But if I wanted to catch up to Adrian, I couldn't stick around and help.

I followed him to the end of the alley. He sniffed the air and then turned left, down another street, before slipping into an alley to his right. I tried to stay close, but he was moving fast and there was something about him that worried me. He was tense, almost as if the scuffle had awakened something in him, something that needed to strike out the moment it was able. I wasn't so sure I'd be safe from it if I was in the way when it broke through.

Adrian slowed as we entered the alley. I caught up to him, miffed about how things had ended with the idiot kids.

"I could have handled myself back there," I said. "You didn't need to hurt them."

"I know." He sniffed the air again and then took off at a run.

I cursed loudly and followed after him. He vanished around the corner and I came out just in time to see him tear down another side street.

I could tell by the way he was acting that he'd caught wind of our targets and that we were close. I drew both my gun and sword and jogged after him, knowing this would probably end in a fight. I turned down the side street and nearly collided with Adrian's back.

I was about to grumble at him about warning me next time when I saw what was happening farther down the street.

The woman was fiddling with her keys, standing in front of a door to an apartment complex. She didn't look harried or rushed any longer. In fact, she appeared to almost be delaying herself on purpose.

At first, I didn't see the man with the briefcase. There was a moment when I feared he realized he was being followed and skipped out. I was rewarded a few seconds later when the man came out of a small cubby across the street. A syringe was in his hand.

He moved so silently, it made me wonder if there was something supernatural about him. I knew the Left Hand were good at sneaking up on supes, but seeing it was almost freaky. The were should have sniffed him out before he came anywhere close, yet she didn't seem to notice him inching ever closer.

The man got within a few steps without her turning. If I let him get any closer, he'd inject her with the serum and we might not be able to get to her in time to save her.

And then he made a mistake.

A small chunk of concrete clattered as his foot bumped up against it. He froze in place, but he'd already been discovered.

The woman spun and saw him where he stood, uncertain. Her eyes flashed yellow and she grinned.

The Left Hand man made a lunge for her. She easily batted the syringe from his hand. It clattered to the pavement, somehow not shattering when it hit. She grabbed him by both arms and head-butted him square in the nose. Blood spurted and he cried out, but not in fear. He cursed her and spit in her face, grinning all the while.

Fur sprouted from around her ears and her fingers extended into claws. Her face started to contort and I could hear the snap of bones and muscle from all the way down the street.

"Shit," I cursed, raising my gun. I wanted the guy alive. "Stop!" I shouted. "Don't kill him."

The were glanced at me and I knew it was already too late. Her snout was almost fully extended now, her eyes wild with blood lust. I had but seconds before she would kill him.

"Adrian," I growled. "Do something."

He stood by, watching the scene. He didn't make a move to help.

"Don't kill him," I said again. "I need him alive." My aim firmed on the werewolf.

She snarled at me and before I could pull the trigger, she spun the Left Hand man around, putting him between us. He screamed once, and then blood splattered the pavement. His scream turned into a gurgle as she tore out his throat.

There was a moment when everything seemed to stand still. The guy jerked a few times in her hands and then fell limp. There were tearing sounds coming from the other side of him and I knew she was feeding.

Adrian stepped forward, putting himself between me and the were. He knew I was going to shoot the bitch the moment she dropped her meal and I think he was trying to protect her. He probably planned on recruiting her.

Just then, the sound of a window opening made me look up.

A face appeared, looking down at me. Yellow eyes gleamed in the faint light.

The woman dropped the dead man to the ground. Blood covered her snout and gristle hung from her teeth. She raised her head to the sky and howled.

The door to the apartment building burst open. A window shattered overhead.

Half a dozen werewolves poured into the alley, ready for a fight.

10

Sharp claws lashed out, just barely missing my fingers. My gun clattered to the pavement a few yards away. The wolf snarled and leapt forward, teeth bared. He was already fully shifted, as if he'd been waiting inside for this very moment.

I didn't have time to think. I sure as hell didn't expect to get into a fight like this tonight. I knew there were places where rogue wolves congregated together, but they were often off the beaten path. Having too many werewolves living close together—or like these ones, living together—would typically draw the eye of the local count. These guys must have been damn near model citizens to still be living together like this.

Until now, that is.

I ducked backward, losing my balance as the wolf barreled into me. Hot breath that smelled vaguely of spaghetti washed over me as he snapped at me. He thought he could overpower me with his bulk, but I surprised him by adjusting my fall and using his momentum to fling him over me. I took a knee to the chin and got up close and personal with his private parts, but otherwise, was unharmed.

As soon as I hit the ground, I rolled to the side. The wolf was up and moving almost as soon as he hit, so I had just barely enough time to spin. I kept low to the ground and swung my sword in a low arc. The werewolf tried to jump, but he was a tad too slow. The blade bit into his leg, just above his left ankle. He crashed to the ground with a yelp.

Normally, I would have finished him off so he couldn't rejoin the fight the moment the silver ran its course through his veins, but I felt something coming at me. I ducked and swung around as the female were came at me. Her clothes were in tatters now that she was fully shifted. Blood splattered her maw and her teeth were stained red from the Left Hand man's blood. There was a chunk of something in her teeth.

She dodged my swing and tried to loop around to grab me. I rolled back and sprang to my feet, sword at the ready. I was out of her reach for the moment, but the wall was at my back now. I'd run out of room.

The wolf grinned and hunched her shoulders as if ready to spring.

That's when Adrian hit her.

Once again he'd arrived to save me when I didn't really need it. He smashed into her side, almost faster than the eye could see. He'd fully shifted at some point while I'd been distracted with my own fight. There were two crumpled bodies nearby. The amount of blood told me they weren't going to be getting up ever again.

Powerful jaws closed around the woman's throat. Their eyes met and something passed between them. The female wolf gave half a snarl before he ripped her throat out in a spray of blood and gristle.

He turned to me, still chewing on the flesh. I could almost see the glee in his eyes, something that was rare for him. He was usually so good at keeping his face calm and blank, it was a surprise to see anything else.

This was what he lived for. This was the sort of thing he reveled in. Violence. Death. It was all a thrill to him.

Which was exactly why I'd never become one of his.

There were two weres remaining. They were watching us, yellow eyes flaring. There was no way they'd run. Once shifted, werewolves can barely control themselves. They had enough sense not to attack their friends most of the time, but it was often a close call. It was damn near impossible for them to walk away from a fight, especially on their own territory.

"Bring it on," I said, wiping at my mouth. There was blood there from where my fangs had extended during the fight. It made me wonder how different Adrian and I really were.

The wolves charged as one. One came at me, the other at Adrian. I felt flattered that the bigger one chose to rush at me.

I braced myself and drew a knife from my belt. The wolf snarled and leapt at me from a few yards away. His dark fur was wet, as if he'd been showering when he'd shifted. Water droplets sprayed from him as he flew through the air, muscles rippling, claws extended.

I waited until the last possible moment before spinning away. Using a backhanded motion, I struck out with my knife. Warmth spilled out over my hand as the blade sank home. I let the knife go and let the wolf fall face-first onto the pavement where I'd just been standing. He convulsed once as the silver began to work through him and then fell still.

Adrian was still fighting with the other wolf, though fighting might not be an accurate description of what was going on. He was toying with the smaller wolf, letting him get in close before batting him away. There was a wolfish grin on his face and his eyes gleamed as if he were laughing.

A scowl spread across my face. I might kill weres and vamps, but I didn't torture them. I finished them off as soon as possible and moved on. Toying with them like this was like a cat playing with a mouse—if the mouse had sharp talons for claws and teeth that could rip through wood.

I glanced around and found my gun lying next to the open doorway. I walked over to it, watching the entrance, as well as the windows above, just in case more wolves decided to show up. I glanced inside the doorway, saw nothing, and picked up my Glock. There was a faint scratch along the side I knew would cause Ethan to complain, but it looked otherwise unharmed.

I turned, found Adrian still playing with the other wolf, raised my gun, and fired. The bullet took the smaller were in the side of the head.

Adrian jumped about three feet back and turned on me. Absolute rage filled his eyes and I turned on him, suddenly worried. His upper lip raised in a sneer and he took two threatening steps forward.

"That's far enough, Adrian," I said. My arm was shaking and a shudder ran through my gut.

It was the Oath. I couldn't shoot him. Even if he charged me and grabbed me by the head and squeezed, I wouldn't be able to shoot him. The best I could do would be to try to get away, but without being able to harm him, I knew I wouldn't get far. To run would more than likely set off his hunting instinct and I'd stand no chance.

"Adrian," I said as he took another step my way, "we need to go." Someone had to have heard the fight. There was a chance the police would be on the way, if not a vampire count come to claim the survivors. Either way, it wouldn't be good. Someone would get hurt.

A groan caused Adrian to stop and turn. The were I'd hit in the leg was trying to crawl away, though the silver kept him virtually paralyzed.

With a snarl, Adrian leapt at him and ravaged the poor wolf. Blood and gore bloomed all around the two almost instantly. It was the single most violent thing I'd ever seen, and I'd seen quite a lot of horrible things. I was forced to turn away lest I be sick.

A moment later, the sound of rending and tearing stopped. There were a few cracks and pops and, a moment later, the sound of bare, wet feet, approached. I turned to find Adrian walking toward me, blood covering his nude form.

"I want him," he said, jerking a thumb toward the wolf who still had my knife stuck in his gut.

I glanced at the remains of the wolf Adrian had just ravaged and wondered if he planned on doing the same to the other. There was nothing left but strings of flesh and gore. It was almost impossible to tell it had once been human.

"Why?" I demanded, my stomach churning. "So you can toy with him like that other were? So you can torture him and rip him apart at your leisure?" I was angry. Adrian was a monster. If I'd ever questioned it in the slightest, I had more than enough proof of that now.

Adrian shrugged, his face back to being blank. "He could prove useful to me."

I scowled. "You're recruiting him?"

"He could find a place in my House, yes."

"You just want him as another foot soldier to do your bidding."

Once more he shrugged. "Better than dead."

I wasn't so sure about that.

Adrian glanced around the alley and then walked toward me. "Watch him," he said, nodding toward the downed wolf. "I need to find something to wear."

Adrian's old clothes were lying on the ground in shreds. There was no way he was going to get back into them.

He vanished into the apartment complex, presumably to rifle through the dead men's clothes. A siren was wailing in the distance, but it was fading—it wasn't coming our way. A few curtains swished in nearby buildings, but if anyone was watching, they weren't getting involved.

I glanced at the incapacitated wolf. Knowing he wasn't about to get up and walk away, I turned toward the Left Hand member, or what was left of him.

Like Adrian's victim, he was a mess of blood and gore. Somewhere in the fight, someone had torn him up a little more than the female wolf had. He was barely recognizable as a man now. His face was gone. Only flaps of flesh clung to the bone.

I knelt beside him, doing my best to control my hunger. Out of everyone there, he was the only one whose blood wouldn't taint me.

But I wasn't about to feed on him. He was dead, which means he wouldn't care, but there was something about feeding on someone else's remains, lapping at cooling blood, that repulsed me in a way a normal feeding wouldn't.

It wasn't pleasant, but I checked the man's pockets in the hopes of finding something that would identify him. Most of the damage to his body was on the upper half, so it wasn't as bad as it could have been.

There were a few coins shoved into his left pants pocket, but nothing else. I checked for a wallet in a back pocket, but it was empty as well. I scanned the ground nearby, thinking it may have fallen out, but if it had, someone had kicked it away. There wasn't even a key on him to tell me where he might have been staying.

I rose and found the cubby he'd come out of. Lying on a low windowsill near the ground was his briefcase. It stood open and the first thing I noticed was the serrated knife resting front and center. It looked as though he'd taken the time to lay it out so he could brandish it at his victim before using it.

There were at least a dozen syringes and vials snugly placed in foam cutouts inside the case. There was an empty spot where the broken syringe had been and a spot that the knife would fit in. Other than that, nothing else.

I had no idea how long Adrian would take to find the bigger were's room and get changed. I wasn't even sure the wolf lived here. Maybe they'd congregated together for a party of some kind. I sort of hoped he came up empty and would have to sneak away, naked. I didn't want him thinking he could follow me home.

I slipped the knife back into its spot and snapped the briefcase closed. Adrian wasn't getting this one. I wasn't even sure I'd take it to Jonathan. Ethan might have better luck figuring out what was in the mixture than Doctor Lei would.

Right. You mean his demon would, don't you?

Adrian appeared in the doorway just as I turned around. He was wearing a plain black shirt that was just a tad too tight and a pair of jeans that looked as if he'd had to sew himself inside them. He looked me up and down, eyes lingering on the briefcase. The faintest of frowns crept over his face before vanishing like smoke.

"We'll have to be cautious taking the werewolf back with us," he said, glancing toward the downed wolf. "We don't want to draw more attention to ourselves."

I still had my gun in hand and I wanted more than ever to raise it and shoot him. "No," I said, angry at him for assuming we were leaving together.

He glanced at me, eyebrows raised. "No?"

"I wanted him alive." I gestured toward the dead Left Hand man with my gun. "I asked you to do something to help and you just stood there and let her kill him."

"There was nothing I could do."

"Bullshit. You didn't even try."

"It wasn't my place to interfere."

Anger boiled. "If you wanted me to trust you, then maybe you should have made it your place."

His eyes narrowed. "She would have killed him the moment I moved forward. You were the one with the gun. You should have shot her."

He had me there. At the time, I'd been afraid of hitting the man. It would have been so much easier if Adrian would have at least distracted her.

"You could have tried to help," I grumbled.

He shrugged. "Next time, I'll know what you prefer."

I laughed. "There will be no next time. I didn't even want there to be a this time!"

Adrian walked over to the were and turned him over with a foot. "You will need to take your knife so as not to draw the eye of those we would wish to avoid. The blood will not help our cause, but I think we can manage it. Others will have heard the fight and we can tell them we are taking him to get help if someone should ask."

I very nearly screamed in frustration. It was like he was oblivious to everything but his own concerns.

I stormed over to the injured wolf. I wasn't going to let Adrian take him in so he could brainwash him into doing his bidding. I didn't think. I didn't let myself be swayed by pity.

I walked up right beside Adrian, raised my gun, and put a bullet right between the eyes of the paralyzed wolf.

The sound of the gunshot reverberated off the buildings on either side of the street. Adrian stared down at the now-dead wolf as I drew out my knife and wiped off the blood on his wet fur. I shoved the blade back in its sheath, knowing the remaining blood would cause it to stick later, but not caring.

"Now we're even," I said as I turned and walked away.

"Where are you going?" He didn't sound even the slightest bit put out that I'd killed the wolf he'd planned on recruiting. In fact, I thought I heard respect in his voice.

I didn't stop walking, though. I knew where I had to go if I wanted to learn more about the Left Hand. I didn't like it, but I had little choice.

"Your place," I said, angry at myself for having to stoop to this. "I need to speak to Davin."

11

Adrian must have beat me to his mansion by at least twenty minutes, thanks to my having to walk all the way back to my motorcycle and find a way to secure the briefcase. By the time I got there, the place was clean and orderly, which surprised me. I doubted a big building full of werewolves stayed this clean. He'd probably called ahead and had them scrub the place down in an effort to impress me.

The hardwood floor sparkled as if it had recently been waxed. The tables just inside the door were free of dust and fresh fruit was set out on them. Even the bullet holes from my last visit had been repaired to the point I couldn't even tell where they'd been.

I kept my hand on my gun as I strolled inside. A trio of Adrian's wolves were waiting. Only one of them had the knot of scar tissue that told me he was once a member of the Luna Cult. I didn't recognize him.

"They're waiting for you this way," Scar said with a slight bow of his head.

Okay, I wasn't expecting that. Then again, I never bothered to see how Adrian actually ran the place. Normally, I'd charge in with guns blazing, not caring what I hit. The wolves would be too busy scrambling around, avoiding my bullets, to show much hospitality.

All three wolves turned and walked toward the staircase leading up into the heights of the mansion. None of them glanced over his shoulder to see if I were following, or perhaps aiming at the backs of their skulls, as I normally would have. I don't know if they truly trusted me, or if they were trusting in Adrian's word that I wouldn't shoot them. I had a feeling they'd been warned to act as if I wasn't dangerous or else they'd suffer his own brand of punishment.

I followed the wolves up the stairs with a scowl. I really wanted to shoot one of them just to prove I wasn't one of Adrian's goons. They *should* fear me. Just because I was bound to Adrian, didn't mean I accepted his Little House of Weres.

Of course, if I were to shoot one of them, Adrian would go after someone I cared about. I might not like it, but we were stuck working together as long as he wanted us to. I was sure if I refused him too much, he'd take it out on someone else.

The weres led me down a long, carpeted hallway to a closed door where another pair of wolves waited. They both bowed their heads as we approached, before turning and opening the doors wide enough for me to enter. My guides stepped aside to let me pass—they weren't going to come in with me.

I hesitated. To walk past them would mean I'd be putting my back to them. If this wasn't on the up and up, they could be on me before I could react.

But Adrian wanted me to trust him. He wanted me to join his little club and work for him.

And to be his mate. I couldn't forget that part.

I rested my hand on my sword hilt as I walked past them. I saw one of the wolves tense, but none of them made a move toward me. The doors closed behind me as I entered the room.

I found myself in a sitting room much like Jonathan's at the Den. There were bookshelves along the wall, but I had a hard time imagining Adrian or Davin actually reading anything. A fireplace separated large windows that looked out over the water out front. A fire had been lit. It crackled serenely, giving the room an air of warmth and comfort.

Adrian was standing at one of the windows, looking out. He'd obviously seen me coming since I hadn't taken my usual roundabout way to get there. I'd parked in the driveway like a normal person this time, which had been weird in itself. Even though he didn't turn to face me, I could tell he'd changed clothes to something more typical of him. He didn't so much as twitch to acknowledge my entrance.

Davin, on the other hand, stood from a chair the moment he saw me. He smiled his gap-toothed grin and stuck his tongue out through the hole where his incisors had once been. He had a wineglass filled with blood in one hand and held a small electronic device in the other. He set it down and took a sip of blood before greeting me.

"Oh, my Lady Death," he said, licking his lips. "Time has flown by, has it not?"

"Davin." I stopped two feet into the room. There was no way I was going to approach either of the two madmen. I wanted my information and I wanted to get the hell out of there.

"How have you been?" Davin asked. He sounded affable, but I could still hear the traces of insanity on his voice. "Have you put to use our gift? Do you know of the power you now possess?"

I scowled at him, not wanting to think about that night. Adrian had dosed me with silver dust, tied me down into his basement, and made me immune to silver at the same time he forced me into the Oath. I wouldn't call that a gift, though even I had to admit that being immune to silver was damn helpful in my line of work.

Davin watched me with eyes that all but shouted insane. He was doing a good job at sounding like he was normal, but he couldn't hide those eyes. He was still so thin it was a wonder he hadn't broken in half from the weight of his own head. His cheekbones protruded from his face like sores. His fingers were long, bony, and were now tipped with fingernails cut to sharp points.

"I'm here to talk about the Left Hand, not chat," I said. "I'm sure Adrian has filled you in."

I expected Adrian to nod or perhaps turn and take over the conversation, but he simply stood there. He was so motionless, it was eerie. It was like looking at a breathing statue.

"He has, he has," Davin said. He went back to his chair and sat down. He drained the glass of blood and set it aside. The red on his lips looked bright against his paleness. "They are a plague, are they not?"

"What can you tell me about them?"

"That they are murderers. They are far worse than anything I would ever have become if left to my own devices." His fingers went to where his incisors had once been. "Do they know?"

"Does who know what?"

"Your Cult. Do they know where I am?"

I clenched my jaw. I really didn't want to talk about this with Davin. It reminded me that I was keeping things from Jonathan, things he should know. I had to keep telling myself I was withholding information from him to keep him safe. If he knew Davin was here, or that Adrian's wolves were immune to silver, or that I was now bound to the former Cult wolf, he'd be here in an instant, ready to kill them all. I couldn't risk him dying because of me.

"No," I said. "That's not what I'm here to talk about."

Davin giggled. His eyes rolled in a head that was bobbing up and down like a demented bobblehead.

"Good, good," he said. "I wouldn't want them to continue their castrations. There are things I wish to keep intact, you know?" His eyes gleamed. "They took only a small part of me, leaving the greater whole. It was a mistake to leave so much of me."

As insane as he might be, I had to remember that Davin was also extremely dangerous. He was a sorcerer far more powerful than Jonathan. I'd seen him do things. He could stop bullets with a wave of his hand, forming a shield that would not only protect him, but also those around him. He'd been the one to oversee the Oath, had manipulated it so that it bound a vampire to a werewolf instead of the other way around. I could only imagine what other powers he might have locked away in that head of his.

And I didn't want those powers loosened on me or anyone else I cared about. Sadly, killing him was out, thanks to Adrian.

"I'm just interested in the Left Hand," I said. I tried to sound as pleasant as possible in the hope it would make him willing to talk. I even managed a smile.

Davin's giggle turned into a chuckle. "I've already told you something of them, have I not? It earned me my freedom, in a way."

"You have," I said, ignoring the last. He was free because of the deal I'd struck with him. I didn't need to be reminded that I was responsible for him being loose. "But I want to know more."

"Such as?"

"Who are they? Do you have any names? What about descriptions of some of the members so I know who to look for? What about their location? Do you have any idea what sort of places they frequent?"

The questions just spilled out of me. I felt so lost. The more questions I asked, the more I realized how little I really knew. How was I supposed to stop them if I didn't know the first thing about them?

Davin eyed me a long moment, that damnable grin on his face. "So many questions," he said. "You ask so much, yet offer so little."

"People are dying," I said. I glanced toward Adrian's back and raised my voice so he knew I was talking to him. "I'm sure yours have been affected."

He didn't so much as flinch.

"People die all the time," Davin said. "They think they are safe in their little homes and then someone comes along and kills each and every one of them. They take them down one by one, ripping out pieces of their soul as they do. It's a way of life."

The urge to walk across the room and smack some sense into the vampire was so strong, I actually took a step forward before catching myself.

"Do you know anything that could help me?"

Davin sighed. "I know many things that would help you greatly in many different ways." He paused and then smiled. "But about the Left Hand—I fear you will not be happy."

"Just tell me anything you know." I wanted out of there in the worst way. I knew his madness wasn't catching, but I felt queasy nonetheless.

Suddenly, he appeared bored. His shoulders slumped and his head drooped down to his chest. He began clicking his fingernails together so they made an annoying snapping sound. He seemed to have completely forgotten about me.

"Davin," I said. It came out sharp and angry.

He glanced up. There was knowledge behind those eyes. "You will not find them," he said. "If it were that easy, they'd have been wiped out long ago."

"That doesn't mean I can't try."

"The city is a big place," he said. "There are many nooks and crannies in which they could conceal themselves from even the most prying of eyes. They could be anywhere."

"So you have no idea where I might look?"

He shrugged. "Somewhere where they will not draw attention to themselves most likely. But that could be in isolation or in the most public of places. They are but Purebloods, are they not? They don't need to hide from those that walk the day. In fact, they may revel in it."

I growled in frustration. As much as I didn't want to believe it, he was right. The Left Hand looked like anyone and everyone. They'd have an easier time blending in than any vampire or werewolf. They didn't have to contend with the bloodlust and urge to kill. They didn't change shape when they became excited. Hell, they could go out under a full moon and walk the streets like any normal, if not slightly insane, person.

Davin was right. They could be virtually anywhere.

"What about a name?" I asked, knowing the answer before I even asked the question.

"I only survived them," he said. "I did not escape them."

A headache started to bloom behind my eyes. Coming here had been a total waste of time. Davin didn't know anything I didn't already know. Either that, or he wasn't going to tell me. I was sure if he truly did have important information, he would have used it as a bargaining chip earlier, back when we had him locked away in the Den.

"Thanks," I said, bitterness marring the word. "I'll see myself out."

"There is one thing I do know," Davin said, sitting up straighter. His eyes were gleaming again.

I frowned at him and crossed my arms. I wasn't so sure I believed he'd tell me anything of value. "What is it, Davin?" I sounded tired and frustrated, something I normally wouldn't have let on, especially to an enemy.

"They have a leader."

"I assumed as much," I said.

"Ah, but it is not a leader like you are used to. There are many Denmasters in the Cult. There are many counts and countesses who are willing to step in and take over the moment another has fallen.

"But the Left Hand . . . they have but one—a single person who guides and controls them all. If he were to fall, there would be no one else strong enough to take his place. He *is* the Left Hand. He travels with them, controls them from within. Find and kill him and you can destroy the group as a whole."

"Wouldn't someone else in the Left Hand take over?"

Davin shrugged. "Perhaps. But they would be severely weakened. From what I have learned, he is the sole reason they exist. Without him, they are nothing."

I nodded, suddenly excited. I had no clue where to look, but if I could somehow find the Left Hand leader, I might very well end their killings without having to eradicate them. Killing Purebloods, even ones who killed on a regular basis, wasn't something I enjoyed doing.

"Thanks," I said, this time with much more conviction.

"I live to serve." Davin bowed his head and then giggled to himself.

I turned to leave, mind whirling. That's when Adrian finally decided to speak.

"May I have a moment?"

I considered just walking out. I wanted nothing to do with Adrian, but I had to admit, he had helped me. Sure, he'd done nothing to keep the Left Hand man alive when I'd asked, but if I'd gone into that alone, I would have been overwhelmed. He could have barred me from seeing Davin as well, which meant I wouldn't have gotten that little sliver of information.

"Five minutes," I said, turning back to him. "No more. I have things to do."

He was facing the room now and he gave me a nod. "Davin."

The vampire stood and walked past me. He winked before leaving the room.

"Okay," I said as soon as the door was closed again. "Talk."

Adrian remained standing by the window, arms behind his back. His face was as blank as ever, but I could see something in his eye. I'm not sure if it was excitement or worry or perhaps he was just trying to keep himself from lunging at me, but there was definitely something there.

"I have helped you," he said, voice dead and lifeless. It was so void of emotion, it actually caused me to shudder.

"You have," I said. "But you've also gotten in my way. I think we're even."

"I have given you much and you have not attempted to once return the favor."

"And how do you expect me to do that?"

A faint smile lit the corner of his mouth before fading away to nothing. "How else? You have something I want."

I clamped down hard on my teeth. I didn't want to antagonize the guy any more than usual, but Christ, how many times did we have to go through this?

"I'm not going to be your mate," I said, voice low and dangerous.

"We don't have to start there," he said. "You could move in here. I have rooms set aside for you. You can bring anyone you please to stay with you. I will give you an entire wing if that is what it will take to bring you to me."

Flashes of red dotted my vision. "I'm not going to move in with you, either."

"It is only a matter of time until you'll have no choice."

I took a step forward. "Is that some sort of threat?"

Adrian's eyebrow twitched in what I took to be amusement. It's hard to tell with him.

"Call it an observation," he said. "You have become a lightning rod for danger. You cannot help but become overwhelmed. If you remain as you are, separate from everyone who cares for you, you will not survive for much longer."

I laughed. "You don't care for me," I said. "You just want the strength I can bring you."

He shrugged, seemingly indifferent. "That is caring in its own way." He turned back to look out the window. "I will see you soon."

As much as I wanted to kick him square on the ass and shove him out the window, I turned and walked away. I doubted I could do it anyway, thanks to the Oath. I had yet to try anything, but eventually, I was almost positive I would. He was too aggravating not to.

I stormed out of the room, past the surprised wolves, and showed myself out. Davin was thankfully nowhere in sight. I wasn't so sure I could keep myself from punching him simply for the satisfaction of hearing his nose break.

I checked to make sure the briefcase was where I'd left it and then mounted my bike. I glanced back toward the window, but Adrian was no longer there. I started up the Honda and sped out of his paved driveway, wanting to put as much distance between us as possible.

But no matter how far I went, I knew I'd still feel him there. The Oath would make sure of that. As long as we were bound, Adrian and I would be connected.

Someday, I'd find a way to break free of him. And when I did, I wouldn't hesitate to put a bullet between his eyes.

12

The television was on, but I wasn't watching it. I sat on my bed, staring forward, and seeing nothing. The blinds were closed to the sun that was nearly down. It would be night soon.

Monday night.

It had been weeks since Baset had a name for me, yet I knew that when I went to the contact spot, she'd have one for me now. I didn't have time to deal with being her assassin. It would only make things harder, add one more item to my already full plate.

I could feel the old frustrations building and was trying hard to suppress them. Now wasn't the time to break down. I'd been doing so well lately, to revert to the always pissed-off vampire I'd once been would only serve to make things far harder than they needed to be. I needed a clear head.

I wished I could simply skip tonight and not worry about it until I took care of the Left Hand. But I knew I couldn't. If I didn't show, someone would get hurt. If I picked up the name and took my time taking care of it, someone would get hurt. If I did exactly what Baset wanted, someone would get hurt—only this time, the someone wouldn't be one of my friends.

A light knock came at my door. I clicked the TV off and leaned back against the wall. I already felt exhausted and had yet to do anything.

"Come in," I called.

The door opened and Jeremy stepped quietly inside. He closed the door behind him and then turned to face me, his expression serious.

"Ethan's still asleep," he said.

I waited for him to go on, but he seemed content to simply stare. I was already dressed, so it wasn't like I was sitting around in a revealing outfit. He was fidgeting with his phone, turning it slowly around in circles in his hand. The sight of that phone had my nerves pinging all over the place.

"Has something happened at the Den?" I asked, sitting up straighter. It would be just my luck to have another body pop up just as I was heading to deal with Baset's man.

Jeremy glanced down at his phone. He gave a nervous laugh and then shoved it into his pocket. He showed me his empty hand. "No," he said. "I just needed something to do with my hand. I don't smoke, so . . ." He shrugged.

"I see."

Jeremy ran his fingers through his hair and then looked toward the covered window. He appeared agitated, which only heightened my own nerves. If he didn't say anything soon, I think I might have been the one to explode.

"Out with it," I said. "What's going on?"

"Tonight's Monday," he said. He took a few quick steps forward and then stopped like he hit an invisible wall.

I scooted over and motioned for him to sit. He hesitated, seemingly unsure about sharing a bed with me, even if we were both fully dressed and sitting apart, but eventually came over and sat down. The bed sagged with his weight.

"And?" I asked as soon as he was seated. No one knew about my deal with Baset except for Jonathan. Had he told Jeremy at some point? If he had, I was going to have to break something. That was my business and I didn't want anyone else involved.

"And I want to come."

"Why?"

"I think I can be of some help."

I narrowed my eyes at him. Jeremy bit his lip and looked away.

"What do you know?"

He cleared his throat and suddenly looked like he wanted to be anywhere else. "I know that every Monday you leave. When you come back, you sometimes have a target for a hunt. I don't know how you get it, but I do know you don't like it." He took a deep breath. "And I think if you had someone else to lean on, then maybe it wouldn't be so bad."

I studied him in an attempt to see if he knew more than he was letting on. I didn't want anyone else to know I was being forced into being Baset's assassin. For one, it could get him into some serious trouble. For another, it was as embarrassing as hell.

"It's too dangerous," I said. "I can't risk you."

His jaw clenched. "I'm not fragile. I want to be of some help."

"You are helping."

"How?" He turned violently to face me. "By sitting around here and waiting for someone to call? By baby-sitting someone who could probably take care of himself without me? What good is that really doing?"

"Jeremy," I said, my heart going out to the kid, "you are helping."

"I thought I could be content," he said with a frustrated sigh. "I thought that being needed would keep me going, but it doesn't help. I see you risk your life nearly every damn night while I sit here on my ass where it's safe. I can't live like this. I really thought I could, but I can't."

I thought back to our drinks at the bar and wondered what had changed since then. I thought he was going to be okay, that he was past his inferior feelings, but it appeared I'd been wrong. Was I really that bad of a judge of people not to have seen his frustration welling? It was clear he'd been thinking about it for a long time.

"I'm sorry," I said, wishing I could say something else. "I need you here tonight."

He looked like he wanted to argue, but instead nodded. He looked down at his hand and smiled weakly. "I figured you'd say that," he said. "I thought I'd at least give it a try." He took a deep breath and looked me in the eye. "Just promise me that you won't leave me here forever. Tell me that one day you'll trust me enough to take me with you."

That one hurt. The sudden pang surprised me and I very nearly reached out to touch his arm to comfort him.

"I trust you now," I said. "That's why I'm willing to leave you here with Ethan when I wouldn't do the same with anyone else."

He nodded again and stood. "Yeah," he said. "I guess." He started for the door, shoulders slumped in defeat.

"Jeremy," I said.

He stopped and glanced back at me. There was a glimmer of hope in his eye.

"One day, when things are a little less volatile around here, I'll take you with me. I promise."

He smiled and gave me yet another short nod. Then, he walked out of my room.

I felt terrible about it, but what else could I have done? If I'd shown up at the meeting spot with Jeremy in tow, Baset surely would retaliate in some way. She might decide to force him into her power, make him eat her flesh. I couldn't risk letting him fall into her hands.

I really wished there was a way I could make Jeremy feel more useful without having to worry every second about whether or not I was going to get him killed. He'd been right when he said Ethan could take care of himself. He spent most nights locked behind bombproof doors in his lab. He didn't need someone to baby-sit him.

Yet despite that, I felt better with Jeremy here. There was a growing number of people who knew where I lived. If just one of them decided to take me out, I'd much rather have someone here to slow them down long enough for me to get back and take care of them myself.

Or at least long enough for Ethan to get away.

And even that made me feel bad. I didn't want Jeremy to get hurt. There seemed to be no good way to do this.

Jeremy was in his room when I finally rose and walked down the hall. Night had fallen and I was ready to get this over with. I could hear him moving around on the other side of his closed door. I considered knocking and telling him once more how important he was. Maybe if I kept telling him, he'd eventually believe me.

Then again, it might just make him feel worse. He already felt useless. Telling him anything different probably wasn't going to help. He'd probably think I was patronizing him.

I headed downstairs for my weapons, thinking of Jeremy the whole way. I could start using him for daytime recon if he was willing to miss a few hours of sleep. Or perhaps I could send him to Mikael for me when I needed information. I was sure Mikael already knew Jeremy was here and that he was watching my house for me, so I doubted it would be a problem.

I threw my coat on over my weapons and headed out to the garage. I hadn't seen Ethan. I didn't even look to see if he was in his lab or still in his room.

The garage door opened and I sped out. There was still a faint light over the horizon, though it wouldn't affect me. I was a little weaker, but it would pass by the time I got where I was going. The sun would be down by then.

I glanced back as the house dwindled. I wondered if Ethan was watching me. I hadn't exactly been hiding the fact I'd been leaving at first dark every Monday night and that I often had the name of someone I needed to deal with when I got back. It was only a matter of time until someone figured it out. It wouldn't have surprised me to learn both of them knew and Jeremy had been the one chosen to say something about it.

The ride to the abandoned building where I always met with Baset's man was long and uneventful. There was an odd mix of Purebloods and supes on the streets. Many were going home after work in the hope of avoiding the violence that inevitably came at dusk. These were the late workers, the ones who risked getting attacked on the way home for a few extra bucks per hour. It was the only way some people could provide for their families these days.

Of course, there were those who reveled in the sense of danger. There would always be thrill seekers who figured they'd rather die doing something exciting than cowering in their homes like the more sensible Purebloods.

There was definitely something in the air tonight. There was a fear, a nervousness that had never been there before. Just looking at someone, I couldn't tell for certain if they were a supe or a Pureblood, not unless they shifted or did something that proved them to be one or the other. But the more I looked, the more I noticed small groups of people who made me think of werewolves or vampires. They were huddled together as if afraid to be alone.

The Left Hand had definitely made its mark. People were scared. It wouldn't surprise me to find out that all of the counts and countesses were hiding away in their mansions, sending lackeys in their stead for things they normally would do on their own. Just because they had power, didn't mean they were invincible.

I pulled up in front of the abandoned building, a sense of foreboding settling over me. While I hadn't been attacked here, one of Baset's wolves had been. I'd found his body inside, blood pooled on the floor. As far as I knew, there could be more bodies inside even now.

I remained seated on the Honda and waited. Baset's second, Henri, was usually the one who met me here when there was a name. When there wasn't, someone else would appear, shake his head, and then walk away. I was hoping for the latter.

A shadow shifted in the alley between buildings and my heart sank. Henri stepped out, eyes hard and angry. He strode over to me and reached into his coat. He removed an envelope and handed it to me.

"You have one week," he said, spilling his hot, rancid breath over me.

I cringed back as I took the envelope. "You should invest in some mouthwash," I said with a grimace. I could still remember the sound of him eating Baset's rotting flesh.

Henri smiled. "You should consider the same."

I tucked the envelope into my coat and looked away to hide my embarrassment. I'd totally forgotten about Ethan's concoction. The awful taste was still there, but I guess I'd gotten used to it.

"Who is it this time?" I asked.

"Someone who needs to die."

"But why?"

He shrugged. "Because Countess Baset wishes it so."

"You know, I do like to know who I'm killing." I sounded sulky. "It seems only fair to give me that."

Henri chuckled. He looked to the sky as if searching for an answer there before he shrugged again. "This man has displeased Baset. He has overstepped his bounds and *used* one of hers wrongly." He glanced at me with a knowing grin. "If you'd heard of him before now, he would have already been on your hit list. You aren't doing anything you wouldn't have done on your own."

There was a moment when I considered whipping out my gun and shooting Henri just to see what Baset would do. When I'd killed her lover, all she'd done was force me to take over Telia's job as her assassin. Maybe she wouldn't do much more if I did the same to Henri. I couldn't stand the guy.

Then again, when I'd killed Telia, she'd tortured Jonathan to get my attention. I couldn't forget about that part.

I sighed. There was no getting around it; Henri was as untouchable to me as was Adrian. To kill him would surely end with the deaths of far too many people.

I revved the Honda's engine and prepared to leave.

"Besides," Henri said, "you have ways to find out the information you seek. Why bother asking me?"

"It would save me a trip."

"Would you believe what I told you?"

I didn't have to think about it. "No," I said, "I guess not."

"Then there is no point to this conversation." Henri smiled. "You have one week. I will be here Monday with your payment, one way or the other."

I knew it was a threat as well as a promise. If I didn't deliver, Baset would kill someone I cared about.

"I'll be here," I said.

Henri only smiled before walking away.

I waited until I could no longer see him before I removed the envelope from my coat. I tore it open and looked at the name on the slip of paper, half afraid it would be a name I recognized.

Thankfully, it was no one I knew. It would be just my luck if Baset gave me Adrian's name or perhaps Nathan's. While I might enjoy killing the first, there was no way it was happening while I was bound to him by the Oath. And for as much as I didn't like Nathan, I didn't want him to die either. Jonathan would never forgive me for that.

I shoved the name into my pocket and rode away. I'd have to take care of it soon enough, but first, there was something else I needed to do.

13

When I walked through the front doors of the Luna Cult Den, I expected there to be more people milling about. Instead, I found only two.

Nathan stood near the stairs with the young girl Jeremy had been talking to. They were speaking in low voices and if Nathan's face was any indication, they were arguing. As soon as they saw me, the exchange abruptly ceased.

"Who is she?" the Cultist said to Nathan, flinging an arm at me. There was an aggression there that surprised me. I knew I wasn't exactly the most popular person here, but quite a few respected me for what I'd done to help the Cult. I guess she hadn't gotten the memo.

Nathan glanced at me and a slight frown creased his features. "A friend." He said it like a curse.

The young Cultist sniffed and rolled her eyes before eyeing me up and down. "She doesn't belong here."

Nathan looked like he wanted to agree, but instead put a hand on the girl's arm. She jerked away from his touch and snarled at him.

"Don't touch me, pig." She turned on me. "Whoever the fuck you are, you should just turn around right now. You don't belong here. We don't want you here. You'll screw everything up!"

I raised my eyebrows at her. I wasn't sure if I should be amused or irritated by her. She appeared to be in her twenties, but I wondered if perhaps she was still in her volatile teenage years and life on the streets had prematurely aged her.

"Mira . . ." Nathan tried to calm her but she was having none of it.

"Whatever. Fuck off." She waved a hand in Nathan's face. I was surprised he didn't bite it off. She glanced at me. "And fuck you, too." She stormed off.

I watched her go, amused despite myself. If she'd done that to me a few months ago, I probably would have knocked her flat on her ass. Then again, most of her anger seemed to be targeted at Nathan. Maybe I'd have applauded her instead.

"New recruit?" I asked, turning to face the scowling were. He waited until the girl vanished and the door slammed before turning to me.

"No," he said, crossing his arms. He leaned against the banister and glared at me. "What do you want?"

"Who is she, then?" I asked, pressing the point. "She doesn't seem to be too happy to be here."

"Mira," Nathan said, glancing toward the door she went through before turning stonily back to me.

"Mira who?"

He shrugged. "Pablo's girlfriend."

I very nearly choked. "What? Pablo has a girlfriend?" I tried to sort it out in my head. I suppose their anger issues were similar, but otherwise, I couldn't imagine them together.

Nathan ground his teeth. "We do have lives here."

"I . . ." I what? It seemed strange to be thinking of anyone inside the Cult having a life outside it. I mean, these were werewolves and werewolf worshippers. I couldn't see any of them being domestic.

"So, what were you two fighting about when I came in?" I asked, unsure I could continue down the other line of thought. Pablo and Mira? Wow.

"Pablo's birthday."

"His what?"

Nathan's eyes flared. "Are you just here to irritate me or do you have something important to say?"

I shook my head. First I learn Pablo had a girlfriend and then that he was having a birthday. That was another one of those things I never even considered. These were people inside the Cult, people who had lives.

I took a deep breath and glanced toward the door Mira had gone through. I guess I could still learn a thing or two about how the Cult operated. My opinion of the Cultists had always been of people who had no real direction in life. They worshipped werewolves and I'd thought that was all they did. The ones on the streets were thugs.

But even they had lives back home; mothers and fathers and sisters and brothers. Some had wives and husbands and kids. Even the vampires and werewolves I killed on a regular basis had families.

It was the first time it really hit me. I mean, I should have thought about it before. My family had been killed by a vampire count and his werewolf thugs. Just because I'd lost everyone, didn't mean it was that way for everyone else.

"What do you want?" Nathan's voice broke into my reflections. He looked beyond annoyed now. He looked downright hostile.

"I need to speak to Jonathan," I said. I could think about Pablo's birthday later. Maybe I should get him a present of some sort. Then maybe he wouldn't spend all his time glaring at me.

"He's busy."

"He's never too busy to see me." I smiled sweetly, knowing it would irritate the big wolf.

He surprised me by smiling. "Tonight, he is."

I couldn't tell if he was just being difficult or if he was serious. I frowned and took a step toward the staircase.

"I need to see him about something important," I said. "Whatever he's doing, he won't mind the interruption."

"I wouldn't be so sure about that," Nathan said, his smile turning almost sinister.

He was finally getting to me. I narrowed my eyes at him. "Let me pass."

"If what you have to say is so important, you can tell me. I will make sure he gets the information when he's done."

I crossed my arms. "No," I said, taking another step forward. "What I have to say, I have to say directly to him."

Nathan straightened and put himself between me and the staircase. The only way I was going to get up there was if I went through him.

As much as I wanted to, I didn't punch him. Instead, I stopped about a foot in front of him and glared up at his smug face. If it came down to a battle of brute strength, there was no way I was going to win. Nathan could pick me up and break me in half without breaking a sweat.

It was a good thing I had my weapons. Brute strength didn't mean much when someone was shoving the barrel of a gun up your nose.

"Nathan," I said, warning in my voice. "Move."

"I cannot do that," he said, still smiling that dangerous smile of his. "I have orders that no one is to disturb him."

"I'm not just anyone."

"But you are the one person I am sure he doesn't want to see right now."

There was a glimmer to his eye that almost made me break down and take that swing at him. He was enjoying this far more than he should. While he'd always been difficult before, he'd never been this bad about it.

"What's wrong with you?" I asked, taking a step back just in case he really was looking for a fight. "I need to see Jonathan. You do know the Left Hand is out there right now, killing people, right?"

His smile slipped the tiniest bit. "Do you have information on them?"

I hesitated. While Adrian and I had followed a Left Hand member, we had nothing to show for it outside the case, and I'd given that to Ethan when I'd gotten home last night. There wasn't anything in it that the Cult didn't already know.

"Not exactly," I said.

Nathan grunted and the smile returned. "Then why bring them up?"

"Because I really need to talk to Jonathan and you're being an ass about it."

He huffed and shook his head. "You are so damn stubborn. I . . ." He frowned and his eyes clouded over for a moment before clearing. "I knew someone very much like you once."

"Really?" I said, anger flaring. "Did she kick your ass like I'm about to?"

He shrugged with one shoulder. "In her own way, yes, she did." The smile was gone. He stared at me with a mixture of hatred and something else I couldn't place. It wasn't love or longing, thank God, but something entirely different.

I took another step back, feeling suddenly uncomfortable.

"What is Jonathan doing?" I asked. "Can you at least tell me that?"

"I can," Nathan said, the smile returning, but this time, it wasn't as spiteful. "But you won't like it."

"Try me."

"He's with Keira."

My breath caught in my throat. My gaze instinctively rose toward the top level. I couldn't see the gilded doors that led to Jonathan's rooms from where I stood, but I imagined them.

"What are they doing?" My voice hitched on the words.

Nathan chuckled. "You figure it out."

My entire body went cold. I dropped my eyes to stare at Nathan. He looked smug, almost happy that he was able to deliver the news. In fact, I think he'd been relishing the idea of telling me since I'd walked in, but wanted to make me work for it first.

"I see."

"They could be a while," he said. "If you'd like to wait, you could sit in the office. I'm pretty sure you won't be able to hear what's going on above you."

My fingers twitched. I wanted to draw my gun, put a hole in the middle of Nathan's head, and march right up the stairs to confront Jonathan. I didn't trust Keira. She could be working for the enemy and I was almost positive she'd been the wolf who'd attacked me when I'd followed Nathan.

My eyes narrowed, but I didn't draw. "Did you put her up to this?"

He looked confused for a moment before chuckling wryly. "I had nothing to do with it."

I was really starting to wonder. Maybe it was my own wishful thinking, but I wondered if perhaps Nathan and Keira were working together against Jonathan. If she'd been the one to attack me while I was following Nathan, did that mean she was protecting him? Could Nathan have been the one to convince her to come to the Den? Had they been in contact before then?

Were they slipping information to the Left Hand?

As much as I wanted to believe it right then, I just didn't see it. I knew Nathan was up to something and the guy was a royal pain in my ass, but that didn't mean he would turn against Jonathan. Add to that the fact he'd saved my ass more than once. It just didn't add up.

But that didn't mean I trusted Keira. She could still be the enemy.

I almost came out and asked Nathan directly about what he'd been doing and how much Keira knew about it. If he wasn't working with the Left Hand and was merely hunting, he knew it would hurt his standing with both Jonathan and me, but I doubted he would deny it. Nathan wouldn't lie like that. He'd probably turn hard and glare more than usual, but he wouldn't lie to his Denmaster. He wasn't the type.

"What do you know about Keira?" I asked instead. It seemed the safest way to start.

"She's a werewolf," Nathan said. "She came to us recently. She has ingratiated herself to Jonathan—as you can see."

"Do you trust her?"

"Do I trust anyone?"

He had me there. "Do you think she could . . . ?" I trailed off, hoping he'd get the idea without me having to say it.

Nathan only shrugged. "I haven't spent enough time with her to know."

"But you're okay leaving her alone with Jonathan."

There was a hint of doubt in his eyes before he answered. "He trusts her. I have no say in it."

"And that makes it okay?"

Nathan gave a nervous chuckle. I heard him laugh more in the last few minutes than in all the time I'd known him. A part of me wasn't so sure he was enjoying this as much as he put on, that something else was going on and the laughter was some sort of defense mechanism.

But what was he hiding?

"Jonathan can take care of himself," he said. "I do recall someone else repeatedly telling him the same thing when he tried to take care of her."

I bit back a retort and let out a frustrated breath. I wasn't going to get anything out of Nathan. Confronting him about what he'd been doing would only result in a fight. Jonathan was "busy" with Keira and I had no idea how long that would take. There was no way I was going to stand around waiting for them to finish.

I felt my face grow hot and turned away, not wanting Nathan to see it. I wasn't sure why I was so upset over this. I'd turned Jonathan down more than once. It was only right for him to seek comfort in someone else's arms.

But it felt too soon. How well could he really know Keira? If she was the reason the Left Hand had gotten so close to the Den, she could be setting him up for a major downfall.

"Would you like me to tell him you stopped by?" Nathan asked. I glanced back to see him still standing at the stairs, but he wasn't smiling. There was a look of concern on his face that vanished the moment he saw me looking at him.

I nodded and looked away. I felt sick. I didn't want to be there anymore. I wasn't even sure I wanted to come back if I could help it. I was wasting my time at the Den, always had been.

But I wouldn't turn completely away from the Cult—not while the Left Hand was killing them.

"Tell him I was here," I said, venom in my voice. "Tell him I have some questions for him when he isn't too busy fucking his girlfriend."

I started for the door.

"Kat," Nathan said, sounding almost apologetic.

I kept on walking.

"It isn't what you think."

Sure it was. That's why he enjoyed it so much.

I pushed through the doors and stormed away. I didn't look back. As far as I was concerned, I was done with the Den and the Cult's games.

The door opened behind me and I quickened my pace. I didn't know if it was some random Cultist leaving for the night or if it was Nathan. I only knew that if I saw anyone from the Den, I'd probably end up hurting someone. I didn't want that on my conscience.

I nearly ran to the Cult garage. As soon as I was there, I threw myself onto my bike and revved the engine. I was breathing hard and my head felt full of cement. I couldn't think; wasn't sure I wanted to.

I tore out of the garage and sped off into the night. My cheeks were wet, but I refused to wipe them dry. To do so would be to admit I cared.

14

Home sounded really good by then, but as much as I wanted to vanish into my room and melt into a sappy puddle, I still had a job to do. Thanks to Countess Baset, I had one more chore to worry about. Just because I was pissed, didn't mean I could blow it off. I needed to get information on the name Henri had given me so I could hurry up and kill the guy. The faster I finished off my target, the better.

I pulled into the Bloody Stake parking lot, mildly surprised to see business had begun to pick up again. While the lot wasn't as full as it used to be, it was a lot busier than the last time I was there. I guesstimated that a little over half the parking spaces were filled.

I shut off the engine and started for the front door, ready to get this over with. I knew Mikael was going to ask about how I got the name—he always did—and I wasn't ready to tell him. I suppose I should be happy he was asking, because the day he stopped would be the day he already knew.

A trio of men stood by the trash bins at the end of the parking lot. They were swathed in shadow, almost as if they were trying to hide. They watched me as I strode toward the bar, only looking away when I opened the door to step inside. I didn't know if they were weres or vamps, but I was pretty sure they weren't Purebloods. They had that look about them that spoke of danger. Their attention made my skin crawl.

Bart looked up as I entered. He gave me a brief nod before moving to the other end of the bar where he went about serving a couple that looked a few years from being legal. The guy might be able to pull it off with his scruffy cheeks and stress lines, but to my eyes the girl looked to be no older than fifteen.

It wasn't my place to judge. I figured Bart knew what he was doing. Just because they looked young, didn't mean they were. Werewolves and vampires did age, but not nearly as fast as Purebloods, thanks to our ultra-healing genes. Those two could be over fifty for all I knew.

I found Mikael sitting in his usual booth with a girl. Before I even took a step his way, he was motioning for her to leave. It looked like he had figured out my Monday routine as well. He didn't take his eyes off me as I crossed the room and slid into the booth across from him.

"It's good to see you again, my sweet."

I grimaced at the pet name, but didn't tell him to stop. Mikael did what he wanted to do. I wasn't sure if all Swedes were like that or just him, though I was betting on the latter. There wasn't anyone in the world like Mikael.

"Been keeping busy?" I asked, glancing around the bar.

As I'd noticed outside, it wasn't as busy as it used to be, but most of the tables had customers. The empty seats actually made me long for the old days, back when there wasn't as much fear going around and the place would be packed. There was something soothing about a bar full of people who wanted to do nothing more than sit back and relax. I knew there were always a few who were there to pick up their next meal, but that knowledge didn't detract from the atmosphere. In fact, it only enhanced the charm.

Mikael grinned. "It depends on what you mean by 'busy.'" He ran his fingers through his greased-back hair and sat back.

I rolled my eyes. "Never mind. I don't want to know."

He chuckled before sighing. "It is good to see you back more regularly, my sweet. There is something to say for normalcy, yes?"

I nodded, wondering if he might have been reading my mind. Hadn't I just thought the same thing?

"But I imagine that isn't why you have come to see me."

"It's not."

"Business, yes?"

"Of course."

Mikael studied me a long moment and then surprised me by waving over to the bar. He raised two fingers once he caught Bart's attention before sitting back to study me again.

"You look as if you could use something to drink," he said. "You look stressed."

"I feel stressed."

Bart appeared at my side and set two bottles in front of me. He hesitated, looking mildly confused, before turning and walking away.

I picked up one of the bottles and started to shove the other across the table to Mikael, but he shook his head.

"They are both yours," he said.

I didn't argue. I was definitely in a two-beer-minimum mood.

"So, why have you come to me this fine evening?"

I took a drink to delay the inevitable. While I knew what was coming, I dreaded it. He didn't know about Baset, that I'd become her assassin. He'd eventually figure it out and when that day came, I was sure he'd pack the information away to use against me someday. Just because we got along, didn't mean I could trust him completely.

"What can you tell me about Boris Stevenson?" I asked.

Mikael's eyebrows rose. "Boris?"

"Yeah."

He laughed loudly. No one in the bar even glanced our way. I wasn't sure if it was out of fear of Mikael or if something else was preventing them from hearing him. Either way, it was odd that I seemed to be the only person who'd noticed.

"Boris is not a good man, yes?"

"I suppose not."

"But he seems . . . strange for your interests." He leaned forward. "I take it you will not be telling me how you came across his name?"

"Nope."

Mikael nodded and sat back again, smiling. "I figured not. You have secrets of your own. But someday . . ." He waved a finger at me. "Someday, I will figure it out."

"We'll see." I forced a smile. I really didn't want Mikael to know that the only way I was able to keep Baset from hunting me down and killing me was to become her assassin. "What can you tell me about him?"

Mikael rubbed at his chin and squinted at the dim lights above our heads. I couldn't tell if it was for show or if he was actually thinking. I had no idea how he managed to store so much information on so many people in his head. Circumstances were changing constantly, yet Mikael always seemed on top of them.

I was beginning to suspect he was more than he appeared. In fact, I was almost positive there was something supernatural about him, though I didn't have an inkling as to what he might be.

"Boris Stevenson is a vampire," Mikael said at last. "But you already knew that, yes?"

I didn't respond in any way. I knew absolutely nothing about my target, but I wasn't about to tell him that. That would be giving too much away. Mikael was fishing to see how much I really knew.

He chuckled before going on. "He hasn't done anything especially horrible in the grand scheme of things. He hasn't tried to take down any Major Houses or bothered any of the counts or countesses. In fact, if it wasn't for his . . . unfortunate thirst, he would be of no consequence."

"What unfortunate thirst might that be?"

Mikael shrugged. "A little of this, a little of that. He is a rogue, but something of a famous one in the right circles."

"Famous?" That surprised me. Until I read his name on the page Henri gave me, I'd never heard of him before. "What for?"

"He makes movies."

I gave him a skeptical look. "He's a movie star?"

Mikael leaned forward, still smiling, though something came into his eyes, something that told me he wouldn't mind if Boris Stevenson came up missing. Permanently.

"These are the homemade sort of movies that you have to search really hard for. Not all of the actors and actresses are strictly legal. Not all of them come out of it alive."

"I see."

"He has a thing for young girls especially, the younger the better. He'll take a young-looking girl in her twenties, sure, but if he can get to them before they are of age, he likes that more."

My teeth started to grind together so I took a long pull from my beer to make them stop.

"He keeps a very low profile," Mikael said. "His fame is spread amongst the sick and the perverted. His identity is kept secret by even the most vicious of vampire counts. He keeps them entertained with his blood porn."

I cringed at the term, but a sense of satisfaction and relief swept over me.

This guy deserved to die. Baset had always sent me after someone I would have gone after on my own if I'd known about them, so it wasn't a surprise that Boris fit the mold. I did wonder how he'd drawn her attention, however. Had he killed someone important to her? Had she tried to bring him into her House, only to be rejected? I knew for a fact that Baset didn't take rejection well.

"The movies are not something anyone should see," Mikael said.

"I'll take your word for it."

"But . . ." He raised a finger. "You might wish to see them. Boris is not a man easily spotted. He spends more time amongst others than he does alone. If you wish to, shall we say, make his acquaintance, you will want to know what he looks like."

I didn't like where this was going. "If I know where he lives, I can take care of anyone and everyone there."

"And if you miss him? He will continue making these movies and you will not know it. He doesn't often stick to one place."

I heaved a sigh. He was right, damn it. It would be far easier if I knew what he looked like.

"Fine," I said, a little too harshly. "What do I need to do?"

"Do you have a computer?"

I shook my head.

"I figured as much." Mikael reached down next to him. I couldn't see anything from my side of the booth. In fact, I couldn't hear anything either. He simply reached down and then brought his hand back up with a slip of paper. I wasn't so sure he hadn't conjured it out of nowhere.

He held the page out to me. "There are two addresses here. Go to the first. I will send word you are coming. Anton will be able to help you."

"And the second?"

"It is where Boris Stevenson calls home on the rare occasions he decides to stay there." He smiled.

I took the page, glanced at the address, and then shoved it into my pocket. I sat back and then began to thoughtfully sip my beer.

I could handle a rogue vampire. Rogues had once been my specialty, but I hated how I was going to have to see some of this guy's atrocities before I could take care of him. I'd prefer to simply waltz in, take the vamp down, and then get out of there before things got too bloody. I was getting tired of all the blood.

"Is there something amiss, my sweet?" Mikael asked, breaking into my thoughts. There was concern in his eyes.

"What do you mean?" I asked, setting down my half-empty bottle.

"You seem . . . distracted."

"It's been a busy year."

Mikael gave me a weak smile. "But there is more to it than that. Something has happened and it has happened recently, yes? It has gotten into your head and snaked its way into your mind. I can tell."

I scratched the back of my head and looked away. "I'm fine," I said. "There's just a lot going on right now and I'm having a hard time keeping everything separate."

"Ah," he said, sitting back and crossing his arms.

"What's that supposed to mean?" I flashed back to how Ethan had had the same smug look on his face when I'd told him about Keira.

"What should it mean?" Mikael asked with a grin.

"This isn't a psych evaluation, you know."

He started to laugh, but was cut off by a scream that came from outside.

The entire bar fell abruptly silent. Bart's shotgun appeared in his hand as if by magic. He was still behind the bar, watching the door.

He wasn't the only one. Every eye was focused on the doorway. There were a few tense seconds when not even a whisper could be heard. Then the door burst open and the young girl I'd noticed at the bar earlier burst inside, eyes wide and frantic.

"It's out there." She collapsed to her knees and broke into sobs.

I was up and out of the booth before anyone else could move. Bart came around the bar to join me, danger in his eyes. He didn't like violence on his property and it was pretty clear something violent had just happened.

"Everyone stay inside," he growled. "Everyone but you." He nodded to me and we headed for the door together.

Bart was the first into the lot. The lights from inside were so dim, it barely illuminated the pavement. The main source of light came from the neon sign above the bar of the woman staking the vampire. It gave everything a slightly red sheen.

As soon as we were in the parking lot, the young man stood. He was standing near my motorcycle, of all places. His eyes widened when he saw Bart's gun was aimed at him.

"He's over here," he said, raising his hands and taking a step back. "We found him. We didn't kill him. I swear."

I followed Bart across the lot. I glanced toward the trash bin where I'd seen the trio of men, but they were gone.

"Fucking shit," Bart said, lowering his shotgun.

My heart just about stopped.

Lying on the ground, right beside my motorcycle, was a body. Blood pooled around him and beneath my tires. Blank eyes stared at the sky above our heads. His throat had been opened from ear to ear and a silver cross lay smoldering in his forehead. He was quite clearly dead.

I didn't have time to see much else. A growl came from behind me and I spun to find half the bar's patrons had spilled out onto the lot. Feral yellow eyes were looking past me to the body on the ground, at the blood that had ceased pumping. The lead wolf's nostrils flared, as he took in the scent.

It pushed him over the edge.

He started to shift.

15

It was like dominoes. The first wolf began his shift and the ones behind him did the same. The combination of fear and the smell of blood had set them off, which was bad news for anyone who wasn't a supe. One man who'd come out with the rest, slipped back inside, his face pale and bloodless.

"Goddamn it," Bart muttered as he raised his shotgun. I placed a hand on his arm before he could fire. If he killed one of the wolves, the rest would attack. He might have dealt with fights on his property before, but I had a feeling he'd never dealt with this many at once.

He glanced at me and then lowered the barrel so it wasn't pointed at anyone, though he still held it in a way that would allow him to fire off a quick shot if needed. There was no way he was going to remove his finger from the trigger. I just hoped it didn't go off accidentally.

"Get back!" I shouted, hand moving to my own gun. I wouldn't draw unless I had no choice. I think Bart would forgive me this time if I were to shoot someone, but I didn't want to risk it if I didn't have to.

A half-dozen shifted werewolves prowled in front of us. Closer to the building, a pair of vampires with blood dripping from their ravaged gums stood, watching. The only Pureblood left outside—if you didn't count Bart—was the young man standing behind us. He looked terrified, and rightfully so. If the weres attacked, he'd probably be the first to die.

Eyes peered out from the windows of the Bloody Stake. It seemed everyone had risen to see what was happening—everyone but Mikael. I didn't see his face in the crowd.

A werewolf snarled and Bart swung his gun around to him without actually raising it. The wolf bared his fangs but didn't charge.

"Blood has been spilled," one of the vampires said. He looked eager for a fight, but was standing well back of the wolves. He wasn't dumb enough to get too close.

"It's none of your concern," I said. "Go back inside."

"Who are you to tell us what to do?" the other vampire said, grinning. His nostrils flared as he drew in the scent of death.

The first vampire braved a step forward. "This place belongs to us," he said. "It's time we took it back for good."

I winced, knowing what was coming next.

There was a loud boom, and the vampire's head splattered against the wall behind him. His body dropped limply to the ground. His buddy flinched and with an oddly chipper smile, vanished back into the bar where he wouldn't be a target.

"Anybody else?" Bart shouted, gun trailing from left to right without actually aiming at anyone.

Two of the wolves at the back spun and loped off, leaving their tattered clothes behind. I noticed a few of the faces at the window had vanished, though I didn't think the vampire was causing problems inside.

That left four wolves facing us. The vampire's blood had started to push a couple of them into a near blood frenzy. They snarled and slavered as they paced. Their muscles were tense, seconds from springing.

I drew my gun. Bart and I could handle four.

One of the wolves stepped forward and I aimed at him. "I wouldn't do that," I said. His eyes were wild, crazed with both fear and hunger. If he so much as twitched in my direction again, I was going to have to put him down.

Another of the wolves slunk off, presumably to find an easier target. While they didn't know I had silver bullets in my gun, they knew a shot to the head could be deadly, even to a werewolf.

"If you ever want to come back here," Bart said, face red with anger, "you better go now. I won't hold this against you."

Another wolf turned and loped off, leaving two.

"I'd do as he says," I said. "He's a pretty damn good shot."

My hand was steady as I drew a bead on what I took to be the leader. In times past, I would have killed him already. This wolf was the first to shift, which set off the rest. My old self viewed that as a killable offense.

But I was trying to be a better person. I've spent time with weres who weren't bad people. I knew now that some could be saved, even this guy. Maybe he hadn't fed for a while and the blood had triggered the monster inside him faster than he could control. It wasn't his fault he was what he was.

The lead wolf snarled, but slowly backed away. I was worried he was heading for the bar where all the Purebloods were hiding, but instead, he turned and ran off, crossing the road without stopping for the light traffic. The last wolf took off after him, either giving chase for a fight or because they were friends. I didn't care. I was just happy they were gone.

Even after they'd vanished, Bart and I stayed vigilant. Just because they appeared to have left, didn't mean they were actually gone for good. I wouldn't put it past an angry were to loop around and try to come at us from another angle.

"Go on," Bart said, startling me. I glanced over to see him talking to the Pureblood guy. "Take your girl and go before they come back."

He didn't need to be told twice. The kid ran for the bar. He barely slowed to rip open the door and stumble inside. A moment later he returned with the pale young girl on his arm. They got into a car and tore out of the lot.

"Know him?" Bart asked, turning toward the body. He'd lowered his gun and took his finger off the trigger, so I put mine away. I kept my hand close to my knives just in case. I wasn't about to believe all of the wolves were gone. I had a feeling we were being watched.

I knelt by the body and studied the face. I almost expected it to be one of the three men I'd seen by the trash bin, but that wasn't the case.

But he was familiar. It took me a moment to figure out where I'd seen him.

"He's a werewolf," I said, swallowing hard.

The guy wasn't shifted and was fully dressed, telling me he hadn't seen his attacker coming. One of his knuckles was scraped where he'd either fallen or tried to strike out at his assailant. The only other wound I could see was the slashed throat and burn from the silver cross on his forehead.

"I don't think I've seen him here before," Bart said.

I hadn't either. In fact, I'd only ever seen him once.

The dead wolf lying in the parking lot was the one who'd helped me when the female wolf I thought to be Keira had attacked me. I didn't know his allegiances, but now I knew he hadn't been following Nathan.

He'd been following me.

"I'm going to go in and close up the bar," Bart said. "I have clean-up to do and can't run the place while I do it." He started to walk away, but hesitated. "Don't leave until I've had a chance to talk to you."

He limped away.

Great. I hoped Bart wouldn't hold this against me. The body had been found next to my Honda, and while he didn't know how I knew the guy, I was pretty sure he'd figured out I was a part of this somehow.

The wolf was actually dressed nicely, as if he'd been planning on heading to an expensive restaurant after following me around a bit. He was wearing a black suit and tie with a white dress shirt underneath. His shoes were scuffed, but I had a feeling if I were to find his vehicle, I'd find a pair of polished dress shoes there.

These weren't the sort of clothes you shifted in.

"Why were you following me?" I muttered as I scanned the area.

I couldn't figure out why he would be after me. He sure as hell didn't look like one of Baset's men and there was something about him that told me he didn't follow Adrian.

So who sent him?

A feeling of dread crept into my gut. If it wasn't Adrian and it wasn't Baset, then I could think of only one other person who'd have someone following me.

Mephisto.

I'd only seen the vampire count once as I'd sped away from his territory, but that one look told me all I needed to know about him.

He was powerful—something I'd already known—but he was also interested in me. He'd stopped his men from coming after me when they had me all but trapped.

"Son of a bitch." If Mephisto had someone following me, I was in more trouble than I'd thought. I knew I'd drawn his interest, but hadn't been sure he'd stuck a tail on me.

And if the wolf had followed me here . . .

I immediately thought of Ethan. Did Mephisto know where I lived? Why didn't I just invite all of the werewolves and vampires who knew where I lived over for a party? Maybe we could hash out our differences with a big old orgy of blood and death. Last one standing inherits the city or some shit like that.

I plucked the cross off the dead wolf's forehead. Blood was splattered across it from where it had sprayed from his throat. It was uncomfortable in my hand, as if my body knew the silver should have affected me, but it didn't burn. I turned it over a few times, wondering how many more people would have to die like this before I managed to stop them.

The bar doors opened and Purebloods started filtering out. I dropped the cross next to the body before rising. I put myself over the body just so no one would get too close. There were quite a few rubberneckers who just about plowed into one another as they drove off the lot, hoping to catch one last glimpse of the body. Bart urged them along, gun still in his hand.

As soon as they were gone, I glanced around, searching for a watcher. I felt like I had a bull's-eye painted on my chest. Anyone could be out there now, watching me. Did Baset have someone following me as well? Did Adrian? Had their men watched the Left Hand kill Mephisto's wolf?

I could feel panic setting in. I mean, Christ, I knew I was in a shitload of trouble, but this was starting to get ridiculous. I very nearly expected to turn around and see the road to Delai appear and Levi come waltzing out to crush me into dust.

"You know the guy?" Bart said as the last of the bar's patrons left.

I nodded. "I've seen him before, but don't know his name or anything."

Bart scowled at the body. "This might hurt business a bit."

"Look," I said, turning to face him, "I'm sorry about this. This isn't my fault."

"I know," he said. "The Left Hand did it."

"So you know of them."

He gave a single-shoulder shrug. "Don't serve 'em, though. They aren't worth the trouble." He heaved a sigh. "Do you think this is a message for you?"

I thought about it. At first, I'd thought it very well might be, but now that I recognized the face, I wasn't so sure. He could have been checking out my Honda, maybe placing some sort of tracking device on it when he'd been jumped. There was no reason to believe the Left Hand even knew who I was.

"I don't think so," I said, eyeing my bike. "At least not a message for me specifically." Could they have known this was Mephisto's man and was warning the count that they were coming for him?

Bart glanced around the now empty lot. "Bad things are coming," he said. "I can feel it in my bones."

I turned to follow Bart's gaze, which now rested on his bar. A curtain fluttered, but I didn't see anyone inside. I wondered if Mikael was still there or if he'd left with the others. I didn't recall seeing him. In fact, I'm not so sure he had anywhere else to go. The guy was always sitting in the same booth at the Bloody Stake like he was glued to it.

"I didn't mean for this to happen." I don't know why, but I felt the need to apologize. "I think this guy was following me and got killed for it."

"But not by you or yours."

It was a statement, but I felt the need to answer anyway. "No," I said. "Not one of mine."

Bart rubbed at his face. "Things like this keep happening. It's almost not worth it anymore."

"I'm sorry," I said. I felt horrible. Every time I came to the Bloody Stake lately, it seemed like someone died.

"This isn't your fault," Bart said. "While this might hurt numbers for a little while, it seems like this might be more problematic for you. I'm starting to get worried about you."

I almost laughed. "I've been worrying about me for a long time now."

"But things have been worse lately, haven't they?"

I sighed. "Yeah," I said, "they have."

"I just want you to be careful. I don't want you to end up dead, no matter what others think."

And with that, he turned and limped his way back to the bar.

I stood there, feeling trapped. When I'd started hunting vampires and werewolves, I never thought it would end up like this. I'd figured I'd go for a few years until I went after someone bigger and better than me and that would be that.

I'd come across quite a few people now who could rip me apart without batting an eye, and yet here I was. Instead of killing me, they're putting me under their thumbs. Before long, I wouldn't be able to move one way or another. And then what would happen? Would they all converge on me as one? Will they tear each other apart trying to lay claim to me?

I knew I'd have to do something about it eventually, but first, I had to deal with the Left Hand. Sure, I could wait and hope they took out Baset or Adrian or Mephisto for me, but I wasn't counting on it. To let them run free would be to put others I cared about at risk, and I didn't just mean Jonathan.

I walked around the parking lot, looking for any sort of clue as to who the Left Hand member might be. Could it have been the trio near the trash bins? I checked the ground carefully there but found only garbage and a few recently used cigarette butts. I found no sign, outside the body, that anyone from the Left Hand had ever been there. There wasn't even a broken or empty syringe.

Bart came out of the bar as I walked back toward my bike. He raised an eyebrow at me. He was carrying an industrial strength trash bag. There'd be no decent burial for this guy.

"You still here?" he said as he strode over to the body.

"Just leaving," I said. Blood was drying under the wheels. It would be a bitch to get out. Traces would more than likely remain for weeks. "Need me to help with this?" I asked, indicating the body.

"Nah," Bart said. "I'll take care of it. I was running low on meat for the burgers anyway."

I looked up, shocked, to find him grinning at me. He winked before kneeling by the corpse and going through his pockets. Maybe if he found ID, he'd contact the guy's next of kin.

As Bart went about bagging the body, I checked over my motorcycle carefully. If Mephisto's man had put something onto it, I was going to find it.

I scoured every inch of my Honda, but found nothing. Either putting something on it wasn't his goal, or he hadn't had a chance to do it. Or perhaps the Left Hand killer had removed whatever was placed there.

In the end, it didn't matter. My bike appeared clean. If Mephisto wanted to track me, he'd have to do it the old fashioned way.

Bart waved as I started up the engine and rolled out into the road. I waved back and aimed for home, hoping I wouldn't find someone lying dead in my front yard.

16

"How'd things go?"

I paused just inside the dining room, coat halfway off. Jeremy was standing between me and the stairs, with Ethan sitting on the couch to my right. I couldn't tell if Jeremy was pissed at me or not about running off without him. If he was still angry, he was doing a damn good job of hiding it.

I sighed and finished taking off my coat. I draped it over a chair and went to work on my belt and shoulder holster.

Ethan walked over to Jeremy. He wasn't wearing shoes, telling me he was done with the basement tonight.

I set my weapons on the table and then looked at them. They'd effectively cut me off from the rest of the house, but no one was saying anything. It was clear they were itching for a talk. I simply wanted to get upstairs to a bath, where I could soak out the worries. I was mentally exhausted.

"What?" I asked, when I'd decided the silence had gone on long enough.

"Are you okay?" Ethan asked, doing his best to look me in the eye, though I could tell he was nervous.

"Not really."

"Care to talk about it?"

"Not really."

"Kat . . ."

I pulled out the chair I'd set my coat on and dropped down into it. "What do you want me to say?" I asked. "It was a bad night. That's nothing new. I'm tired. I just want to go upstairs and cool out for a little bit. Is that too much to ask?"

Jeremy and Ethan glanced at each other. Something passed between them before they both turned to look at me.

"We're worried," Jeremy said.

"Is this an intervention?" I asked with an irritated laugh. Neither man smiled.

"No," Ethan said. "But we do want to talk to you."

I waved a hand at them to go on, too exhausted to talk. I'd dealt with far too much that night without actually having to kill someone. What I really wanted to do was to blow them off and go straight to my room, but knew I needed to hear them out. The old Kat was the type who would tell anyone and everyone to piss off. I wasn't that person anymore.

Or at least, I was trying not to be.

"You can't leave without telling us where you're going." Jeremy spoke carefully, as if making sure he chose his words correctly. I guess he still felt the need to treat me like my old self. "We need to know in case something happens. We might have to come looking for you and it would be nice to know where in the hell you are."

"It's not safe out there," Ethan added with a shudder and glance toward the back door.

"Has it ever been?"

"Well, no." His face reddened. "But it's worse now."

I couldn't argue with that.

"It's just . . ." Ethan trailed off and looked to Jeremy for help.

"We sit here, waiting for you to get home night after night." Jeremy shifted his weight, looking decidedly uncomfortable. "We don't know if you're alive or dead. Someone could have you locked away somewhere. We just don't know."

I looked down at my hands. They might not call it an intervention, but it sure as hell felt like one. They were making me feel like a teenager who'd been sneaking out at night to see her metalhead boyfriend.

I knew I should be more upfront with them, but it was hard. I'd kept things to myself for so long, it wasn't easy to open up to people, even my friends. I didn't always know whom I could trust. I feared getting people hurt, myself included.

"You don't have to tell us *why* you're going wherever it is you go on nights like these," Jeremy said. "We just want to know where it is you're going just in case something happens."

"Okay," I said.

"Okay?" Ethan sounded surprised. I'm not sure there was a time I didn't argue with a request like that.

"Yeah," I said. "I need to start trusting you more." I glanced at Jeremy. "Both of you."

I think I caught both of them off guard because they both looked at each other as if they'd had this big speech planned and I'd totally wrecked it. Jeremy looked worried, like he thought I was trying to trick them somehow. It was almost funny.

"So, you're not mad?" Ethan asked.

"I am," I admitted. "But I realize it isn't you I'm mad at. I had a real shitty night and, well, you know what it's like living with a monster inside you." I directed the last at Jeremy. "It's easy to lose control and lash out at people who don't deserve it."

There was a moment of silence, as if they still didn't believe me.

"I'm serious," I said. "I'll tell someone where I'm going whenever I leave. I promise."

"Great," Ethan said with a shaky laugh. He clapped his hands together and cleared his throat. "Now that that's settled, there's something else we want to talk to you about."

I didn't like the way he said that. I narrowed my eyes at him and he took a step back. He ran his fingers through his hair and continued to clear his throat as if something was caught in it.

"We were thinking it wouldn't be such a bad idea to take Jonathan up on his offer," Jeremy said, drawing my eye.

"Which offer?"

"You know, the one where we go hide out at his place for a little while," Ethan said with a weak smile.

"You can't be serious."

"It would be safer," Jeremy said.

"I'm not so sure about that."

This time, it was Jeremy who narrowed his eyes. "And what do you mean by that?"

This was it—the big test. I could go back to my old ways and refuse to tell him anything, or I could tell him that I thought someone at the Den was feeding the Left Hand information. I could tell him about my concern over Nathan and Keira. He might not live at the Den, but Jeremy was still part of the Cult.

Then again, telling him might cause some serious damage. He might hate me for even considering such a thing, or he might start to distrust those who took him in. Either way, he wouldn't be happy with it. It would be far easier to try to do this on my own so that when the shit eventually did hit the fan, I'd be the only one standing in front of it.

Why did trusting others have to be so damn hard?

"I have some concerns about a few people at the Den," I said, meeting Jeremy's eye.

"Concerns? About who?"

I rubbed at the back of my neck. "Nathan, for one." I winced as I said it.

"What about him?"

"Do you know where he's been sneaking off to?" I figured I might as well go all out and see what Jeremy knew. If I were going to accuse Nathan of something, it would be far better to get as many facts as I could.

"Sneaking off?" Jeremy looked genuinely confused.

"Yeah. I was heading in one night and caught him driving off on his own. I followed him, curious, and he went to some house and just watched it. Before I could see what he was up to, I got jumped."

"By Nathan?"

"By someone else. I . . . I think it might have been Keira but I can't be sure."

"Wait, what?" This time there was anger in Jeremy's voice. I'm not sure if it was directed at me or at the other weres. I'm not so sure it mattered. One-armed or not, Jeremy was still a werewolf with a monster inside him that could cause irrational bouts of rage in an instant.

I carefully moved my hand next to my gun, just in case. I doubted Jeremy would attack me, but it was always best to be safe around a were. I wouldn't shoot him, but I hoped the threat would cause him to hesitate if he were to wolf out on me.

"She was shifted when she attacked, so it might not have been her," I admitted. "And Nathan was gone before I could question him. I don't think he saw me."

"Jesus." Jeremy rubbed at his forehead and started pacing. "Do you think Nathan and Keira have anything to do with . . ." He shook his head. "No. I refuse to believe it. They wouldn't help the Left Hand."

"I agree that Nathan wouldn't," I said, surprising even myself. I moved my hand away from my gun. Jeremy looked agitated, but not so much that I was worried he'd shift. "It isn't his style. But how much do we really know about Keira?"

Jeremy remained silent.

"Are you sure there's something going on with them?" Ethan asked. "I mean, could it have all been a coincidence?"

"Sure," I said. "But Nathan looked nervous. He was up to something. And I sure as hell don't trust Keira."

Deep down, I knew my distrust was rooted in how close she seemed to be with Jonathan, but there was nothing that would get me to admit that to either of them. It just seemed too convenient for her to show up just as the Left Hand started killing people. She had to be connected somehow.

"We should talk to Jonathan," Jeremy said, reaching for his phone. "He'll know what to do."

"I tried," I said. "Nathan stopped me."

Jeremy looked troubled and eased his phone back into his pocket. "Why would he do that?"

"I guess he was with Keira. She . . . she may have gotten to him."

The room fell silent, which was okay by me. The thought of Jonathan and Keira together had my stomach twisted into knots. The bath sounded better than ever now. I wasn't even sure I could keep talking about this without breaking down like a love-struck teenager.

Is that what I was? Could I actually be in love with a werewolf?

I stared down at my hands, which were shaking. I wasn't sure what was happening to me. I truly didn't want Nathan to be up to something devious. We'd never gotten along, sure, but he was always there when I needed him. He could have let me die more than once, but he always saved me.

But Keira . . . I had no connection with her. In fact, I almost hoped she was the one who was feeding the Left Hand information.

It would suck for Jonathan, but at least I'd get the pleasure of putting her down for him. Things would be so much easier if she weren't around.

I sighed. Once again, I wasn't sure which part of me was talking.

"What can we do?" Ethan asked into the silence that had fallen.

I shrugged. "I'll talk to Jonathan as soon as I can."

"I can call him," Jeremy offered, reaching for his phone again.

"No. I think this needs to be done face to face."

"When?"

"Soon," I said. "I'd do it tomorrow, but . . ."

"It's okay," Jeremy said, actually managing something akin to a smile. "We understand."

Our eyes met. I could tell he truly did understand. He wasn't going to ask me about where I'd been or what I've been doing every Monday since I'd dealt with Baset. He trusted me to do what was right.

God, I hoped that trust wasn't misplaced.

"I'm going to get some rest," I said. "I've got something I have to take care of tomorrow, but as soon as that's done, I'm going to go talk to Jonathan."

I rose and both men stepped back. While some things had been settled, there was a whole lot of unease going around.

"Don't bring any of this up to him if you talk to him tonight," I told Jeremy. "I'd like to make sure I'm not leaping at shadows here. Maybe Nathan has a good reason for doing what he's doing. Maybe I'm wrong about Keira. If anyone is going to bring these concerns up to Jonathan, it has to be me, all right?"

Jeremy nodded.

"Okay." I heaved a sigh and headed for the stairs. "I'll see you two tomorrow night."

I paused by the stairs as another thought hit me. I turned back to face Ethan.

"Did you happen to find anything out about the stuff in the syringe?" I'd given him the briefcase last night as soon as I'd gotten home. I figured he might have some luck identifying what was inside. I'm not sure how it would help, but the more we knew about the Left Hand, the better.

"Not yet," he said. "I'll keep working on it."

I nodded and continued upstairs.

I entered my room and closed the door behind me. I leaned against it and sighed. I might have come clean with a few things, but there was still quite a lot I'd left out. They deserved to know about Baset and Mephisto.

About Adrian.

I could feel him out there and wondered if he was thinking about me. I knew his intentions were impure, knew that he was far more dangerous than a lot of people gave him credit for, yet there was a comfort there, knowing he'd protect me even if I didn't actually need it.

I'd never become his mate. He could take that dream and shove it up his ass for all I cared. I doubted I could even bring myself to like the guy. He was a pompous ass who was as creepy as hell with his blank stares and emotionless voice.

But maybe, someday, when I wasn't so preoccupied with everyone trying to control me, I could learn to trust him. Stranger things have happened.

17

Anton Green lived in a surprisingly nice neighborhood. The lawns were manicured, houses were of moderate size, and welcome mats sat on nearly every doorstep. There were motion sensors outside all of the houses, and I caught a glimpse of something near one door that looked like the barrel of a gun poking out of shrubbery.

Needless to say, the people here were prepared.

When Mikael had given me Anton's name and address, I immediately thought about movies in which the guy with all the info lived in a basement with computers hanging from every available space, where you had to duck beneath wires, and step over empty soda bottles. You'd find all of this after saying your pleasantries to his mother.

One look at the property and I knew that wasn't the case.

I parked behind a blue Chevy in front of a white house with black shutters. The glow coming from inside told me someone was home and they were looking at either a television or computer screen. I glanced around and noted that many of the other houses were the same.

But despite the fact that they gave all appearances of being unafraid, I could smell blood in the air. I wasn't sure if it was Pureblood blood or if it was the blood of a supe who'd strayed too close, but it was there. Across the street, someone peered out of an upstairs window and I caught a glint of light that could only have reflected from a gunsight.

I decided the blood must have been from a supe.

I walked slowly past the Chevy truck and glanced inside. There were a few discarded napkins on the passenger seat and a plastic bag stuffed with wrappers sat on the floor. Otherwise it was clean. There were no guns laying inside or blood splatter, or even a few stray wires from a computer. It looked like anyone's truck, really.

The light from inside suddenly went out. I paused beside the truck and studied the windows. I couldn't see past the curtains to tell if someone was moving around inside or not; they were too thick.

Mikael had said he'd tell Anton I was coming, but how much had he told him? As far as I knew, Anton knew just as much as Mikael, which meant I was still a threat to him and his neighborhood. He might not be happy to see me.

The back of my neck itched where I could still feel the gun pointing from the house across the street. I had a feeling there were more eyes than that on me. It wouldn't surprise me to learn that Anton was sitting inside, gun in hand, waiting to put a bullet through my eyes the moment I came too close.

I kept my hand away from my weapons as I strode toward the door. I couldn't show fear here. I had a feeling fear was met with violent and abrupt force in the guise of a bullet through the head. The seemingly peaceful neighborhood was definitely not as peaceful as it first appeared.

A ceramic cat with the word "Welcome" painted across its chest sat beside the door. The door itself looked welcoming, outside of the peephole that looked to me to be a little too large and a little too dark. I had a feeling I was staring straight into the barrel of a gun.

With nothing else to do, I knocked on the door. If Anton was going to blow my head off, running wouldn't do any good. He'd just shoot me in the back if I tried.

"Anton?" I called through the door when it didn't open. "Mikael sent me."

Four quick clicks sounded and the door opened. Standing just inside was a man who looked as if he'd spent most of his life in the gym. He was wearing tight bicycle shorts and a sleeveless shirt that exposed biceps bigger around than my leg. His head was shaved bald and a faint scar cut through one eyebrow.

He gave me a smile that could light up a room. "Come on in," he said. "I was expecting you."

I stepped past him, noting he stood a good two heads taller than me. He wasn't wearing shoes and I vaguely wondered if he could even *find* shoes that would fit him. His feet were bigger than most people's heads.

He closed the door and took a moment to hit the safety on the gun built into the door, right where the peephole should be. "Can't be too careful," he said with a grin as he turned. "Let's head to my office."

He led the way across a room that looked as if his grandmother had decorated it. The television sat across the room on top of a doily. In fact, every surface was covered by white crocheted doilies. Even the chairs and couches had them draped over their backs.

Anton must have seen something in my face because he paused long enough to run his fingers over one. "It's a hobby," he said. "Keeps my fingers nimble."

He waggled huge fingers at me before turning and walking deeper into the house. With a grunt and one last look around the room, I followed him.

We went up a flight of stairs—dispelling any illusions that he would take me into his basement hideaway—and went to the first room on our left. He opened the door and flipped on the light.

It looked like any other office. The window was covered so that no light could possibly seep out, and if I didn't miss my guess, the glass would be tinted as well. A pair of computer chairs sat in front of a large desk. In place of the mass of wires and computers I'd expected were two seemingly innocuous laptops sitting side by side on an otherwise clean desk.

He took the first chair and leaned back. He was still smiling and even though I was positive he knew I was a vampire, he seemed completely unconcerned. I glanced around, thinking he had some other weaponry he could trigger in a heartbeat if I were to attack, but there didn't appear to be anything. And there sure as hell wasn't anything hidden on him. There'd be nowhere for him to hide it.

"How do you know Mikael?" I asked when my scan of the room was complete.

Anton shrugged. "Saw him at the Bloody Stake a few times. Offered him my services."

I glanced at the computers and he laughed.

"Not that kind of services."

My brow started to crease and then I shook my head. I really didn't want to know.

"Do you know why I'm here?" I asked instead.

"I do." Anton's smile fell. "I can't say I like it. This isn't the sort of thing I like finding, but what can you do?"

"So I take it you get information for Mikael?"

Anton laughed again. I'd expected it to be a deep rumble, but it was more of a pleasing chuckle than anything. I could listen to him laugh all day and not get annoyed.

"More like he tells me where to find stuff and I extract it for him. If anything hits the net and he has even the slightest interest in it, I get a call from him."

"I see."

"Please," Anton said. "Take a seat." He gestured toward the other chair.

I considered declining. If I were sitting, I'd be in a more vulnerable position. If Anton had some other trick up his sleeve, I'd want to be prepared.

But Mikael wouldn't have sent me here if he thought Anton was a danger to me. I was sure the guy could take care of himself, or else I wouldn't be here. This was probably one of the few places I could go and actually be safe.

I sat down and let my coat fall open. The hilt of my sword poked out and Anton's eyes widened for a fraction of a second before he was grinning again.

"Now," he said, "this isn't going to be pleasant."

He opened his laptop and a video player was already up. The screen was dark, but I could tell it wasn't just a black screen. It looked as if he'd paused the movie just as it was fading in.

I braced myself. Mikael had said this wasn't something anyone should watch. I wasn't looking forward to this in the slightest, but I definitely could use a visual description of my target. It would make my job far easier, especially if Mikael was right and I wouldn't find him alone.

"Ready for this?" Anton asked, finger poised over his mouse button.

I nodded.

He clicked Play.

The screen rolled dark for a moment and then came into focus. It showed an empty room that looked to be some sort of hotel room. The bed was stripped of its sheets and pillows. They'd been tossed into a chair and left there, telling me this wasn't exactly a high quality production.

There was faint music playing, but I couldn't make it out. I wasn't sure if it was supposed to have been heard on the video or if Anton had the volume turned way down. It didn't seem like the right kind of music for a porno, even a blood porn like this was supposed to be. The music sounded like it belonged in a dance club or perhaps a party house somewhere. The pulse-pounding beat caused my own heart rate to pick up despite the fact I couldn't really hear it clearly.

"They always start like this," Anton said. "And are always in the same room." He pointed to a spot on the screen. "Bloodstains," he said, indicating a darker spot on the wall.

I grimaced. "How long before he shows up?"

"Not long," Anton said. "The guy thinks this is his establishing shot. Needs a lesson in moviemaking, if you ask me."

I continued to watch the screen. I scanned the room, hoping I could make something out that would help me, but there really wasn't anything to see. I could make out the bloodstains on the wall, and the mattress itself looked as if it had seen its fair share of blood, but otherwise, there were no identifying features that would tell me where the film had been shot.

Before I could ask Anton if he knew, a girl walked over to the bed and sat down. She was pale and shaking. Her eyes were terrified as they found the camera. She stared pleadingly into the lens, as if hoping that someone would see her and come rescue her. She couldn't have been any more than fifteen.

I almost told Anton to shut it off. I was *not* going to watch this girl get defiled by anyone, even if it would help me take the man down. Rushing out and searching for Boris Stevenson wouldn't do a damn bit of good for her, though. I was pretty sure the girl in this movie was already dead.

"You won't have to watch him hurt her," Anton said. "I chose this one because it takes him some time before he gets into it enough to bite." Anton cleared his throat. He looked as uncomfortable as I felt. "But you do get a good look at his face, which is what you wanted, right?"

I nodded. I felt sick to my stomach. The girl's eyes were jerking back and forth, like she wasn't sure if she should be staring into the camera or looking at the person approaching. I could hear the sound of his feet on the carpet, but he'd yet to walk into the frame.

"Death is just another form of life."

The voice coming out of the speakers made me jump. It was louder than I'd expected. The girl hadn't made a peep and the music stayed just faint background noise. I'd been positive the volume had been turned way down, but I guess that wasn't the case.

"That's Boris," Anton said.

A moment later, a nude man strode into the frame.

He wasn't muscular or all that well built, to be honest. He had a bald spot on the back of his head and while he wasn't overweight, he looked flabby. Just because someone is a vampire, doesn't mean they suddenly become ripped. This guy looked like he enjoyed sitting around eating potato chips far more than doing anything strenuous.

He walked toward the girl, who cringed away from him on the bed, but she didn't try to run. I'm not sure if she'd wanted to do this or if she was being compelled somehow, because if it were me, I'd have kicked him in the nuts and bashed his face in by now. I don't care if there was a guy standing off screen with a gun aimed at my head. If I was going to die, I was going to go down fighting.

My hands were clenched into fists as I waited for Boris to move so I could get a better look at him. I wanted this over with already.

He sat at the edge of the bed, back still to the screen. He was facing the girl who was trembling so badly, I was afraid she might die of fright right then and there.

Boris reached out a hand and gently touched her cheek. She winced, but didn't pull away.

"I'll take you to your new life," he said and the girl nodded.

"How much longer?" I asked through gritted teeth.

"He turns in a sec."

I bit my lip. Why couldn't Anton have simply paused the video on a shot of Boris and left the rest to my imagination? I really didn't need to see this to know the guy needed to die.

Boris pulled back his hand and then turned. He looked directly into the camera, giving me a perfect view of his face. He was showing fang with his smile. He had a bad goatee that was uneven on the right side, as if he accidentally shaved too far up and didn't bother fixing it. His eyebrows were thick and bushy above beady little eyes. His nostrils were huge black holes in his face. The guy's nose was as big as a Buick.

Anton reached out and hit Pause. "I'm guessing you don't need to see any more?"

"No," I said. "This is good." I couldn't take my eyes off the vampire. I wished I could reach through the screen and wring his neck.

"It isn't pretty," Anton said. I glanced at him and noticed he was pale. "I had to watch a few of these for Mikael. I didn't eat for a week after."

"I can imagine."

Anton turned in his chair and looked hard at me. I tore my eyes away from Boris's smug face and met his gaze.

"Are you going to kill him?" he asked.

"Yes."

"Are you going to make him suffer?"

"I am."

Anton pressed his lips together and his eyes became hard. He suddenly looked like someone who could crush a man's skull by simply thinking about it. No wonder the neighborhood appeared mostly untouched. They had a terrifying protector.

"Good," he said finally. "I want him to scream for mercy."

So did I, but I kept that to myself.

Anton sighed and then turned back to the screen. "Can I shut this off now?" he asked. "I can't stand looking at him any longer."

"Yeah." I stood. "I'm done."

Anton hit the keys like he was trying to hurt Boris through the computer. The screen went dark and he lowered the laptop lid.

"I hope you get him," Anton said. "You look like someone who can take care of herself."

I wondered how much he knew about me. It didn't sound like he knew who I was exactly, which suited me just fine. I didn't want anyone to know I was the one whom the supernatural world called Lady Death.

"I can." I took a deep breath and started for the door. "I can show myself out."

Anton didn't follow me as I left his office and headed downstairs. I glanced at the doilies strewn about his living room and it only made me angrier. Why couldn't more people be like Anton? Why did there have to be people like Boris, whose hobbies included butchering young women in front of a camera for profit?

I just about tore Anton's door from its frame as I stormed out of his house. I wasn't waiting around.

Boris Stevenson was a dead man. He just didn't know it yet.

18

Boris's house was in a part of town I knew well. The place was thick with vampire rogues who had too little power to advance through the ranks. None of them had Houses of their own. They simply did what they could to make a living for themselves. More often than not, they were killed by counts or countesses when they fed from someone in the wrong territory. Many died when they refused to join a vampire House as a mere minion to someone far more powerful.

But just because the vampires here were rogue, it didn't mean they were any less dangerous. In fact, if I made too much of a scene when taking Boris down, I could have a dozen angry vamps descending on me.

I smiled as I approached the address Mikael had given me. Rogues used to be my bread and butter. Thomas and I worked together to take them down, one by one. We occasionally went after the Fledgling Houses, but that was about our limit. When we'd tried to go after a bigger House, it had ended up with both of us becoming something other than human.

The smile slid away at the memory. Thomas was no more. I was doing this on my own.

I could see the lights of High Street glowing over the tops of the buildings as I turned onto Boris's street. Brownstone tenements had gone up here recently, yet they looked as if they'd been built over a hundred years prior. Shattered windows were covered with plywood to keep out the light, as well as the cold. Crumbling foundations had become home to graffiti of all sorts, including the kind painted in blood.

Eyes watched me from open doorways, many of them bloodshot. While drugs didn't affect vampires and werewolves like they would a Pureblood, it didn't mean the supes couldn't still try to reach that high. Often, they'd pump their bodies so full of narcotics, they'd fry their brains long before they ever felt the effects. Addicts had it hard when turned.

I knew some of the people watching me were Purebloods. The vampires would feed on them in exchange for more drugs, and sometimes more victims. These were the type of people who got high on being fed upon. They reveled in the pain, of the feeling of their lives being drained from them. It gave them a perverse pleasure I never understood.

But while they watched me as I rode past, I knew none of them would do anything to stop me. Half of them were too dazed to do much more than keep breathing. Those that could would only bother me if I started trouble.

Which was exactly what I was there to do.

I wasn't sure who ran this part of town anymore. I'd lost track long ago. When I'd stopped hunting rogue wolves and vamps as my main targets, I'd let things go. Even without me killing them, the vamps and wolves here didn't last long. No one did. This place was a wasteland of life.

Boris's house came into view and I slowed down. I couldn't just leap off my motorcycle and go charging in unless I wanted everyone to be waiting for me when I came back out. I coasted slowly by and took it all in, looking for a weakness I could exploit.

The house looked much like the other single-family homes in the area. It was standing, which was a plus, but looked as if it hadn't had anyone even try to keep it from collapsing. The grass—what little of it there was—was brown and dead. The wooden front porch was leaning, as if slowly sinking into the concrete foundation beneath. The windows had bars on them and the front door looked sturdier than the rest of the house. I had a feeling I wouldn't be getting in that way.

I sped up once I was past the house and turned down a side

street. There were a few people here, but they weren't paying me any mind.

I found an abandoned gas station and pulled in behind the crumbling structure. I shut off the engine and sat there a moment, contemplating my course of action.

Boris's place wasn't going to be easy to get into. I hadn't seen the back, but I figured it might be just as tough. But it might very well be the only way I could get in without being seen. There were too many people on the streets, watching.

Which was exactly why he'd chosen the place as his headquarters, I was sure. If the guy was famous in the vampire circles, then he could afford someplace better. I didn't know if the house was the place where he took his victims or if he actually lived there. I just hoped he was there when I made my move.

I didn't like this at all. It was too public. Baset had yet to put me in a situation I couldn't handle, but this was the first time I was going to have to take care of someone where others might see me. I couldn't kill them all. Doing this was putting myself at risk and I'd be damned if I was going to get myself killed for Baset.

Still, I had to try.

I dismounted and began the short walk back to Boris's street. I checked to make sure no one was watching me, and then continued on past the street. An alley ran along the back of the buildings. A graffiti-filled brick wall blocked the rest of the view. If I were careful, I could reach his back door without anyone seeing me.

I hesitated outside the alley to make sure I wasn't being followed. No one was in sight. I darted into the alley and kept low as I ran the rest of the way to Boris's house.

The back looked as secure as the front. All windows were barred, so I wasn't going in that way. There was a back door, but it was three feet off the ground and there were no steps. I had a feeling it was bolted on the other side, if not completely walled off. I couldn't see even a hint of light through the tiny window in the door.

I frowned, considering my options. I could try to shoot the lock on the door and hope I could get in that way, but a gunshot would announce my presence. I had a feeling a person like Boris Stevenson had an escape plan. By the time I'd get in through the back, he'd be out the front door and halfway down the street.

There might be a basement in a house like this, but I couldn't find any windows—at least not from the back. I doubted they would have forgotten to bar the windows to the basement, so I wasn't sure what good it would do me if I'd actually found any.

That only left the front. If I was going to deal with Boris here tonight, I'd have to walk right through the front door, kill him, and figure out how to get out of there before others were on to me.

I worked my way around the side of the house to get a better look at the front. I could see people standing out there, talking among themselves. The moment I stepped out of the small space between houses, they'd all see me.

I was at a total loss. The best I could hope for was that Boris would come outside and take a lonely stroll out back where I could kill him without anyone else knowing.

Right. I'm sure if I waited long enough, that was going to happen.

I crept back into the shadows. I wasn't sure Boris was even there. I leaned in close and tried to hear through the walls, but it was useless. If he was inside, he'd have to be just about shouting for me to hear anything. My hearing might be better than an average Pureblood's, but that didn't mean I could hear through walls.

I decided to wait it out. I moved so I could keep an eye on the street. If the people chatting out front decided to move on, I might make a go of it. Otherwise, I'd see what I could learn and then come back another day with a better plan in place.

Cars occasionally went down the road, but none of them stopped outside Boris's house. I heard a door slam inside once, telling me someone was home, but I had no idea if it was Boris or someone he associated with. As far as I knew, there could be a dozen people inside.

I was just about to give up and leave when the front door opened. Voices filtered down to me and I stepped back into the shadows. The wooden porch creaked as a pair of men came walking down the stairs.

"I'm heading to Avril's." I instantly recognized the voice as Boris's. It wasn't as sinister sounding as it had been on the video, but it was definitely him. "See that you get a good deal, all right?"

"Of course." The other voice belonged to a man who sounded like he'd smoked all his life. It was either that or he'd gargled razor blades as a kid. "Need me to pick up anything else while I'm out?"

"Nah," Boris said. "I won't be back tonight. If I need anything, I'll get it myself when I'm done."

Two shapes appeared and walked past the gap between houses. Neither looked my way, much to my relief. If either one had glanced down the gap, they'd surely have seen me. There wasn't enough room for me to swing my sword and by the time I drew my gun, they could have gunned me down.

"Do you think you can bring me back some . . . ?" The gravelly voice trailed off.

"You know I can't do that for you, Ray."

"But man . . . I need it. Can't you just get me a little? I'll pay you for it."

"I'm sorry . . ." The voices trailed off.

A moment later, a car door a short way down opened and closed before an engine started up. Another car engine revved a few moments after that, and a piece-of-shit convertible putted past. I caught a glimpse of the driver. He was bald with a ratty beard. My best guess was it was the guy Boris had been talking to.

I waited five minutes longer before heading back into the alley. I knew where Avril's was, so I didn't have to tail Boris to know where he was going. I could take some time to formulate something of a plan before I got there.

Of course, even the best laid plans typically fall apart moments after execution. In the end, I didn't care how I did it. I only knew that tonight would be Boris Stevenson's last.

19

Avril's sat square in the middle of the worst stretch of High Street. The nightclub had once been a concert hall, but now was used more often for raves and parties. Vampires and werewolves were the main patrons, along with Purebloods who let the vamps drink from them. While there were rules against killing the willing sheep, accidents did happen.

I'd always left the place alone, figuring if people wanted to throw their lives away by becoming blood slaves to vamps, they didn't deserve saving. And as long as the vampires and wolves were coming here to feed, they weren't out on the streets, killing innocent victims. It wasn't an ideal situation, but it was one I could live with.

A bouncer stood just outside Avril's front doors. He was wearing the requisite sleeveless leather that displayed biceps that were more than likely chemically enhanced. His eyes scanned left and right, lingering on girls in the skimpiest of clothes. A woman leaning beside him didn't seem to mind.

I was sure Boris had already gone in, but I couldn't be sure. Just because he'd told the other man that he'd be going to Avril's didn't mean he was telling the truth. He could have been misleading the man for one reason or another.

But the place fit. The pulse-pounding music I could hear coming from Avril's every time someone opened the door was similar to the background noise I'd heard in the video. Could Boris be filming his movies here? Did the owner of the nightclub know?

I didn't see how he couldn't. Chances were good they provide Boris a room where he could conduct his business without interruption. The owner probably got a cut of anything Boris made with his movies. Where else could the filmmaker find so many willing victims to exploit? It wasn't like Avril's catered strictly to the legal.

A man wearing a loud pink suit poked his head out of the nightclub. He said a few words to the bouncer and then ducked back inside. The woman gave the bouncer a quick kiss on the cheek before heading in after the guy in the pink suit.

I was torn on what to do. I didn't want Boris to get away, or worse, kill someone while I waited outside. But I also knew that confronting him in such a public place, especially one where the people were more than likely on his side, was just asking for trouble. If I waited, I might be able to take him out as he walked back to his car, but that would mean standing around on High Street for who knows how long. The guy might decide to spend the night in there.

There really was no other choice. Waiting would more than likely mean someone would die. If I wanted to make sure it was Boris Stevenson who met his end, I needed to be proactive.

I crossed the street and approached Avril's warily. I'd seen a few people go into the club and none of them had been patted down for weapons. The bouncer had simply nodded and let them pass without another look. I had no idea if that meant they were regulars or if anyone could go in and the bouncer was simply there for show. He might be their way of weeding out the weak. If someone was afraid to approach the club because of the big guy out front, there was no way they could handle what went on inside.

Just as I stepped onto the sidewalk, the woman returned. She leaned against the wall beside the bouncer, grinning from ear to ear. Her lips were a little redder than before she went in.

The urge to whip out my gun and shoot her was so strong, my hand actually moved toward my coat. I stopped myself, plastered on a smile, and sauntered up to the pair, hoping they wouldn't take a look at my outfit and decide I was a danger. If one of them so much as touched me, I'd be forced to fight. A sword isn't an easy thing to hide.

I didn't need to worry. The bouncer glanced up long enough to give me a quick nod before turning back to the woman. I thought I caught him sniff, telling me he was likely a werewolf, put there to sniff out trouble. I walked past them and opened the doors to Avril's.

Music blasted into me the moment I was through the heavy doors. The lights were so dim, only a vampire or werewolf could see without tripping all over themselves. I walked down a short hallway, into the main section of the club. The dance floor itself was a large open space near a stage where a DJ bounced in a red haze caused by light filtering through mist. The dance floor was surrounded by a raised section where tables were bolted to the floor, sectioned off from one another.

The place was packed nearly wall to wall. There were multiple feedings going on at the sectioned off tables and a few were happening by the walls. Nothing expressly violent was happening—if you discounted the blood dribbling from wounded necks and fangs. The dancers on the floor below seemed happy, if not in something of a daze.

I scanned the room, hoping I'd spot Boris, but it was nearly impossible to make one face out from the next. The mist was coming from beneath the DJ. It seeped over the crowd, especially those at the front, further masking the features of those reveling in the loud music and blood.

Hunger and disgust warred inside me as I moved farther into the room. The place felt cramped. No matter which way I walked, I ended up passing someone who was bleeding. I wanted to slit the throat of every vamp and wolf in the place, to punish them for feeding on people like cattle, yet I also wanted to join them. Blood seeped into my mouth where my fangs began to protrude.

I couldn't stay there. The hunt might have started with Boris, but if I stayed in the midst all of the feedings going on around me, I'd end up giving in to my monster.

I backed out into a narrow room I'd passed coming in. A bar ran along one wall, serving what looked to be actual liquor instead of blood. I decided it might be the best place to start my search. Boris was a familiar face here, and if I was right, he was using Avril's to film his movies. The nightclub had an addition built on over the last few years, adding another couple of floors to the building. If I didn't miss my guess, Boris might very well be upstairs with a victim even now.

Walking to the bar was a test of my control. Even out here, there were people being fed upon. I very nearly stepped on a woman's hand who was apparently having some sort of pleasure seizure. She stared up at me with glassy eyes and smiled as her entire lower half vibrated. Another woman—this one a vampire—was feeding from the bottom of her foot.

I grimaced as I stepped around the pair. Foot blood was the same as any other blood, yet something about it made my stomach curdle. My disgust very nearly quieted my hunger.

There were no stools at the bar. It was standing room only and I could tell that it was a favorite hangout for a lot of people. I had to squeeze my way between two leather-clad women wearing fake fangs. A blue light shone up from the floor behind the bar, casting strange shadows on the two barmen behind the bar. One of them saw me slide up and moved my way.

"I'd like something to drink," I shouted. The music was so loud, I could hardly hear myself think, let alone speak.

The barman seemed to have heard me just fine and he ducked away to make me something. I figured he knew what he was doing and left him at it. I just wanted something that would help ease the hunger inside me. If it had a little fire to it, all the better.

He returned a moment later with something red in a glass. For a split second, I thought it was blood, but it didn't move right. I sniffed it, decided it wasn't going to hurt me, and drained the glass. It burned going down, but it did its job. The hunger was still there, but it was now more of a faint pulse in my gut rather than the raging beast it had been.

"Anything else?" the barman asked. His voice carried well over the noise and it made me wonder if they specifically found someone with the right cadence to be heard over the music or if he was a sorcerer of some kind.

"I'm looking for someone," I shouted, hoping no one in the immediate vicinity was listening. They all appeared to be absorbed in their own conversations. "He came in a little while ago."

The barman shrugged in a way that told me I'd have to do better than that. He picked up my empty glass and it vanished behind the bar, presumably to be washed later.

"His name is Boris Stevenson," I said, keeping my voice as low as I could and still be heard. I really didn't want to have to say his name, but if I wanted to find him, I had no choice.

The barman hesitated a moment before leaning forward. "How do you know Boris?"

I shrugged with one shoulder and gave the man a sideways grin. "We go way back," I said. "I was going to meet him here, but was held up in traffic. I'm not sure where he's gone."

"Really now?" the barman said, his smile hardening. "How come I've never seen you here with him before?"

"I'm from out of town," I said, the lie not quite stumbling from my lips. I managed to hold my smile in place and look him in the eye while I said it.

The barman studied me for a long moment, as if deciding whether or not I was telling the truth. I felt the need to press him a little harder and hoped I wouldn't go too far.

"We were supposed to look for someone for the next flick," I said, casting a look around the bar area as if I was on the job even then. "Boris wanted me to be a part of this one." I waggled my eyebrows at him. I felt like an idiot.

The barman's smile turned genuine. "Really?" He eyed me up and down. From the look in his eye, I knew he was picturing me without my coat and clothes. "He always did have good taste in women, even if you are a little old." He glanced to the side. "Hey, Cal, is Boris upstairs?"

Cal—the other barman apparently—nodded without glancing our way.

"He's upstairs," my barman said, needlessly. "I think he's already chosen tonight's star. She's a little older than what he goes for, but I guess since this one's for you, he made an exception." He laughed. "She was a little pushy for my taste. She practically begged him to take her somewhere private."

My gut tightened. Had Boris already started filming? Was his victim still alive?

I thanked the barman and started to turn away. I stopped myself and turned back before the barman could move. "How do I get upstairs?" I asked, giving him a toothy smile. My fangs were still showing a little bit.

He eyed them with something akin to hunger. I didn't think this guy was a supe of any kind, outside of maybe a little sorcery. I couldn't see any fang marks on his exposed flesh, but that meant little. There were quite a few places a vampire could feed without leaving telltale signs. I had a feeling this guy was someone who enjoyed his bites in those sorts of places.

"That way," he said, gesturing toward the entrance. I vaguely remembered seeing a pair of staircases, but they'd been blocked off. "There's an elevator around the corner, just past the restrooms. Tell Yancy you're here for Boris and that I sent you over. He'll send you up." He leaned forward and gave me a hungry smile. "My name's Dom, by the way."

I think he was hoping I'd offer to take him with me to see Boris, or at least, take him home afterward. I thanked him and turned away with a faint shudder. My smile fell away and I put on my game face.

I pushed through the crowded room and stepped out into a small open space. The stairs were indeed there, but sheets of plywood had been placed on them, leaving only a flat surface that would be next to impossible for most people to crawl up. Large barrels were placed in front of the stairs, effectively blocking them off to anyone who didn't get the hint.

The elevator was right where I'd been told it would be. I hadn't seen it when I'd come in because the guy standing in front of it was the size of a truck. He stood at least seven feet tall and I swear he had to be near four hundred pounds. He grinned at me as I approached, exposing wolfish teeth.

"Dom told me I could find Boris upstairs," I said, trying to look casual.

"Did he now?" the man I took to be Yancy said. "And what is a little thing like you going to do with him, hmm?"

I huffed out an annoyed breath. "I'm late," I said. "We were going to do this one together. I don't have time for this."

Yancy's eyebrows rose and his grin widened. "Oh really? That sounds . . . tasty." He chuckled and rubbed his chin. "I might have to see this one."

God, I hoped not. Taking out Boris in a place like this was going to be hard enough. I just had to hope the rooms were private enough I could kill him and get out before anyone was the wiser. From the video, I knew the rooms weren't soundproof.

Yancy stepped aside and ran a card down a slot reader. The doors to the elevator slid silently open and he motioned for me to go in.

"He's in room two, I believe. Just press the button by the door and let him know you're there. If you get lost, Clem will show you the way."

I walked past the giant and stepped into the elevator. It was obviously newer than the rest of the building, though the walls were stained with what I knew to be blood. There was the faintest of hums as the doors slid closed and it started to move. A moment later, the doors opened and I was looking down a long hallway with doors on either side.

I stepped out of the elevator and nearly yelped in surprise when a guy that was Yancy's opposite spoke. He was all of three feet tall, if that, and was so thin, I thought I could lift him with my little finger. He was sitting in a chair in the corner, out of sight of the doors, reading a magazine. Clem, I presumed.

"Who ya looking for?" he asked, grinning. His mouth was lined with tiny little teeth that were all pointed and sharp. For the first time in my life, I wondered if leprechauns were real.

"Boris," I said. "I was told room two."

The little man nodded. "Right there." He gestured toward the first door on the right. A number two was painted on the door in red paint. "Bell's by the door."

I thanked him and walked to the door. Clem had put a kink into my plans. I didn't want to have to kill him, but would if left no other choice. I wasn't going to let Boris violate another girl, even if she wanted it.

But I knew Boris wasn't going to let me in if I buzzed—he'd be too careful for that.

I cleared my throat and pressed the button anyway. Maybe he'd decide two was indeed better than one. I heard a faint buzzing from inside, but no other sound. I didn't see an intercom anywhere, telling me he'd have to open the door to talk to me.

I waited for a long moment and nothing happened. I glanced

back at the little man. He was watching me with that grin on his face. He winked.

I glanced down the length of the hall. There were at least a half dozen doors, all closed. Who knew how many people were there?

This time, I pretended to press the buzzer. I tapped my foot, mind racing. How could I do this without anyone noticing? I looked toward Clem and decided I'd have to deal with him after all.

"I think something's wrong with the buzzer," I said. "He's not answering."

With a sigh, he put down his magazine and walked toward the door. I stepped aside, moving so I was behind him. As soon as he reached up for the button, I grabbed his wrist, spun him around, and with my other hand, grabbed the back of his head and pushed downward toward my rising knee. The impact was jarring. I let him go and he crumpled to the ground, out like a light.

No one came running out. I picked Clem up and carried him back to his chair where I set him down. Blood ran from one nostril so I tilted his head so it wouldn't be seen by anyone coming down the hall. I stepped back and moved his head a little more until I was satisfied it looked as if he'd simply fallen asleep.

That done, I turned back to the door. It didn't look to be all that well made. A good kick would more than likely rip it free, but it would be loud. The music thumped beneath my feet, which might mask some of the sound, but not all of it.

I tried the knob in the hopes it would be unlocked. When that didn't work, I very nearly kicked it in, but stopped myself.

A keycard. The slot was right by the door. Boris would have one. The guy downstairs had one for the elevator. Would the guy up here have a keycard as well?

I hurried back to the unconscious man and rifled through his pockets. I found a card in his pants and prayed it would open the door. I went back, slipped it into the reader, and was rewarded with a green light and a click.

I drew my gun as I pushed the door inward. I stepped quickly inside, ready to fire if Boris made so much as a move toward me.

Turned out, he was in no condition to do much of anything.

Boris lay on the bed, still fully clothed. His head was tilted so I could see his wide, frightened eyes. He made a sort of grunting sound, but did little else. He wasn't tied down and nothing was stuffed in his mouth, yet he was incapable of moving.

A fully clothed woman was straddling him. She glanced at me and smiled.

And then she drew the sharp serrated blade she held across Boris Stevenson's throat, putting an end to his moviemaking days forever.

20

Blood spurted across the bed and the walls.

I froze for an instant, shocked by both Boris's death and the sight of the blood. My hunger raged inside me, tried to force me to act without thinking. I needed to feed, needed to kill.

The Left Hand woman darted from the bed and dove for her purse, pulling me back into the moment. The knife was still clutched in her hand. Blood dripped from the blade, staining the already stained carpet a deep red.

I swallowed back the hunger and sprang into motion. I knew what she had in that purse. If she got hold of another syringe, my blood could be spilled next.

The room wasn't terribly large, so there wasn't much distance between me and the woman. Two quick strides and I was on her. Her hand closed over the purse straps just as I yanked her back and threw her against the wall. She hit with a thump, but didn't fall. Before she could move, I closed the short distance, grabbed her by the arm, and twisted.

The knife fell to the floor and she shrieked. "Demon spawn!" she wailed before spitting in my face. "I will not let you taint me with your filth." She tried to swing her purse at me, but the angle was wrong. It thumped lightly on my back.

She shrieked again and dropped her purse as I grabbed her other wrist.

She was too loud. Someone had to have heard the first couple screams and if they came to investigate, I'd have more trouble to deal with. I just had to hope screams were common here or the music pulsing beneath us was loud enough to drown most of them out.

The woman grinned at me and clenched her jaw. A sudden fear swept through me. I couldn't let her get away. She might be able to lead me to the rest of the Left Hand and there was no way I was going to lose this chance. If she had something in her mouth, a capsule in her tooth or something, she could kill herself.

I let go of her wrists, grabbed the side of her head, and cracked her skull hard against the wall. She gave me a dazed look and started to smile, so I did it again, harder.

This time, she went out.

I dropped her to the ground and quickly checked her over. Other than the knife, she didn't appear to have a weapon on her. She was wearing shorts so tight there was no way she'd get anything inside a pocket. Her shirt showed her midriff and she wasn't wearing a bra.

No wonder Boris had taken her in. She was eighteen, if that. She was little more than a kid, really. She had all the looks in the world and had obviously known how to use them. I wondered how many other vampires or werewolves she'd lured into rooms just like this one.

I ran my finger along the inside of her mouth. When I found nothing, I moved to check her teeth. There was nothing there as far as I could tell, but then again, I didn't really know much about how those suicide capsules are made. I wasn't sure if the Left Hand even used stuff like that. As far as I knew, if she'd had anything in her mouth, she might have already swallowed it.

I was tempted to shove my fingers down her throat to make her vomit, but that would take time and might wake her up. It was only a matter of time before someone saw the open door and wondered what was going on.

A gurgle from the bed brought my head around. Boris was still alive, but barely. Blood ran freely from his throat. He couldn't do much more than keep his fading eyes on me as his life slipped away. He was completely paralyzed and probably terrified out of his mind, yet because of the stuff in the syringe, he looked almost serene.

There was a moment when compassion almost made me finish

him off. Then I remembered the video with the girl and instead turned away. Boris deserved an ugly death for an ugly life.

My eyes fell on a camera next to the far wall. The little light told me it was on. I walked over to it, considered it a moment, and then smashed the damn thing into tiny little pieces. I made sure there was nothing left that anyone could come back and look at, though it would serve Boris right if his death had found its way to the Internet.

Once I was sure there'd be no visual evidence I'd ever been there, I slung the Left Hand woman's purse over my shoulder, shoved her knife inside, and then hoisted her to her feet. There were no windows in the room and I imagined most of the rooms upstairs were like that. It was unlikely I'd find a way out that way. Chances were good the elevator was the only way in or out so Avril's staff could keep an eye on their patrons.

I closed room 2's door behind me and dragged the woman to the elevator. I slid the card I'd taken from Clem through the reader and then slipped it back into his pocket as the door opened. I dragged the woman inside and as the doors closed and we started downward, I tried to come up with a plan.

I wasn't sure how I was going to manage to get out without drawing attention to myself. The woman was quite clearly unconscious and more than one person knew she'd gone upstairs with Boris. They also knew I'd gone in search of him. If I left with the woman he was supposed to be brutalizing, someone would surely notice. I was just thankful she wasn't heavy. I could walk quickly and hope no one would pay too much attention.

The elevator came to a halt. I plastered on an embarrassed smile as I dragged the woman out. Yancy's eyebrows rose as we emerged.

"She couldn't handle it," I said. "I'm taking her out for some air before heading back in. We're going to try someone with a little more stamina, I think."

His brow started to furrow, but quickly smoothed out. "Whatever," he said with a sigh. "Isn't like she's the first." He sniffed at her. "At least this one's still alive. The last didn't make it more than five minutes before stroking. And I don't mean that in a good way." He winked.

I bared my teeth at him in what I hoped looked like a grin. I turned away before he saw the anger in my eyes. I'd have to remember to come back for him someday.

Surprisingly, no one so much as looked at me as I worked my way through the room with the unconscious woman on my arm. It must not have been an uncommon occurrence in a place like this. I could see multiple men and women who looked as if they were about to collapse. There were probably dozens of people dragged through the room on a nightly basis.

We made it outside without incident. The man at the door gave me a surprised look, so I gave him the same excuse I'd told Yancy. I doubted he had any idea I'd been in to see Boris, but it was best I kept it simple. He just grunted at me and looked away; it wasn't any of his business.

I'd thought I'd run into trouble getting the woman back to the parking garage where I'd parked my Honda, but not a single person stopped us. We got some pretty odd looks, but nothing to be concerned about. Once I got to the garage, I frowned at the motorcycle. I had a problem.

"I need a fucking car."

I had no idea how in the hell I was going to get her to the Den. If she woke up while I was on the road, her struggles would probably tip us over. A crash wouldn't kill me, but it might her.

I didn't even have a cell phone to call Jeremy or Jonathan to come get her. I was sure I could find a pay phone somewhere, but that meant dragging her back out onto High Street and wasting more time. I had no idea how long she'd stay unconscious. I'd hit her head against the wall pretty damn hard, so I was hoping it would be a while.

Then again, I didn't even know Jonathan *or* Jeremy's number to call them. So even if I found a phone, there wasn't much I could do with it.

With a sigh, I heaved the Left Hand woman onto my bike and slid onto the Honda behind her. I had her sitting up so I could use my arms to keep her from sliding off. I could see and turn as long as I didn't drive too fast. I just had to hope she didn't wake up before I got there.

She snorted as the motorcycle started up, but otherwise didn't stir. I tested my range of motion, prayed I wouldn't splatter us all over the highway, and then took off out of the garage. I very nearly tipped making the first turn, but quickly righted myself.

I sped past Avril's without a glance, putting the club and the dead filmmaker behind me. By the time I was done with the Left Hand woman, she was going to wish I'd killed her too.

21

I have no idea how I managed to get to the Den parking garage without crashing into something. The damn woman kept sliding to the side. She nearly knocked my hand from the bike once, which would have dumped her unceremoniously onto the road and more than likely sent me into a sideways crash.

But somehow, I made it. I parked in the garage and then picked the woman up like a child. Her purse swung behind me, smacking me in the back of my legs as it kept sliding down to my elbow. How in the world could women carry these things all of the time? A part of me was glad I never lived the sort of life to need one. I'd have gone insane in minutes.

By the time I reached the Den, my arms were aching and I was ready to throw the damn purse into the nearby lake. The woman hadn't started out heavy, but I was wearing down. The adrenaline from finding her had worn off long ago. Now, all I wanted to do was get her inside and into a cell before she woke up.

I reached the top of the stairs and the doors opened for me. Pablo was glowering as usual, but he moved aside to let me pass through without us touching. I think he wanted to say something smart, but wisely held his tongue. I was in no mood for his insults tonight.

As soon as the Den doors closed behind me, the office door opened and Jonathan emerged, flanked by Keira.

"Who is it?" he asked, hurrying my way.

"I don't know her name," I said. "But I caught her killing a vampire. She's a member of the Left Hand."

His eyes widened for a heartbeat before he took her from me. "Let's get her downstairs."

Keira led the way into the office and pressed the button to open the hidden door. Jonathan took the stairs first, walking sideways so as not to crack the woman's skull against the wall as he went. I followed close behind him, hoping Keira would stay upstairs. I didn't need her wolfing out and accidentally killing the Left Hand woman before we got any useful information out of her.

Of course, the werewolf couldn't resist and followed us down.

"What happened?" Jonathan asked as he wedged open a cell door with his foot. He carried the woman inside, set her carefully onto the floor, then backed out. He closed the door and, using a key in his pocket, locked it.

"I was on the trail of someone," I said, not wanting to mention who I was after or why. "When I reached him, she was there. I knocked her out after she killed him."

Jonathan frowned. He crossed his arms and studied the frail thing. "Are you sure she's of the Left Hand?"

I handed him the purse. "I'm assuming her kit is in there. She cut the guy's throat, but I didn't see her use a syringe or anything. He wasn't fighting back, so I'm pretty sure she'd already injected him by the time I showed up."

Jonathan glanced into the purse before handing it to Keira. "Take that upstairs and go through it. Tell me if you find anything we can use to either question her or find out where she came from."

Keira hesitated as if she didn't want to leave before turning and walking away, purse clutched tightly in her hands.

"She doesn't look like much," he said as soon as Keira was gone. "I can't imagine her killing anyone."

I had to admit, he was right. She looked so tiny, it was hard to imagine her overpowering anyone. Then again, she'd had the help of her syringe. I leaned down a little and studied her face. She reminded me of someone, but I couldn't place the face. I wondered if I'd seen her around town before.

The woman groaned and started to stir. I straightened and

waited for her to rouse herself. I had quite a few questions I wanted to ask her and I wanted to do so before she had all of her wits about her.

She came to with a sudden jolt. She sat up, grabbed her head, and groaned. She looked at us through eyes barely open. She smiled through her pain and worked her way to her feet. She was wobbly, but determined. The look of zealotry I'd seen in every Left Hand person I'd ever seen was in her eye.

"Who are you?" Jonathan asked, taking the lead.

"Demon spawn." She spat through the bars. "I will not speak with your kind."

"Just tell me your name," he said with a kind smile. "I'm not going to hurt you. If you have family, I could call them, let them know you're okay."

She laughed. "I know your kind. By His hand, I will smite thee."

Jonathan gave her a sympathetic look. "You won't be smiting anyone from inside there." He nodded toward the bars.

She snarled and crossed herself. She backed into the far corner and pointedly looked away.

I took a step forward, but Jonathan touched my arm to stop me. He shook his head slightly and I backed off. I really wanted to know how she knew what I was the moment she'd seen me, but it could wait.

"I'll see if I can find you something to eat or drink," Jonathan said. "Is there anything else you'd like?"

She spat on the ground again in answer.

"Let's go," Jonathan whispered to me, turning toward the stairs.

I wanted to protest. I'd caught the woman, so I deserved a chance to interrogate her. I wanted the Left Hand stopped just as much as anyone—if not more so—and this was the perfect opportunity to learn something about them. All we had to do was get her to talk. I was sure I could break her.

Jonathan cleared his throat and I turned to follow him. He wanted to try a different tactic, I was sure. Perhaps kindness would get her to see not all supes are bad people. I doubted it, but the Den was Jonathan's territory. It was his call.

We went back upstairs in silence. Keira was sitting at the desk with the purse's contents spilled out before her.

"Anything?" Jonathan asked, closing the door behind him.

"Just this." Keira held out a plastic case that could have been a large makeup case. The serrated knife lay on the corner of the desk.

Jonathan took it and snapped it open. Instead of makeup, two filled syringes sat inside. He snapped the case closed and tossed it back onto the desk.

"Any sort of personal identification we can use? ID? Credit cards?"

Keira shook her head. "Not even a driver's license or a receipt."

He sighed and walked over to the door. He poked his head outside. "Pablo, bring some water and food to take down to our guest." He closed the door and with another sigh, walked over to the desk to stand beside Keira. She instantly reached out to touch his hand.

Something in my gut clenched, as did my jaw. With everything that was happening, I'd almost forgotten about how much I didn't like the female were.

"Where's Nathan?" I asked. I'd much rather deal with his snarky comments than watch Keira touch Jonathan.

"Busy," he said, looking distracted. "He should be back later."

"So you know where he is?"

He looked up at me. "Of course."

"And what about her?" I nodded my head toward Keira.

She stood, hand never leaving Jonathan's own. Her eyes narrowed, but she kept her mouth shut.

"What about her?" Jonathan asked, looking annoyed.

"Do you always know where she is?"

"This isn't a prison," Jonathan said. I could tell he was growing angry. He kept clenching and unclenching his jaw and there was the faintest twinge of yellow to his eye. "She can come and go as she pleases, just like you."

"And what about three nights ago?"

Jonathan frowned. "What about it?"

"Where was she then?"

The door opened and Pablo stepped inside, carrying a tray with a plastic cup of water and some tuna on a paper plate on it. He didn't look my way as he walked past. Keira pressed the button to open the hidden door for him.

"Let's continue this upstairs," Jonathan said, voice tight.

I motioned for him to lead the way and we went up to his rooms.

I was pissed beyond belief and really wasn't sure how it had happened. I had no proof Keira was the wolf who'd attacked me when I was tailing Nathan, yet I couldn't help but hope it was. It would make things so much easier. I'd know whom to blame.

"Now, what is all of this about?" Jonathan said as we entered his sitting room. He crossed his arms and leaned against the wall.

Unfortunately, Keira came in and moved to stand on the other side of the door. I really wish she would've stayed behind.

"I was out three nights ago and came across Nathan," I said. "Before I could talk to him, a werewolf attacked me. She reminded me of Keira."

"I never attacked you," Keira said, taking a step my way. Her eyes flashed yellow.

I smiled at her, daring her to attack. If she shifted, I'd know for sure whether she was responsible or not. I'd yet to see her fully wolf out.

"When was this exactly?" Jonathan asked, brow furrowed in concentration.

"Three nights ago."

"Then it couldn't be her," he said.

"And why the fuck not?"

"Because she was with me."

My heart just about plummeted through the floor. My legs were weak and I rested my hand on the back of a chair to steady myself. "Oh."

"We were—"

"I don't want to know," I said, cutting him off.

"I—"

"I said, I don't want to know." I turned away, angry at myself for caring. If Jonathan tried to tell me they were just sitting around talking, I'd probably rip out his throat.

Jonathan gave a frustrated sigh. "I'm going to go down and talk to our guest," he said. "I want you to stay here in case I need you. Can you do that for me?"

I very nearly told him to shove it up his ass, but nodded instead. I couldn't let my own personal issues get in the way of what needed to be done.

"Keira." He motioned for her to leave ahead of him. She glared at me for a moment before storming out of the room. I had to give her credit; she could have lost control and shifted. It would have been more than enough reason to kill her.

"Kat," Jonathan said, stopping just outside the sitting room doors. "I'm sorry for all of this. I'll figure out who attacked you."

"Don't worry about it," I said. "I'll take care of it."

"Please . . ."

I looked over at him and saw pain painted all over his face. Something stirred deep inside of me. Looking at him like that brought all kinds of pains and fears to mind. I suddenly became terrified I'd lose him, that I'd be forced to deal with all of this on my own.

I don't know what compelled me, if it was something outside my influence or those parts of myself that I tried so damn hard to hide, but the next thing I knew, I was walking briskly across the room. I stopped right in front of Jonathan, our faces inches apart.

He opened his mouth as if to speak.

I silenced him with a kiss.

He stood rigid against me for a moment before softening. His hands found my back and he leaned in to me, kissing me back so fiercely, our teeth nearly scraped together.

But I didn't let up. All I wanted to do was drag him back into the room and keep him locked inside with me until the danger had passed. I wanted him to protect me as much as I wanted to protect him. If we were together, we could do that.

And then sense slammed into me. I broke the kiss, breathless. I took a step back, confused. Scared. I licked my lips and could still taste him on them.

"I'm sorry," I said. I was shaking. I wanted to throw myself at him again.

Jonathan opened his mouth and I realized that whatever he said would probably send me over the edge. I'd end up giving myself to him, would let him do with me as he pleased.

So I did the only thing I could do to keep myself from giving in to the emotions fighting for dominance in my head.

"I can't," I said.

I closed the doors before he could speak.

22

I could hardly stand the wait. Part of me wanted to run away, to slip right out of the Den so I wouldn't have to face Jonathan again. I wasn't sure what had compelled me to kiss him like that, if it was jealousy or fear, but strangely, I wasn't entirely unhappy about it. The kiss had felt right in more ways than one.

Which was exactly why I was suffering so damn much. It shouldn't have felt right in the slightest. We were two different creatures, monsters whose blood would contaminate the other and drive each other insane. We couldn't survive together.

Add to that the fact I was so used to pushing everyone away, I didn't know what to do with myself. I was suddenly stuck in a situation where I couldn't continue to push him away. I'd let him slip in through the cracks in my mental armor and I knew there'd be no way to get him back out.

A knock at the door stopped my pacing. Jonathan entered with Nathan right behind him. I stiffened at the sight of the big wolf and turned away, hoping he wouldn't see my anger at him. Right then, I didn't want a confrontation.

"We couldn't get anything out of her," Jonathan said, closing the door. It had been a little over an hour since he'd left me alone in the room, telling me they'd worked pretty hard. Normally, werewolves could get people to talk within minutes, if they were determined enough.

"I'm not surprised," I said, moving to look out the window. It was still dark outside. It was strange to think that anyone who might be out there watching the place couldn't see me standing framed in the window thanks to Jonathan's glamour.

"She talks less than the last one," he went on. "But when she does speak, all she does is scream about how we are demon spawn. It's the same thing over and over." There was a weary frustration in his voice that made me turn to face him.

"We'll get it out of her," I said. "Let me have a go."

Nathan gave me a grin that said louder than words that he doubted my ability to get the Left Hand woman to talk. Sadly, I felt the same way. I just couldn't sit there any longer letting everyone else do what I should have been doing in the first place.

"We might have a better idea," Jonathan said. He motioned toward the chairs and couch.

I really didn't want to sit; not with Nathan in the room or after what had happened with Jonathan. I was afraid I'd have a hard time keeping myself from blurting something out about the kiss in front of the Denmaster's second, which would only make things more strained between us.

But I sat. I wanted to end the fight with the Left Hand. Maybe once that was taken care of, I could worry about my conflicting feelings toward Jonathan and what it might mean for my future.

I took the chair closest to the window. Jonathan took his usual spot on the couch. Nathan, of course, stood behind his Denmaster, acting the part of guardian. I thought it funny he was doing it now when Keira wasn't around. He should have been by Jonathan's side every second he was with the female wolf.

"I'm thinking we should let her go," Jonathan said as soon as we were seated.

"What?" I sat forward. "Why?"

"We aren't going to get anything out of her by talking to her. She is too staunch in her beliefs to ever betray her people. Pain doesn't sway her in the slightest. In fact, it only makes her call us names that much more." Jonathan sighed. "I felt like a monster allowing it."

I could tell by Nathan's satisfied smirk, he'd been the one delivering the pain. No matter how close I'd become with the werewolves of the Cult, they still had that demon inside them that reveled in hurting others. I couldn't hold it too much against them; it was inside me, too.

"So why let her go?" I asked. "She'll just go back to her people and tell them who we are, where to find us."

"That's the point."

And that's when I got it. "You plan on following her."

"Of course." Jonathan sat back looking pleased.

"She won't fall for it," I said. "She would have to know that we're letting her go so we can track her. She'll just hole up and wait for our guard to slip."

"That's why we won't simply let her walk out the door. We'll stage an attack and allow her to escape."

I thought about it. There were so many ways something like that could go wrong, but it would make the woman think she was getting away on her own. She might run straight back to the rest of the Left Hand, leading us right to them.

"It might work," I said, liking the idea more and more.

"We'll tell her we're transporting her to a more secure location, somewhere we can hold her better. Once we are a safe distance away, we'll be attacked by weres we know, allowing her to escape."

"And you're sure she'll buy it?"

"What other choice do we have if we want to get to the Left Hand now? I'm tired of chasing ghosts. This way, she'll lead us right to them and we can finish them off without having to track them down on our own."

"We could turn her."

Both Jonathan and I turned to Nathan.

He shrugged. "She believes we are monsters, so why not turn her into one? Perhaps seeing what we are from the inside will convince her to work with us. She'll have little choice once the hunger sets in."

"Or she'll try that much harder to kill us," I said.

"I agree." Jonathan shook his head. "It's far too risky. If we turn her and she comes at us, we'll have a harder time putting her down. Besides," he said, turning back to me, "I'm not one who turns others lightly."

I had to agree. Jonathan's refusal to turn the Cult was why Adrian had left him in the first place.

Nathan frowned, but didn't otherwise argue. I could see he still thought turning her was our best bet, but like a good dog, he bowed to Jonathan's wishes.

"Keira believes we'll be led to where the Left Hand congregates. In the mad flight to escape, she'll think of nothing other than to get back to those she trusts."

I felt my face darken. "Keira, huh?"

Jonathan nodded, so lost in thought, he didn't appear to notice my glower. "She's the one who came up with the idea of releasing her. When given a chance, she can prove quite useful." He leveled his gaze at me.

I shrugged it off. I guess he wasn't as oblivious to my dislike of her as he appeared. "It *is* a good plan," I said, begrudgingly. "If we can pull it off."

"I think with the three of us following her, we'll be fine."

I shook my head. "I should go alone."

"Kat . . ."

"If too many of us try to track her, she'll surely notice. We'll scare her off. I have a feeling if she even *thinks* someone is following her, she'll step in front of a bus just to keep us from getting to the rest of her people."

"She's human," Jonathan said. "She doesn't have a wolf's nose, our senses. She won't know we're there."

"But she does have years of paranoia and hatred for our kind," I said. "Do you think they haven't figured out how we move, how we think? Even if she buys the attack, she'll still be cautious about being followed. Do you think, even for a second, she won't be watching for that?"

Jonathan rubbed at his temples. "With three of us, she'll have a hard time losing us."

"She'll also have an easier time spotting us." I crossed my arms, standing firm. I knew what I was talking about. She wouldn't risk taking others down with her; it wasn't the Left Hand's style. I might hate what the group stood for, but that didn't mean I'd underestimate them ever again.

"She has a point," Nathan said, surprising me. I figured he'd contradict me out of spite.

"I know she does," Jonathan snapped. "I just don't like the idea of letting Kat go alone."

"I've done this sort of thing before."

"It's too dangerous."

"You were the one who said they're just humans," I said. "How dangerous could they really be? They aren't going to be sneaking up on me this time; I'll be the one sneaking up on them."

Jonathan heaved a sigh and looked skyward. "Why can't you work with me on this?"

"I am," I said. "I just think it's too risky to send too many people after her."

"Then we compromise," he said. "Two of us go. You and I will follow her."

It was tempting, but I shook my head. I had a feeling that being left alone with Jonathan right then wouldn't be conducive to me paying attention to what I was doing. We'd lose her for sure.

"I have to do this alone."

"Goddamn it, Kat . . ." He trailed off as a brisk knock at the door was followed by Pablo's entrance. He hadn't even waited for Jonathan to answer.

"I'm sorry for the interruption, Denmaster," he said with a slight bow of his head. "But I have an important message for you."

"Can it wait?" Jonathan asked. He was clearly miffed by my stubbornness, but I wasn't going to relent on this. I knew I could follow the woman unseen. If I had someone else with me, I couldn't vouch for their silence or skill.

"I don't believe so."

Jonathan heaved another big sigh and stood. "I'll be right back," he said. "This isn't over."

He strode out of the room, full of purpose. As stubborn as I was being, Jonathan looked as if he was prepared to top me.

My gaze turned to Nathan and I found him staring at me. Neither of us spoke. We simply stared, studying each other. I kept hoping I'd see something in his eyes that would tell me what was going on with him. I was afraid he'd started hunting humans again, killing innocents instead of taking what the Den provided—whatever that was. It was the only thing that made sense. Why else would he be so secretive?

Nathan appeared to be attempting to read me as well. I kept my face blank, not wanting to give anything away. I was sure he suspected I was on to something. I just didn't want him to be sure of it. If he was insecure, he might make a mistake.

"You don't give up easily," he said with a grim smile.

I wasn't sure what he was referring to, but I smiled at him anyway. "Of course not. That's what I do."

"I've always enjoyed stubbornness," he said, smile faltering. "There is something endearing about it."

I snorted, but never got a chance to reply. The door opened and a harried looking Jonathan returned. He strode across the room and whispered something into Nathan's ear.

The big wolf paled and ran out of the room. I'd never seen him look that terrified in my life.

I stood, hands reflexively going to my weapons. "What's going on?"

"It's nothing," Jonathan said. He was running his hands incessantly through his hair. He looked white as a sheet. "We'll stage the attack tomorrow. We're running out of time."

I didn't like the sound of that. "That doesn't sound like nothing. What's happening?"

Jonathan took a deep breath and closed his eyes. He stood like that for a long moment before letting his breath out in a huff. He opened his eyes and looked at me.

"Go home," he said. "Get some rest before tomorrow. Be back here just after first dark. We'll get you set up to follow her. Keira and I will work on the details during the day. I'll make sure you have everything you need before we start."

"I'm going alone?"

He nodded.

"What's changed?" I moved to stand in front of him. "Something has happened. I want to know what it is."

"I . . . I can't." He shook his head and looked away. "It's not my place."

I wanted to rear back and hit him. He was keeping something from me and I was worried that what I didn't know might come back later and bite me in the ass—especially if that something was Nathan.

"I'm sorry," he said, gaze returning to mine. I could tell he truly meant it.

My heart did a little hiccup. There was pain in those eyes. Pain and pleading.

"Okay," I said, looking at my hands so I wouldn't have to see the pain any longer. I felt like a bitch for pressing so much.

"I wish I could tell you," Jonathan whispered. He rested his hand on my cheek. "It's just not my place."

I bit my lip and nodded.

We stood like that for a long moment. His fingers brushed down my cheek before his hand dropped away.

"I really do have to go," he said. "I'll see you tomorrow."

I looked up and caught indecision in his gaze. I think he wanted to lean forward and kiss me good-bye, but he was afraid how I'd react.

Right then, I wasn't sure what I'd do. I felt somewhat betrayed by his refusal to tell me what was going on with Nathan. If he was in trouble, perhaps I could help. If he was doing something he wasn't supposed to, then something should be done. I mean, I was the one who was supposed to be struggling with being honest and forthright with my friends. I didn't expect it from others.

"I'll see you then," I said, turning away.

I walked to the door, shoulders tense. I didn't go quickly. What I really wanted was for him to stop me, to rush across the room, grab me, and pull me into his arms. With that one gesture, I knew everything could be all right.

But he didn't. Deep down, I knew he wouldn't—*couldn't*—do something like that.

With a heavy heart, I left the Den—and Jonathan—behind.

23

Sometimes, not having to sleep is a curse.

If I could have simply lain down and fallen asleep, I wouldn't have spent the following day staring up at the ceiling, thinking. I didn't know which way was up anymore. I wanted to believe Jonathan knew what he was doing, that he wasn't letting Nathan do anything harmful, but they were both werewolves. How could I completely trust them to do the right thing?

I kept telling myself that it was the old me talking, that Jonathan had earned my trust long ago, yet I couldn't stop thinking it. I was pretty sure Keira was part of the problem. If she weren't around, then my faith in the Luna Cult wolves would've been solid. Her presence was making me irrational.

Just before the sun went down, I decided to get ready for the night. I got up, showered, and changed. I wanted to be at the Den as soon as possible, meaning I'd be leaving while there was still a hint of light in the sky. If I could take care of the Left Hand tonight, it would go a long way to making my life easier. Maybe I'd start thinking clearly again.

Ethan was standing in the hall as I left my room. He didn't speak; didn't need to. He knew something was going on, though I had yet to explain it to him. By the time I'd gotten home last night, he'd already been in his room, as had Jeremy. I was pretty sure the werewolf already knew the plan. Jonathan would have called him. I'd leave it up to him to let Ethan know what was going on.

With a slight nod of his head, Ethan reassured me everything was okay, before heading into the bathroom for his evening shower.

From there, I gathered my weapons, threw on my coat, and headed out to the garage. The sun was but a glow on the horizon as I pulled out of the garage on my bike. I felt weak from the last remaining rays, but they wouldn't otherwise harm me. By the time I got to the Den, it would be full-on night.

My nerves were on high alert as I pulled into the Luna Cult garage. I kept telling myself that it was because of the Left Hand and our plan to find them. I knew deep down it wasn't the case—I was worried about seeing Jonathan. Did he understand what was happening between us? Did I?

I hurried to the old library that was now the Luna Cult Den. My brain kept going back to that kiss the night before. Had it been a mistake? Sometimes, it felt like it was. At others, it felt like the best thing that had ever happened to me.

It was almost a relief to reach the Den. I forced my mind to shift gears. I needed to focus. I couldn't let myself get distracted by mooning over a werewolf. If I wasn't careful, the Left Hand woman might get away and all would be for naught.

I pushed through the doors of the Den. Bright lights speared into my skull, causing me to blink rapidly to clear my vision. I no longer hesitated when I stepped through the glamour, but it still fucked up my sight every damn time.

Pablo was waiting for me by the stairs.

"The Denmaster is downstairs with the woman now," he said through gritted teeth. "He's telling her we plan on moving her. I am to tell you what to do and where to be. Once you find out where she goes, you'll return here and let us know. From there, the Denmaster will figure out how best to attack."

I nodded distractedly. Was Jonathan avoiding me? Why wasn't Nathan the one giving me the details? Hell, right then, I'd have taken Keira over Pablo.

"Where's this happening?" I asked instead. I needed to focus. I was sure Jonathan had his reasons for doing it this way.

"Near the garage," Pablo said. "There will be a car parked a little past it. We will be walking her toward it when the werewolves attack."

I nodded. "And where will I be?"

"There is a building across from the garage. You can hide next to it. She will flee in that direction. She'll have no other choice."

I knew the building. I'd seen it every single time I'd come to the Den. The windows were gone, meaning I could hide inside in the shadows and still have an easy way out.

"What if she takes the car?" I asked.

"She won't."

"How can you be sure?"

Pablo sneered. "I will be at the car, as will a few other Cultists. We will not be engaging in the fight. We'll give chase when she runs, forcing her in the direction we choose. Once she's running, we'll get attacked and will seemingly lose her trail. That's where they need *you.*" He just about spat the last.

I nodded and pointedly checked my gun. I'd made sure it was loaded before leaving, but needed to do something else with my hands so I didn't hit him. I still wasn't sure why he hated me so much.

"Don't fuck this up," he said, turning toward the office.

"Hey, Pablo," I said, suddenly feeling the need to try to patch things up. If I was going to spend time in the Den, I really should try to get along with the people that lived here.

Pablo turned, impatient.

"Happy birthday."

Surprise flashed over his face. He opened his mouth as if he wanted to say something, but closed it and shook his head. He huffed and walked away.

"Asshole," I grumbled, as I turned and left the Den.

I jogged toward my hiding spot, wanting to get there well ahead of everyone else. The longer I was there, the better I could hide. It would give me a chance to settle in and find the best spot to keep an eye on the action.

I was a little nervous about following the Left Hand woman on foot. I didn't know what I'd do if she were to try to hitch a ride from someone. I could run pretty damn fast when I wanted to, but not so fast as to run down a car. I just had to hope that if she did get into a car, she would do so where there'd be heavy traffic or a car of my own I could nab.

Lights across the campus drew my eye as I approached the building across from the parking garage. The woman wouldn't be driven toward the populated part of the campus, but what if she looped around that way? I doubted college kids were ready for an all-out battle between weres and the Left Hand. Too many innocents would die that way.

With a sigh, I forced my gaze away. If that's where she went, we'd have to deal with it. Maybe that's how the Left Hand knew where the Den was in the first place. If they were hiding out on the campus somewhere, it wouldn't be too hard to imagine them coming across someone who was heading to or from one of the supposedly empty buildings. Hell, I was rarely careful about sneaking around here these days. I could have led them right to the Den's front steps without knowing it.

The door to my hiding spot creaked as it swung open. The room smelled of mildew and rot, but thanks to the broken windows, it wasn't overwhelming. The floor crunched as I walked across the small front room, to a window I could peer out from. It gave me a good view of the garage and a quick escape when I needed to start after my prey.

And then I waited.

Time ticked by slowly. It felt like hours, though I knew it had only been a few minutes. There was little to no movement anywhere, not even in the garage where the werewolves were supposed to attack from. I expected to see someone huddled in there, preparing for the staged attack, yet it appeared as if no one was there at all. I sure as hell hadn't seen anyone when I arrived.

Doubt trickled in. Could this be some sort of trick? Was Jonathan planning on following her himself and had he sent me here to get me out of the way?

I very nearly rose, but just then, Pablo came into view. Two Cultists I didn't recognize were walking beside him. They were talking quietly among themselves, more than likely going over last-minute instructions if Pablo's aggressive manner was any indication.

The two Cultists stopped outside the garage as Pablo went in. A moment later, a black car pulled out and parked a little way down the street. Pablo turned it so the car was blocking off most of the road. It would make it hard for the woman to run that way without going through the car and if she tried to use it as a getaway vehicle, she'd have to work to get it turned in the right direction.

Pablo got out of the car and the Cultists moved to stand next to him. His eyes flickered in my direction, but in no other way did Pablo acknowledge my presence.

More time passed. Pablo and the Cultists looked anxious, as if they really didn't want to be standing exposed out there. I didn't blame them. The Left Hand *was* out there killing people. There was no telling where they might be.

A group of three men came walking from the direction of the Den. They were wearing clothes that would be easy to remove—the sort of things werewolves would wear. They waved once to Pablo and then vanished into the garage, presumably to ready themselves for the attack. I recognized two of the wolves as ones who had come with Keira.

Uneasiness swept over me once more. What if Keira was indeed responsible for the Left Hand knowing where the Den was located? Could we really trust her and those other weres not to go too far in the attack?

In the end, it wasn't my choice. I was here and ready. If something went wrong, I sure as hell wasn't going to let the Left Hand woman escape. I'd kill her first.

From there, there was more waiting. By the time I heard loud voices approaching from the direction of the Den, I was just about itching for action. I could clearly make out Jonathan's voice, followed by the sound of the Left Hand woman's rambling. A few moments later, they appeared.

Jonathan was in the lead with five others behind him, including the woman. She was being held by Keira and was otherwise unbound. They were flanked by three Cultists in their robes, looking scared out of their minds.

I tensed and slipped back into the shadows a little more. I knew it was unlikely the woman would see me even if I was crouched right next to the window, but I didn't want to take any chances. This might very well be the only chance we'd get to find the Left Hand hideout—if there actually was one.

I knew it was coming, yet I actually jumped when the fully

shifted werewolves charged out from the garage. Jonathan shouted out a warning just as he went down under the weight of one of the wolves. Keira pushed the Left Hand woman to the ground as she leapt into the staged fray.

One of the Cultists screamed and blood splattered the ground. He fell in a heap and I wasn't sure if he was breathing or not. The blood that hit the pavement looked like blood, not paint or anything. The fighting looked real enough, yet I knew Jonathan wouldn't allow one of his people to get hurt just so we could follow the Left Hand woman.

I drew my gun and eased closer to the window. Had I been right about Keira? Was this staged attack not so staged after all? I had to hope that Jonathan would be able to take control of the situation if it wasn't.

The Left Hand woman lay on the ground, watching the battle with wide eyes. She seemed frozen to the spot, as if she was afraid to move lest she draw attention to herself.

"Come on," I whispered, hand tightening on my gun. If she didn't run soon, I'd have to do something.

Finally, she pushed herself to her feet. She took two quick steps back, toward where I hid, and then turned to run.

Pablo shouted after her and the group of three Cultists started running after her like he said they would. It was clear they weren't trying too hard to catch her. I mentally cursed Pablo and hoped the woman wouldn't notice their lack of effort. It would be a dead give-away.

The woman ran a few feet past me, eyes wide with terror. She might have put in with a group who killed monsters for a living, but I don't think she'd ever seen them this way. She preferred her kills quiet and quick. This was anything but.

A howl lit up the night and one of the wolves broke off the fight and ran down Pablo and the other Cultists. I very nearly shot him out of reflex. His maw was stained red and he was slavering.

I scurried away from the window, into another room where I waited by the window. The woman tripped just as she came into view and spun back to see what was happening behind her. She scrambled backward, mouth opening and closing like she wanted to scream but was afraid to. Finally, she found her feet again and turned to run. As soon as her back was to me, I was out the window and after her.

The abandoned portion of the campus made it almost too easy. I stuck to the shadows, darting behind buildings and debris so that whenever she glanced over her shoulder to look the way behind her appeared clear. She refused to go anywhere near any of the buildings, as if she were afraid of what might be inside them. Quite frankly, I didn't blame her. Who knew what could be lurking inside?

She eventually made it off the campus and slowed down. I stayed well back, knowing she'd probably look back. Almost as soon as I thought it, she did. She scanned the campus behind her and then broke down into a sobbing laugh. She took a deep breath and took off at a jog.

Here, I had to be more careful. There was light traffic on the roads and a few pedestrians could be brave Purebloods or even werewolves and vampires out looking for a snack. I wouldn't know until I got close and by then it might be too late.

The Left Hand woman seemed to realize the same. Any time she saw someone, she made it a point to cross over to the other side of the street. No one broke off to follow her, though a few did stop to stare. It would have been just my luck for her to come across an ultraviolent count out on an evening stroll with his retinue.

I was forced to let her get well ahead of me, which I didn't like at all. If she saw me, she would know she was being followed. I'd been the one to capture her. I was pretty sure she wouldn't forget my face.

Eventually, the terror ebbed from her and exhaustion took over. Her pace slowed and more than once, she stopped to catch her breath. We were walking away from the campus, for which I was thankful, though I didn't know where we were heading.

We walked past a few buildings that could have housed a large group of people, but she kept walking past them without a glance. It wasn't until we passed a large warehouse that she slowed and began checking behind her every few seconds.

We were close. I could tell by her body language that she was both relieved to have gotten to a place of perceived safety and terrified about what she'd just escaped.

She went a few blocks farther and then stopped in front of what had once been a restaurant. It had been abandoned for years, though graffiti on the walls told me it had become a hangout for kids. She walked slowly across the parking lot and knocked on the door. There was a call from inside to which she answered, but I couldn't make out the words from as far back as I was. She seemed to be arguing with whoever was inside. After a few moments, the door opened and she was yanked inside.

I watched the place from across the street, almost hoping someone would come outside so I could get a good look at them. The building's windows were boarded up and even the glass doors had plywood on them, making it impossible to see inside. There had been a flickering light when the door had opened, telling me they were more than likely using candles to see by. There'd be no power here.

Minutes passed and nothing else moved. I saw no guards walking the parking lot, nor did I see anyone on the roof or around any of the corners. Nearby, there were a few other abandoned buildings, as well as a few that were not so abandoned. I could hear laughter coming from a gas station down the street, but otherwise, hardly anyone was near.

Pablo had told me to return once I found out where the woman went, but I wasn't so sure I could do that. Just because she'd come here didn't mean the entire Left Hand was here. This could be just one of a dozen similar places throughout the city. Since she thought she'd escaped, she might be nervous about staying here. Chances were good the entire group would up and move, just in case she had been followed. It would be the smart thing to do and as much as I hated the Left Hand, they'd proven themselves smarter than the average Pureblood.

I couldn't let them get away.

Going in alone would be stupid, I knew. The Left Hand might work in the shadows, using syringes and knives to do their work, but I didn't believe they wouldn't use guns if it came right down to it. They had silver for their injections, so silver bullets weren't too far out of the question, either.

Then again, as long as they didn't hit anything vital, it wouldn't slow me down too much.

I took a deep breath and held it. This might be stupid, but it might also be the last chance I'd get to put an end to the Left Hand. I could take out this base of operations, capturing someone to interrogate later.

I checked down the street, saw no one that appeared to be watching, and then made my move for the building I knew held members of the Left Hand.

24

I darted across the parking lot, gun in hand. My eyes scanned the lot and the front of the building, fully expecting a shot to ring out. This was the Left Hand. They wouldn't leave their hiding place undefended in the middle of a big city overrun with werewolves and vampires. They had to have some sort of protection.

But no shots were fired. I reached the front of the building without incident. I might have been seen and the people inside could be ready for me, but at least I'd gotten this far without getting killed.

I pressed myself against the wall between a boarded up window and the door. I could just make out the sound of voices inside.

"You know you aren't supposed to come here until daylight!"

"But I—" The sound of a slap cut her off.

I tensed, listening. It sounded as if the other members of the Left Hand weren't so happy about the woman coming back to them. I hoped I could somehow use that to my advantage.

"What if someone followed you?"

"They didn't."

"How can you be sure?"

There was a long moment of silence. I could hear other faint sounds—the scrape of a chair on hard flooring, a feminine cough. I couldn't tell how many people were inside. So far, only the girl I'd followed and the man who was yelling at her could be heard.

"We're going to have to move." This was a new voice. The guy sounded big, but that could be misleading. I'd heard small people with extremely deep voices before.

"We can't go. My sister . . ."

"Will be fine. She's doing what needs to be done."

I slid closer to the door where I could hear better. I waited for them to go on, but the sound of shuffling began, as if a lot of people had started moving around. There was still talking, but I couldn't make out another word.

My mind raced. Going in might very well end in my death, but it sounded like I'd been right when I'd thought they'd get up and leave when she returned. If I went back to tell Jonathan now, we'd lose them for sure.

I couldn't let that happen.

With deliberate slowness, I reached down and tested the door. A faint, unpleasant, sensation coursed through my hand where I touched the doorknob. When I pulled my hand back, there was something on it. With a sniff, I quickly determined it was a thicker version of the stuff they injected in their victims. If a normal werewolf or vampire had touched the door, the silver in the mixture would have caused them immense pain.

It's a good thing I wasn't normal.

This time when I tried the door, I didn't pull away. The door rattled slightly in its frame, but otherwise was locked.

"What was that?"

All sounds inside ceased.

It looked like I was going to have to do this the hard way.

I took three quick steps away from the door. Out of the corner of my eye, I saw a small section of plywood at one of the windows move aside, exposing a single eye.

Knowing it was going to hurt, I charged the door.

Glass shattered as I slammed into it with all the vampire strength I could muster. The wood on the other side didn't stand a chance. It tore from the frame as I went through the doors and crashed to the ground amid a shower of glass and splinters. The harsh scent of silver dust just about choked me as I hit. I could feel it stinging the cuts all over my face and hands from the shattered glass.

I rolled to my feet almost immediately. There were at least a dozen shocked faces staring at me. A man who had to be in his sixties stood at the window, hand still on the piece of wood that had created his peephole.

My gun came up, but I wasn't sure where to aim. Everyone was standing completely still, looking at me as if waiting for me to act first. I don't think they expected anyone to make such an extreme entrance, especially someone not affected by the silver they'd coated everything in.

"It's her." The woman drew my eye. She was trembling beside the counter. "She's the one who captured me."

And that was all it took.

The entire room burst into motion. Cases of various types sat around the room. I knew each and every one contained syringes, serrated knives, and that damnable mixture the Left Hand used to paralyze their victims.

"Stop!" I shouted at a man to my right. He already had his syringe in hand and was running toward me. I gave him two more steps and when he didn't stop, I shot him between the eyes.

Coldness swept over me as his blood splattered the floor. My hunger flared. I was suddenly aware of how pure their blood was, how plentiful. I had yet to feed. There were enough people here to sate me a dozen times over.

I turned and shot the older man, just as he reached out to stab me with his syringe. My ears were ringing from the sound of gunshots. I felt a twinge of guilt for killing someone of his age, but it was quickly swallowed by my rage, my beast.

Fangs extended, I grinned. I was losing control. The monster was coming out to play and I was practically helpless against it. It was commanding me to kill, to feed on every last one of them. The urge to throw down my weapons and charge bodily into them was so strong, I actually took a step forward before I regained some of my composure.

Besides, I didn't need to charge. They were coming to me.

I spun to the side just as the Left Hand woman I'd followed tried to flank me with a serrated knife in hand. She had time to widen her eyes and open her mouth to scream before I was on her. My instincts had taken over. I knocked the knife from her hand and wrenched her head to the side. I bared my fangs.

And then I struck.

Hot warmth sprayed into my mouth and down into my gullet. I sank my fangs deep into her neck; so deep, there was no chance she'd survive this. I sucked hard, filling my essence with her life. She shuddered against me and her legs gave out. I held her in place so she wouldn't fall.

Ecstasy made me dizzy. I pulled her close to me and drank. The world around me vanished. All I knew was the blood.

A loud bang caused me to jerk back. The woman, who should have still been alive, fell from my hands, dead. She had a gaping hole in her head, mere inches from where my own head had been.

I turned, snarling. Blood dripped down my chin, covering the front of my black leather. I still had my gun in my hand, but I wasn't thinking clearly. I needed more blood.

A middle-aged man stood next to the counter. Fury lined his features as he did his best to aim at me. His hand was shaking so badly, I wasn't sure he'd manage to hit much of anything if he fired. I think hitting the girl had been an accident.

"Monster," he said. The remaining Left Hand members stood nearby, syringes and knives at the ready. He was the only one with a gun. "Gabriel is right. You are nothing but monsters."

Our eyes locked. I knew that if I moved, he would fire. There was no way I'd get my gun up in time.

"You're no better," I said, slowly licking the blood from my lips. I was starting to regain my control. My beast wasn't quite sated, but it was calming. "You kill, heedless of who you hurt."

"We hurt those who defy Him in his greatness. We kill those who cannot abide the light of His creation." His arm tensed and I knew he was going to shoot.

I moved quickly, darting to the side, just as he pulled the trigger. The bullet hit the plywood behind me, went through that, and shattered the glass on the other side. Someone screamed at the deafening sound.

I dropped low to the ground, rolled past a table and came up next to a woman standing off to the side. I grabbed hold of her, thinking it might buy me some time, but the man shot at me anyway. The bullet took the woman in the belly. I let her go as she fell, screaming.

I darted for the counter, thinking I might be able to use it as cover. This time, his shot was true. The bullet hit me in the shoulder as I leapt for the counter. I spun and fell hard on my back as pain seared through me where the bullet had gone in. It was like fire blooming from the impact, and I knew it wasn't a normal bullet.

I didn't get up right away. Part of it was the pain and part of it was the knowledge that if I rose now he'd probably put a bullet in my head. I couldn't survive that.

"Silver bullets," the man said, coming around the counter. "Who would've thought that all those silly movies had gotten it right?" He set his gun on the counter and held out a hand. Someone slapped a syringe into it. "It's so easy, you see. Your kind have weaknesses. We exploit them. Thanks to His guidance, we know exactly what needs to be done."

He took a step closer. I held completely still, acting the part of a paralyzed victim. I could feel the silver working through my veins, but it wasn't doing anything more than burning ever so slightly.

"I don't know how you managed to avoid getting infected when you burst in here, and I don't care. You showed us our defenses might not be as secure as we thought." He knelt beside me. "I will pray for your soul." The syringe moved toward my neck.

I brought my gun up and pressed it against his chest. He had a moment to look surprised before I pulled the trigger.

Blood splattered my face as he jerked backward. He fell off me, landing hard on his side. His eyes were already starting to glaze.

Pain ripped through my shoulder as I rolled to my feet. His shot hadn't hit anything important but it hurt like hell. I was going to be feeling this one for quite a while.

The remaining Left Hand members were staring at me in shock. One of them made for the counter where the gun sat. I grabbed the gun despite the flare of pain it caused in my injured arm. The man stopped and raised his hands, taking a single step back, though his eyes told me he was ready to charge again the moment I let my guard down.

"Funny thing, silver," I said, turning the gun over in my hands. It was a little bigger than my gun, a little heavier. "It doesn't work on all of us anymore."

A guy who looked no more than sixteen screamed and charged, knife raised above his head. I actually felt bad for shooting him. The boom of the gun was so loud, I didn't even hear the knife clatter to the ground.

"Any more?" I growled. Pain and bloodlust had me seeing red, but at least I was in control. If I gave in, the remaining four members would be dead in seconds. I could revel in their blood, feed until sated.

But I needed them. I didn't know if I'd found their leader or if there were more of them roaming around. I needed to know.

"How many more like you are there?" I asked, eyeing the group.

A woman darted to the side, grabbed a purse, but before she could so much as open it, I shot her in the head. She dropped without a sound.

"Gabriel!" I shouted, hoping to draw him out. I hated killing Purebloods, even ones who were out to kill me. I was tired of it. I just wanted answers.

"He's our leader."

I turned to the speaker. She was maybe twenty, though she looked haggard, as if this life wasn't quite right for her. She, of everyone there, looked the most terrified.

"Is he here?"

She shook her head. "He will know what has happened here and won't return. He knows everything."

"Where can I find him?"

"Aubrey . . ." The man who spoke reached out to grab her. I shot him.

Aubrey screamed as blood splattered her face. She trembled, eyes closed. Tears streamed down her cheeks, mingling with the blood.

Guilt seeped into me, but I pushed it away. I couldn't take it easy on anyone here. Given the chance, they'd all kill me. Aubrey might be the only one who would regret doing it, but I wasn't under any illusions that she would spare me.

"Where can I find him?" I repeated.

"He doesn't stay here with us," she said, voice wavering. She was seconds from a breakdown. "He keeps his own place and checks on us when he has a target for us. We rarely see him otherwise. He has important things to do."

"Where is he staying?" I was growing impatient. I didn't like the way the last two men were looking at her.

Aubrey squeezed her eyes closed and took a deep breath. "I

can't betray him," she said. "He works through His grace, guides us on the right path."

"Do you think all of this death is truly the right path?" I asked, knowing how it had to sound coming out of someone who had just sucked the life out of someone.

She shook her head, refusing to look at me. "I can't."

"Aubrey," I said as gently as I could. "Tell me. I won't hurt you. I'll let you turn around and walk right out of here. You can make a life for yourself, a real life."

Her eyes opened and I saw hope there. "He's sta—"

A pair of screams caused her to stop. Both men charged her at the same time. I shot one before he made it more than a step. His head snapped back and he fell hard on his back, dead before he hit the ground. I swung my aim toward the other, but wasn't fast enough.

Aubrey cried out as he grabbed her from behind. He raised his hand and swept it across her throat. Blood bloomed as the knife he held bit into flesh. He wrenched her head sideways, back into the knife, and slammed the blade home. It nearly severed her head from her body.

She gurgled something inarticulate and then collapsed, blood pumping onto the ground.

The man looked at me and grinned. Aubrey's blood covered his face. "He will avenge us," he said.

"Not if I find him first." My hand trembled where I held the gun. I wanted to shoot him in the worst way, but I needed him. He might not think he'd talk, but once I was through with him, he wouldn't have a choice.

"No," he said, grinning. Blood dripped into his mouth, staining his teeth red. "He'll find you."

And then, before I could stop him, the last member of the Left Hand plunged the knife directly into his own eye.

25

Bodies lay scattered around the room like debris. Blood covered just about every inch of the floor, causing my hunger to stir. The flickering candlelight gave the illusion of movement to the corpses lying in various poses. And that's all it was—an illusion. Everyone was dead.

Bile ripped its way up my throat and I spun to the corner. I fell to my knees and my latest meal spewed against the wall, adding to the liquid mess. I leaned my forehead on a bare patch of wall and breathed in and out slowly, trying to regain some semblance of composure.

Killing had never hit me this hard before—it was mostly that I'd blown my chance of taking out the Left Hand leader and not the actual deaths that had me so upset. I should have killed the two men while the girl was willing to talk. She'd still be alive and I'd have the information that I needed.

Thoughts of Aubrey made my stomach churn. She might have been a member of the Left Hand, but in the short time I'd talked to her, I'd felt something from her, a detachment that separated her from the others. She could have been saved, I was sure. If only I'd been smarter, faster.

I rose to my feet and wiped my arm across my mouth. I was covered in blood and smelled like a slaughterhouse. I wanted a shower in the worst way, but I couldn't leave just yet. There might be something around the hideout that could point me in the direction of the Left Hand leader, Gabriel.

It took me a moment to fully push away my anger and frustration so I could go about checking the bodies. I looked through pockets and bags, places where personal items should have been but were lacking. Instead, there were more syringes and knives. The closest I came to finding anything was a pack of cigarettes stuffed in one young man's back pocket. Otherwise, nothing.

I scanned the room. There were five candles placed around the room, still lit. Two had been on the counter, but had been knocked over during the fight. The wax had already hardened. In the dim light, it looked like blood.

I turned away and made for the back room. It had once been a kitchen, but was now an empty room filled with cots and blankets. There were nearly two dozen of them, telling me I hadn't killed them all. I wasn't sure how many of these cots had lain empty for more than a few days. I knew for a fact a few Left Hand members had died before tonight's slaughter.

It was dismal work, but I began sifting through the sheets and dirty clothes lying beneath many of the beds in bags. There was little of value anywhere in the room. It appeared the Left Hand took things of value from their members, leaving them with clothing, a few pieces of jewelry, and that was about it. I didn't find a single piece of ID, new or old.

I was just about to give up when I heard a crinkle of paper as I set a pillow down. I opened the side of the pillowcase, found a tattered piece of paper, removed it from its hiding place and opened it. I could tell by how thin the paper felt that it had been well read. The writing in some places was smudged, as if someone had run their finger over the words a few dozen times.

Everything is set. Just waiting for the right moment. I love you.

A sudden fear stabbed through me. Could the short note be from someone in the Den? The writing was definitely feminine. Could it be from Keira?

I had no proof that the note had anything to do with Jonathan or the Luna Cult, but a part of me was certain of it. Keira had been the one to suggest letting the Left Hand woman go. Had she also planned the fake attack? The fight had looked real enough. The werewolves who'd joined the Cult with her had been the ones who'd attacked.

I bolted, dropping the letter without thinking. Jonathan could be lying dead in front of the garage even now. The Cult could have been destroyed while I'd been following the woman. I might return to nothing but blood.

My head pounded as I ran. Maybe the Cult had won the fight. Jonathan had some serious fight in him. Maybe he'd only sustained a few injuries and taken care of the problem. Everything had to be okay.

I leapt over an overturned bench and bolted across the empty campus. I could feel eyes on me and prayed that whoever was out there, they were on my side. If the escape had indeed been a setup, it could be Keira, waiting for my return so she could finish me off.

I reached the garage and a wave of relief passed over me when I saw the emptiness. There were no bodies. The car Pablo had driven was gone.

Still, there was blood on the ground. It didn't look like much, but that didn't mean anything. If the fight had been real, the wolves could have fed, drinking most of the blood and then cleaning up after themselves so as not to alarm anyone else who might come along.

I changed course, this time heading straight for the Den. I'd get answers there.

The old library came into view and I ran even faster despite the nagging pain in my shoulder. I knew I wouldn't see any lights from the outside, yet the bleakness of the building sent a new spike of fear coursing through me. As far as I knew, everyone was already dead inside. The bodies could be piled up like cordwood.

Or worse—crucified.

Jonathan has to be alive. If he died, the glamour would be gone.

It was a comforting thought, but not enough to slow my pace. He might still be hurt, dying. The glamour could flicker out like a sputtering candle at any moment.

I burst through the Den doors, not even bothering to shield my eyes against the bright light I knew was to come. I had my sword and gun in hand and didn't even remember drawing them. It took only seconds for my vision to clear and I found Keira standing at the bottom of the stairs, talking to a Cultist I didn't know.

"Where is he?" I demanded, stalking forward. I had my gun up and aimed right between her eyes.

"Who?" Keira said, motioning for the Cultist to leave. She tried to keep her face calm and composed, but her eyes gave her away. There was anger there. Anger and a flare of yellow telling me her wolf had awakened.

"Jonathan," I said through clenched teeth. Just let her shift on me. It would give me an excuse. "Is he alive?"

Keira gave me an odd look. "Of course he is. Why wouldn't he be?"

"Then where is he?"

She looked suddenly uncomfortable. She glanced to the side as she spoke. "He's out."

"Out where?"

"I'm not sure."

"What about Nathan? Did he finally decide to make an appearance?"

"He's not here either," she said. "He's with Jon."

My teeth felt as if they might break, I clenched them so hard. "Where have they gone?"

"They have business to take care of," she said. "I don't know much else. I was told to assist you upon your return." She glanced at me and her eyes flared for an instant before she turned away.

I took a step closer to her. My arm was trembling from holding up my gun. "He wouldn't leave now," I said. "This is too important. Why would he leave you here when he knew I'd be back with information on where the Left Hand woman had gone?"

I had to admit, Keira was holding up well to my threatening tone and posture. Not everyone could keep from lashing out or cowering when they had a gun pointed at their head. She faced me down, the anger simmering in her gaze, but didn't make an aggressive move.

"I don't know why he had to go," she said. "He told me to wait for you. He said he knew you would take care of it on your own and when you're back, get what I could out of you."

Somehow, that sounded like Jonathan. He wasn't stupid. He had to have known I wouldn't hold back when I found the Left Hand hideout.

"So," she went on, licking her lips and swallowing like her throat had gone dry. "What did you learn?"

"I'm not telling you a thing." The urge just to shoot her was so strong, I was forced to drop my aim. I kept my gun pointed in her general direction and I still had my sword in hand, just in case she made any sudden moves. I didn't want there to be any accidents.

I took a step closer to her, seriously invading her space. If she started shifting, I could ram the blade through her gut before she so much as sprouted fur. She might be quick, but I was just as fast.

"Back up," she said, her voice deepening to a near growl. She might have been able to handle me threatening her from a few steps back. She wasn't doing such a good job of it with me up under her nose.

"Not until you tell me what I want to know."

Her nostrils flared and her eyes shifted into full wolf. "You smell like blood," she growled. "Back up if you don't want me to lose control."

Okay, she had a point there. I felt as if I'd bathed in blood and while I'd partially sated my hunger during the fight, I had no idea when Keira had last fed.

I took a couple of steps back. I kept my eyes on her. If she so much as flinched, I wasn't going to hesitate to shoot her. I wouldn't kill her—not yet anyway—but I could wound her. The silver would drop her without me having to hit anything vital.

"I don't like this," I said, almost to myself. "Jonathan should be here."

"I'm sorry, Kat," Keira said. She was leaning against the banister, panting. The smell of blood had really gotten to her. Chances were good, she was still struggling with the urge to attack, but at least now I wasn't shoving it up her nose.

"For?"

"For him not being here," she said. "I don't like the idea of him taking off like this any more than you, but from what I can tell, it was important enough he was willing to risk missing you. You know him; he wouldn't go unless he felt he had to."

I nodded. That definitely sounded like Jonathan.

Still, I didn't like it.

"I take it you took care of the Left Hand?" she asked, eyeing me up and down. The hunger was clear in her eyes.

"Most of them," I said. "They weren't happy to see me."

The adrenaline from my panicked flight to the Den must have worn off then, because pain from the wound in my shoulder hit me like a truck. I groaned and leaned against the wall, feeling tired enough to sleep for a month.

A flash of concern passed over Keira's gaze, but she didn't make a move toward me. "Do you think it's over with?"

I shook my head, wincing at the pain it caused. "No," I said. "I was given the name of their leader. Something tells me he's not the kind of guy who'll walk away."

"Really?"

I looked into Keira's eyes, wanting to gauge her reaction when I told her the name. If I so much as suspected she knew it, I'd put her down right then and there.

"His name is Gabriel."

She didn't flinch, but instead, looked thoughtful. "Was there a last name? Something we could use to pinpoint him?"

I really wanted to blame Keira for the Left Hand, but I was really starting to wonder. She wasn't one who had control of her beast. I seriously doubted she could pull this off so casually without letting something slip.

"No," I said with a heavy sigh. "I'm not even sure they meant to let his name slip." I noted the strange look on Keira's face and my suspicions came roaring back. "Why?"

"It's nothing," she said with a slight shake of her head. "The name Gabriel and the Left Hand go so well together, it makes me wonder if it's an assumed name." She shrugged. "It's something I learned from church when I was little. I don't think it really has any bearing on whether or not we find him."

I sighed. Of course the name might be bogus. If I was going to run a group who went around killing monsters who were far stronger and far faster than we were, I wouldn't want them to be able to give me up either. Why couldn't anything about this be easy?

"There was something else there," I said. "I'm not sure it means anything, though."

"Oh?" Keira's eyes had bled back to their natural brown. She was taking shallow breaths and wouldn't look directly at me, but I could tell she was gaining some semblance of control over her wolf.

"A note," I said. "It didn't have a name and it didn't really say much, but it made me think that perhaps the staged fight outside the garage wasn't so staged after all." I paused. "I thought I saw blood before I followed the woman."

Keira gave a grim smile. "We set that up," she said. "We had some blood donated so that we could use it to make the fight seem more realistic. We wanted her to panic and blood has a tendency to do that."

It made sense. "I don't know. The note could be nothing."

"What did it say?"

I told her, once more watching her carefully for any sort of reaction. *Everything is set. Just waiting for the right moment. I love you.* Keira listened, frowned, and then shrugged.

"I don't know," she said. "But it does sound like something has been planned. Maybe it has to do with Philip's crucifixion."

"Yeah," I said. "Or maybe it has nothing to do with us at all."

"Maybe." Keira ran her fingers through her hair. "Look, Kat," she said, "I'm sorry about whatever it was I did to cause you to distrust me. I would never do anything to harm Jon or the Cult. I'm here because I want to be, not because I want to hurt someone."

I really wanted to believe her, but just couldn't. Whether it was my doubts about her motives, or simply the fact that she'd grown so close to him so fast, I didn't know. I just knew I didn't want her here.

"Make sure Jonathan knows about the note and the leader's name," I said. I sheathed my sword, but kept my gun in my hand. "And we'll want to make sure someone is waiting at the hideout when the sun comes up. I heard them talking about how she shouldn't have returned until the morning, meaning others might arrive."

"I'll see to it," she said.

"Make sure whoever goes knows the Cult well. Make it someone Jonathan would trust with his life." I grimaced. "Pablo would be a good choice. If the mole shows up, then perhaps we'll have our man."

She nodded. "Do you have the note?"

"No," I said. "I dropped it back at the hideout. I'll go back for it."

"I'll have someone look for it," she said. "You should get cleaned up. I have a feeling Jon will be needing you soon."

I grunted. Lately, I wasn't sure how much he really wanted me around. He had Keira. Why would he need a goddamn vampire mucking things up for him?

I gave Keira the address to the Left Hand hideout before turning and walking out of the door. I wasn't positive she'd do what she said, but at least I'd know if I could trust her or not. If she did as she was supposed to, then perhaps I'd have to cut her some slack. If not, well then, I'd have to let my gun do the talking.

26

The landscape seemed to taunt me.

I knew that coming to look out over the spot where Delai used to be would be pointless, but I had to go somewhere, and home wasn't it. There was a kind of peace, a void that allowed me to breathe just a little easier here. I knew things were probably going to get worse long before they got better, but here, in the nothingness, I could relax.

I'd pulled to the side of the road and walked a bit toward where I'd once seen the town. I could sense the animals around me, yet never saw a single one move. None of them were dangerous. I was the danger here. The animals were a reminder of a world that once was, of a peace that probably never truly existed.

I heaved a sigh and looked to the sky. I was being cynical again, but it was hard not to. I had no idea where Delai really was anymore, what dimension it resided in, but I had to look somewhere. I thought of Sienna and of Eilene, wondering if they were okay.

And I thought of Levi.

"If you hurt her . . ." I spoke aloud in the hope he could hear me. He'd guided me to the town before, which meant he'd know what I was. Maybe he was keeping tabs on me now. Maybe he was waiting for his moment to strike.

I was actually sort of glad I got no response. If Levi had come strolling out of the surrounding trees, I wouldn't have been able to do a damn thing to him. He was an angel. There was nothing I could do to stop him.

But soon . . . I would find him. I would stop him. It might mean giving in to my darker nature, allying myself even more with a demon I despised, but I would *not* let Levi win. Once the Left Hand was truly gone, once I'd dealt with Baset, I would find him.

And I would end him.

The thought galvanized me. Nothing could happen to me until I'd taken care of Levi and Delai. I refused to let it. It gave me something to strive for, something far greater than myself.

I turned away and went back to my Honda, actually feeling better than I had when I left it. I wasn't sure if it was lingering effects from the town that had once soothed me so much or if I'd simply calmed down from the fight with the Left Hand and the confrontation with Keira. Either way, I was ready to head home.

My hair hung limp against my back as I put the emptiness behind me. I was still covered in blood and the pain in my shoulder steadily increased the longer I left the bullet lodged inside it. I really should have gone straight home from the Den, but this little side trip had done me some good. It wasn't a weakness to seek a few moments of solace in the insanity. It actually showed strength to step away from everything to catch your breath. It's not always easy to relax when people are dying.

Turning into the driveway, I realized something was off. I felt a presence nearby, just ahead of me. As the feeling hit, I saw him standing just outside the trees. Movement behind him told me he wasn't alone.

I stopped at the bottom of the drive and drew my gun. It would be useless here, but it made me feel better to have it in my hand.

"I can see you, you know," I said, putting as much irritation in my voice as I could.

"I wanted you to," Adrian said. He took two strides my way before stopping again. Davin came out of the trees behind him, grinning his manic grin.

"I should have known you couldn't just leave me alone," I said, angry at myself for not noticing him sooner. The Oath should have warned me, yet I kept ignoring it. I needed to start paying better attention to it before Adrian decided it was time to force me into something else.

Adrian glanced at the gun in my hand. "You do not need to fear me."

"I like holding it."

"I could take that as a threat," he said. "Neither of us would like that."

I sighed and holstered the gun. There was no reason to keep it out. Thanks to the Oath, I couldn't shoot him. And thanks to his threats, I couldn't shoot Davin without putting people I cared about at risk.

"What do you want?" I asked. "It's late and I'm a mess. I want to get cleaned up."

"I could feel your agitation," Adrian said, face as impassive as ever. "I was concerned."

"Right." I very nearly laughed. "You're so worried about me, you had to come here to make sure I was okay. It has nothing to do with you fucking stalking me."

He shrugged. "I only wish to protect my investment."

I snorted. "I can take care of myself, you know."

"I do," he said. "But I also wish for you to accept me as an ally. I want only what is best for you. I'll do whatever it takes to make sure that happens. I feel it is the only way you will finally trust me."

This time I did laugh. "You only care about yourself and your own wants. I just happen to be the object of your latest desires." And I meant that in more than one way. Just the thought was enough to make me want to puke.

He shrugged again. "It is one and the same, really. If something happens to you, then my plans will need to be reevaluated. I do not wish to go down that route. So . . ." He shrugged. "I am here."

"Fine. Whatever." I sighed and rubbed my temples. Couldn't he have chosen another day for this? "I just want to go inside. If there's nothing else, would you please just go away?"

"I can accompany you within your home so we can continue discussions further," he said.

"The hell you will."

Adrian actually flashed an amused smile before all semblance of emotion bled away. "At least tell me why you are so agitated. Perhaps I can find a way to be of help while you . . ."—he looked me up and down—". . . get cleaned up."

Davin giggled, drawing my eye. He stood just slightly behind his master, hunched over like some movie henchman. He watched me with a gleam in his eye that was disconcerting. He knew something I didn't, I was sure. He might be insane, but he wasn't stupid.

"It's complicated," I said, turning back to Adrian.

"As are you," he responded. "Yet I have taken great pains to understand your complications. I believe I can handle whatever troubles you may have."

I sighed. What would it hurt to give him a little more information? It wasn't like he didn't already know about the Left Hand. He'd practically dragged me into a confrontation with one of their members, telling me he knew what I was working on.

But no matter how much of a help Adrian might be in dealing with the Left Hand, I couldn't trust him. He might go and kill twenty innocents, just so he could get at one man. He might do more damage than good.

And then another thought struck me. There was something I wasn't so sure he knew. Hell, I wasn't even sure I was right about it, but it couldn't hurt to bring it up. Maybe he'd try to do something about it and would end up getting himself killed, ridding me of yet another problem.

"Count Mephisto had someone following me recently," I said.

Adrian went motionless. "I see."

"I never would have noticed him if it weren't for finding a body beside my motorcycle at the Bloody Stake a few nights ago."

This time he frowned ever so slightly. "You did not kill him, then?"

"Nope. Someone found him, throat cut. I didn't see the guy until he was already dead." Of course, I wasn't going to tell him the guy had saved me from a wolf attack when I'd followed Nathan a few nights back. It would only confuse him. Hell, it confused me.

"The Left Hand?"

I only shrugged. He could figure it out for himself.

Davin shuddered and seemed to shrink, as if the thought of the Left Hand was enough to send him screaming into the night.

"I will keep an eye out for those that might follow you," Adrian said. "I did not know Count Mephisto had such a great interest in you."

"I don't like *anyone* following me for any reason," I said, hoping he understood.

Adrian, as usual, simply shrugged.

"What I want to know is, how did his wolf manage to find me?" I asked.

"It isn't too hard to pinpoint your location when you frequent the same places. All anyone has to do is wait. You will eventually arrive."

"Yeah, but you've been able to find me without watching my every move. You've had people show up in places I've never gone before. How?"

"We have the Oath."

"And before that?"

Adrian glanced at Davin, who finally joined the conversation.

"We've had something of yours for a long, long time, Lady Death. I've used it to track you."

Adrian turned back to me. "Which means Count Mephisto has something of yours. If he is truly tracking you . . ." He added the last as if he wasn't quite sure he believed me.

I almost told them that it was impossible. How would Mephisto have gotten hold of something of mine?

And then it hit me.

My gun. One of Mephisto's men had knocked it from my grip and I'd lost it beneath a vehicle when I'd gone to his mall in a boneheaded attempt to announce my return. I knew I should have tried to grab it before taking off, but I hadn't been thinking too clearly back then. In fact, I'd been a downright mess. I was only starting to claw my way back out of the messes I'd made for myself.

"Son of a bitch." I had no idea how I was going to get the gun back short of charging right into Mephisto's hands.

"He will be able to find you wherever you go," Adrian said. "He will know where you live. He could have someone here even now." He glanced around at the trees surrounding my property. Anyone could be hiding in them and I wouldn't know it unless they wanted me to.

"Great," I said with a sigh. So much for my relaxed mood. "Everyone wants to watch me. I feel so fucking special."

"Ah, but you are." Adrian smiled again. I was beginning to wonder if maybe he was getting too comfortable around me. He'd never showed this much emotion at once in my presence. "I just don't think you understand how special."

I didn't like the gleam in his eye. I knew what he wanted from me and there was absolutely no chance in hell I was going to give it to him.

"I'm going in now," I said. "I'd appreciate it if you would get the hell out of here and never come back."

"Would you be averse to my checking the grounds?" Adrian asked, all seriousness. "Neither I, nor my wolves, will bother you. We will simply make sure no one else is nearby."

I almost told him to shove it up his ass, but changed my mind. While I could send Jeremy out to scout, he was only one man. If there were more than one wolf out there, he wouldn't stand a chance. And while I could help him look, it would take time—time I didn't have.

"Fine," I said, hating it. "But after you make sure no one else is around, I want you and all of your people gone."

Adrian bowed. I thought I caught a glimpse of a smug smile as his head dipped. He was taking this as a victory.

I revved the Honda's engine and tore up the driveway, spraying gravel in my wake. I hoped I pelted him a good one. The asshole was really getting on my nerves.

I looked back about halfway up the drive, thinking I'd find him watching me, but when I looked, both he and Davin were already gone.

27

"Kat, I . . ." Ethan trailed off as I stepped into the dining room. He held a glass in his hand. More blue liquid that didn't smell quite as bad as before sloshed around inside.

I couldn't look at him. I'd fed on a Pureblood even though I knew Ethan was still trying to come up with a mixture that would sate my hunger. While my victim might not have exactly been Mrs. Innocent, she'd still been human.

"Oh," he said, followed by a strained laugh. "I suppose I can work on it some more. I still don't think I have the taste down. We wouldn't want to have a repeat of last time, would we?" Another strained laugh.

I gave him a stiff nod, still unwilling to look at him. I'd never been embarrassed about what I was before. I've hated it, sure, but never felt like I was just caught in the backseat of a car by my mom. I really had tried to wait for him to come up with a solution before feeding, but the monster inside of me had taken control.

"I'll see you tomorrow night." He turned and walked away.

I slumped against the wall, smearing blood all over it, but right then, I didn't care. I felt exhausted, both mentally and physically. I hadn't been fighting as much or as hard as I used to, yet it was getting to me more and more. It was as if the years of killing were finally catching up to me.

I closed my eyes as a weak groan slipped through my lips. I hurt like hell. The thought of walking up the stairs was not appealing. Each step was going to jar the hell out of my wounded shoulder.

"You okay?"

I opened my eyes to see Jeremy standing on the stairs. He was watching me like he thought I might leap at him.

"I suppose," I said.

"Want to talk about it?"

"Not really." I sighed and almost said more, but stopped myself. No sense dumping on the were. I could handle things right now. Maybe when things got worse—and I was damn sure positive they would—I might consider asking for his help. Until then . . .

"Well, I'm around," Jeremy said, as if reading my thoughts. "Just in case."

He turned to walk away and I very nearly called out to him. Would talking to him really be such a bad thing? If nothing else, I could have him call Jonathan and demand to know what in the hell was going on with Nathan. They both should have been there, waiting for me, tonight.

Jeremy vanished up the stairs. A moment later, his bedroom door closed. The house felt oddly empty and silent.

I took the stairs carefully, doing my best to keep my shoulder level. I kept forgetting how badly it hurt. Being a vampire, I have a high tolerance for pain, so when I'm running around like a maniac, I often forget I'm injured.

Of course, it seems like all the pain comes slamming into me later. High tolerance or not, I felt like shit and wanted nothing more than to soak in a long bath and forget all about the Left Hand.

I made it to my bedroom without crying out and closed the door behind me. I pulled off my coat, frowned at the hole in it, then tossed it in the basket for my bloody leather. Next came my shoulder holster and belt, followed by my pants.

I stood there, in nothing but underwear and shirt, wishing there was another way to get my top off. It was going to hurt like hell taking off the shirt. The fabric had dried to the wound made by the bullet, meaning I was going to have to rip it off.

I bit my lower lip and yanked my shirt upward, over my head, and then threw it across the room. It hit the wall with a wet slap and slid down, trailing blood in its wake. My breath was locked in my throat. I was afraid if I tried to breathe, I'd scream.

It took a few moments, but the pain ebbed. I gasped out a few sharp breaths, wishing I had some pain meds that actually worked. Doctor Lei had something, I was sure. I crossed the room and peeked out my bedroom window. The woods seemed dark and foreboding. Anyone could be watching me out there, even now. I hoped Adrian had rounded up any and all watchers and was gone by now, though I doubted it. Chances were good a thorough search would take all night.

I let the blinds fall closed and plastered them to the wall so no light would seep in once morning came. I went into the bathroom, looked at the tub, and realized I couldn't take a bath—not unless I wanted to lie in bloody water. With a groan, I stepped under the shower and started it up.

The water washed over me, giving me a jolt of energy. I closed my eyes and let the spray cleanse me. I'd wash off eventually, but just standing there felt good, though I had to be careful of the hole in my shoulder. If the water pounded into that, I wasn't so sure I could stop a scream.

The wise thing to do would have been to have someone help. I could have gone to Doctor Lei to have the bullet removed. Hell, I could have asked Ethan to take care of it. This wasn't the first time I'd ever been wounded. He'd taken care of me before.

Yet somehow, this time felt different. I didn't want to drag Ethan into this. I didn't want him to know how badly I was hurt. The skin around the wound was inflamed and the longer I waited to get the bullet out, the more it fucking hurt.

I leaned out of the shower and opened a drawer beneath the sink. I blindly felt around until I found the tweezers. I clutched them in a fist that was already starting to tremble in anticipation of the pain and returned to the shower. I stood there for a long time, head down, eyes closed, breathing in and out slowly.

Once I was calm and mentally ready for it, I bent the tweezers so that they opened a little farther than normal. This was going to hurt like hell, but I wasn't going to take the time for someone else to do it for me. I was positive the bullet lodged in my shoulder was made of silver. I wasn't ready to answer all the questions that would follow the moment anyone else realized what I'd been shot with.

I pressed the tips of the tweezers to the wound. Pain instantly seared through my shoulder, taking my breath. I jerked my hand away and gasped a few choice curses into the water. Gritting my teeth, I sank down into the tub, pressing my back against the far wall to brace myself. The water sprayed onto my knees, sending cascades of water into my face. It helped wash away the sweat that was already beading my brow.

This time I braced myself for the pain. I took two deep breaths, held the last, and then clenched my teeth harder as I pressed the tweezers into the wound.

It was like nothing I'd ever felt before. This wasn't someone jamming claws or knives into me. I was doing this to myself. My mind kept screaming at me to stop before I did even more damage to my wounded shoulder. Ethan wouldn't care what kind of bullet it was. He'd come in and help and would keep his mouth shut about what he found. It wasn't as if he had anyone but Jeremy to tell.

But the thought of anyone knowing how deep into Adrian's grip I was kept me going. I pressed deeper into the wound. The tips of the tweezers hit something hard. It sent shudders through my body as they scraped against the bullet, pushing it the tiniest bit deeper.

I hadn't hit it dead on, so I was forced to move the tweezers around until I was able to slip the ends past the bullet. I could feel resistance where I was pushing against flesh, but at least I wasn't scraping bone.

It took me forever to get the bullet out. The tweezers kept slipping off the surface. I managed to wiggle it a little farther each time, until I was finally able to get a good grip on it. I yanked it free with a cry of pain. The bullet dropped into the bottom of the tub where it rolled into the drain.

I just about collapsed into the shower. If I thought I'd felt exhausted before, I was near dead now. Blood stained the running water crimson as the wound started bleeding again.

It took me a good ten minutes before I was finally able to force myself to my feet. The water was getting cold, which was fine. It numbed me where the pulses of pain radiated from my shoulder through the rest of my body. I grabbed the soap, figuring I best get it over with, and scrubbed myself clean.

I shut off the shower and the fumbled around in the drain until my frozen fingers wrapped around the bullet. I took it and gingerly dried it off. Thankfully, the towel was already red, so it wouldn't show the remnants of blood. I tossed it into the hamper with the rest of my bloody clothes before heading into my bedroom. I plopped down onto my bed and looked at the bullet.

Silver; just like the man said.

I turned it over in my hand slowly. If it weren't for Adrian, I'd be dead right now. Maybe I was being too hard on the wolf. Sure, he was a royal prick and intent on making me his mate, but he'd also made me immune to silver. He'd even saved my life a few times. Was it really so bad being sworn to him? I was beginning to wonder.

A knock came at my door. I looked at the bullet in my hand a moment longer before slipping it beneath my pillow.

"One sec," I called. It took all my remaining energy to stand so I could get dressed. From the tentative sound of the knock, I was sure it was Ethan. He wouldn't want to come in and see me naked, though it wouldn't have been the first time. I might have called him in just to see the look of shock on his face if it weren't for the wound in my shoulder. I didn't want him to know I'd been hurt.

The hole was oozing blood, so I hurried into the bathroom, found some gauze, and taped it in place before slipping on an old T-shirt. I threw on a pair of sweats and then sat down on the bed before calling for Ethan to come in.

He opened the door and stepped inside. "Can we talk for a few minutes?" he asked.

"Sure," I said. I scooted up farther onto the bed so that I was propped up against the headboard. I wasn't so sure I could stay sitting upright much longer.

Ethan glanced around the room briefly before closing the door. He crossed the room and sat at the foot of the bed, facing me. He looked troubled.

"Is everything okay?" I asked.

"I don't know," he said. "I . . . I've been thinking a lot lately." He looked down at his hands, which were busy trying to break one another. "Do you think you'll do it?"

"Do what?"

"You know . . ." He bit his lower lip. "I mean, it has to be enticing, right?"

"Ethan, I have no idea what you're talking about."

He glanced up at me and I saw real concern there. "Beligral's offer."

Oh, hell, I'd completely forgotten about the demon and his offer.

I closed my eyes and leaned my head back. I was so not ready to think about this.

"It's just . . ." Ethan sighed. "I don't know. I'm scared. What if he can do it? What if you go through with this? What becomes of me?"

"What do you mean by that?" I looked him up and down. He looked terrified, like he thought I was ready to run away again. His fear made me hate myself just a little more. I never should have done that to him.

"If you're human again, you couldn't do this." He spread his hands wide, as if to encompass the entire city. "I wouldn't want you to. You might survive for a little while, but sooner or later, someone would get to you."

"They might get to me now."

"Yeah, but you're strong now. You can match their strength. What happens when that's no longer the case?"

He had a point, one I'd thought of on my own.

"Look, Ethan," I said, forcing myself to sit up straighter. I suppressed a groan as my shoulder flared. "I won't leave you alone to fend for yourself."

He nodded and looked away. "I know that, but . . ."

"There's no buts here," I said. "I won't leave you like that *ever* again. If I someday decide to take the demon up on his offer—which is unlikely—I'll do it when it suits all of us. I won't risk people dying for my own purposes. I will not let it hurt you, Jeremy, or anyone else."

"But your humanity . . ."

"Isn't worth your life."

He looked at me then. Tears glistened in his eyes.

"I know I've fucked up a lot lately. This . . . *thing* . . . has gotten inside my head, made me careless. I'm truly sorry about that. I will *never* let that happen again. I promise you, I'll be more careful. I'll try harder."

My mind flashed to Thomas lying buried out back. If Ethan and Jeremy weren't enough reasons to try to be better, then what I'd done to my own brother sure as hell was. I wouldn't let my friends end up like him.

"Okay," Ethan said. He tried to smile, but it didn't come anywhere close to reaching his eyes. "I should probably go." He stood.

"Ethan," I said. I started to reach for him, but hissed in a pained breath instead. My shoulder felt like someone was stabbing it with a hot poker.

He waved me off. "It's okay," he said. He nodded toward my wounded shoulder. "You should stitch that up before you go to bed. Otherwise, it'll seep through the bandage and stain the sheets."

I gave him a surprised look, at which he only laughed. Ethan turned, gave me a knowing wink, and walked out of the room.

28

Ethan and Jeremy were sitting at the table when I came downstairs the next night. There was an empty plate in front of one of the chairs. I sighed and sat down. I really wanted to get to the Bloody Stake and see if I could pry any more information out of Mikael, but it could wait. My friends came first.

"Eggs?" Ethan asked, rising.

"Sure."

He scooped up my plate and scurried off into the kitchen.

"You doing okay?" Jeremy asked.

"As well as can be expected."

He glanced at my shoulder and I winced. It still hurt, but had already started to heal. I think if I'd have had someone else extract the bullet, it wouldn't still be aching, but what's done is done.

"Are you getting close?"

"To what?" I asked as Ethan set my plate down in front of me. It was filled with scrambled eggs mixed with shredded bacon and onion. I scooped a forkful into my mouth and just about melted into my seat. "This is good," I said, chewing.

"To the Left Hand," Jeremy said. "Are you closing in on them?"

I realized then I hadn't told either of them what had happened. If Jonathan hadn't called to fill them in, all they knew was that I came home the night before covered in blood.

I shrugged my uninjured shoulder and continued eating.

Jeremy took the hint and ate the last three bites of his breakfast in quick succession and rose. "I've got some things to do around the house tonight," he said. "I'll see you later?" This last was aimed at me.

"Yeah," I said. "I'm hoping to get some more information tonight. I shouldn't be out too long."

He nodded, frowned slightly, as if unsure I was telling him anything, and then walked away with a shrug.

Ethan opened his mouth to speak, but I cut him off.

"I know," I said. "I shouldn't keep everything to myself. But right now, I don't think I can talk about it. I just want to eat without thinking about blood and guts and the people who'll more than likely end up dying before this thing is done.

He hesitated and then nodded. "Okay," he said. "Just don't shut us out too much." Ethan rose. "I'm going to get some coffee and head on down to my lab. Do you need anything before I go?"

"No," I said. "I'll go down and grab some weapons just in case, but I'm really hoping that tonight is just an information run. I could use a night off."

He dropped a hand onto my good shoulder, squeezed, and then walked away.

I set my fork down, no longer hungry. I hadn't meant to, but within five minutes, I'd pushed both men away. I should have told them something—anything at all that would let them know I wasn't going to go running off to my death. Even the tiniest interaction would have helped.

But right then, I just wanted to forget about everything for a bit. It was bad enough I was going to have to talk to Mikael about what was going on. After that, I planned on hitting up Jonathan at the Den to get some answers from him.

It was going to be a real shitty night.

I rose and headed down into the basement. Ethan was already hard at work downstairs and I inwardly hoped he wasn't summoning his demon. I might be free of the marks, but that didn't mean he was. If we could find a way to get him free, we could put Beligral behind us forever.

Of course, I'd probably have to retire if we did. He supplied us with the silver for my weapons and as much as I hated to admit it, he'd helped me with a few problems I wouldn't have been able to handle on my own. Demon or not, he'd been invaluable.

On that happy thought, I grabbed a fresh gun, checked to make sure it was loaded, and then slammed it home. The sword and knives came next. I ran my finger down the sword blade before sheathing it, marveling at how it didn't burn like it should have. Even Adrian had proved himself invaluable lately.

Once armed, I put on my coat, patted the big door that led down into Ethan's lab, and then headed for the Bloody Stake.

The parking lot was practically empty as I pulled up next to the door. There was no sign that anyone had died outside. The blood had been washed away, leaving behind only the faintest trace. It would take a really good werewolf nose to smell it.

I entered the bar to find a somber crowd. Except for Bart and Mikael, who were always there, only two other people were inside. They sat close to the door and actually jumped when I walked in.

"Slow night?" I asked, turning to Bart.

He glowered as he got me a beer. "What do you think?"

I took the bottle and forced a smile. "I guess a murder can do that."

The two patrons suddenly stood and walked briskly out of the bar.

Bart grunted and wiped down the already spotless bar. "Thanks," he said with a sigh. "You'd think a death here would be a draw. Always had been. But now, people are scared—more scared than usual."

"It'll get better," I said. "I can promise you that."

He eyed me a moment before nodding and turning away.

I took a long pull from the bottle and then turned toward Mikael. He was alone tonight, looking forlorn. He watched my approach, smiling now that he wouldn't be alone.

"Oh, how good it is to see you, my sweet."

I sat down and set the bottle between us. "Want anything?" I asked. He didn't have a drink of his own. It bothered me that he'd just been sitting here with no girls, no drink or food. It was almost as if he knew someone would be needing his services. I had a feeling he knew it would be me.

"The death counts have been rising," he said, ignoring the question. "I've heard there was a big killing recently, one that left numerous people of questionable quality dead. You wouldn't know anything about that, would you?"

"The Left Hand," I said. "At least, most of them."

He smiled at that. "I see. Should I assume we'll be hearing less of them in the coming nights?"

"I hope so."

"I've also heard a rumor that a filmmaker has made his last film. I take it Anton was able to get you what you needed?"

I thought back to the video he'd shown me and my stomach squeezed. "He did." I didn't bother adding I'd been too late to make the kill myself. Somehow, I figured he already knew.

Mikael spread his hands. "It seems I've done my part, yes?"

"You have." I leaned forward and lowered my voice. While no one else was in the bar with us, I didn't want anyone—including Bart—to overhear anything I had to say. "I have a name."

Mikael raised an eyebrow. "Oh, really?" he said, matching my tone. "What sort of name are we talking about here? Another of your mystery kills? Is it Monday already?"

"Not this time," I said with an inward wince. Did everyone know about Mondays? "I believe this name belongs to the leader of the Left Hand."

That definitely sparked his interest. "What is it?" he asked, almost greedily.

I wasn't surprised. This was a man who made his living dealing in information. If I could supply him with something he didn't know, then it had to be worth something to him, right?

I smiled. "If I give you this name, you'll tell me everything you know without worrying about how much it costs. And I don't just mean money."

"Of course," he said, as if it was a given. "Tonight, everything you ask of me will be free in all ways." His eyes gleamed. "Now . . . the name?"

"Gabriel."

He blinked. "A last name?"

"None that I've heard."

His smile faded. "The messenger?"

"I don't know what that means."

"In the Bible," Mikael said with a sigh. "Gabriel is the messenger of God."

"We're not talking about an angel here, are we?" Fear shot through me. If Gabriel was anything close to Levi, I was in some serious trouble. There was no way I could stop him.

"I don't think so," Mikael said. "If an angel was in town, I would know about it."

"Okay, then, we're dealing with a human. That means he'll leave some sort of trace, one you can follow."

"I might."

"So what can you tell me about him?"

He spread his hands in an apologetic way. "Not much without a last name or more information about him. I know of a Gabriel who once spent his time here, but he has long ago left the city. I doubt he has anything to do with leading the Left Hand. It isn't his style."

I sat back, frustrated. "So, I'm pretty much stuck with a useless name?"

He shrugged. "I wouldn't say that, my sweet. You've taken out a large number of the Left Hand, if rumors are true. That will make a difference."

"But if the leader is still out there . . ."

"Then he might kill others, yes? He might recruit more people to his ranks." Mikael gave me a smile. "Which means he'll be forced to put himself out there, leaving a trace, as you say. I believe he would do it here, where so many of his own have met their end. From what I can tell, this man will not give up easily. He will do whatever he can to exact his revenge."

I took a drink and mulled it over. At least he didn't think Gabriel had left. I wasn't sure what I'd do if he packed up and looked for greener pastures to recruit new members of the Left Hand. I doubted he'd stay away for long. I much preferred him here, where I could catch him in the act.

"Thanks," I said. "I'll see if I can dig up anything more about him."

"Sorry I could not be of more help."

I started to slide out of the booth, but stopped. "What can you tell me of the activities of Nathan LaFoe?"

Mikael's eyes widened at that. "Looking into one of your own now?" he asked, sounding vaguely amused.

"Let's just say, I'm curious."

He shrugged. "I am sorry to tell you, but I cannot give you the information you seek."

"He has you in his pay?"

Another shrug. "He has things he wishes to be kept on top of. And while your name gives me something to work with, it isn't enough to betray my clients." He gave me a "what can you do" gesture.

"What about Keira Emery?"

"What about her?"

"Can you tell me anything about her? Where she came from? Who she is? What she wants with Jonathan and the Luna Cult?"

"I could." He crossed his arms in front of him.

"Will you?"

Mikael studied my face for a long time before speaking. "Have you asked yourself why you would want this information?"

"Because I want to make sure she's safe to be around."

Mikael laughed. "Safe? A werewolf is never safe, even if she has joined up with the Luna Cult."

"You know what I mean."

"I do," he said. "I also know that you do not ask this because you think she is up to something. You ask for another reason entirely. It is all over your face."

I looked away. I hated how everyone seemed to be able to read me so well, lately.

"Oh, my sweet," Mikael said, leaning forward. "You are in uncharted territory—for you. You think you have things under control, but I can see the cracks forming. You are troubled because you refuse to allow yourself to express yourself fully. You want to keep everything bottled inside so much, you are shielding yourself from everyone and everything. If you do not let yourself break free, you will eventually shatter."

A part of me wanted to draw my gun and show him how easily I could express myself. A gun did quite a lot of talking without all the words.

But I sagged in my seat instead. I knew he was right. Keira might not be my favorite person in the world, but deep down I didn't really think she had anything to do with the Left Hand. I hated her simply because she was close to Jonathan, closer than I ever seemed to come.

Right then, it was decided. She was better for him. She could give him things I couldn't. Hell, I didn't even know if Jonathan and I would be compatible. We were two different monsters. We didn't mesh well with each other. You just had to mingle our blood together to see that.

"Thanks," I said, standing.

"Anytime," Mikael said, leaning back. "If you figure things out, please let me know. I'll be interested to see how this plays out."

I nodded and walked away.

I'd planned on going to the Den to ask more questions about Nathan and Keira, but now, I was going to go for an entirely different reason. I'd tell Jonathan everything I knew about the Left Hand, would tell him I was going to keep working on the problem until they were no longer an issue.

And then I was going to tell him not to worry about me. I would stop interfering. He and Keira should have their chance to connect without me lurking around, causing a rift.

I left the Bloody Stake and made for the Den.

29

It was a long ride to the Luna Cult garage. I wasn't sure I was ready to talk to Jonathan, especially about Keira, but it had to be done. They had been in the back of my mind since I'd seen them together. It was becoming a distraction. If I wanted to focus on finding Gabriel, I needed to put everything else behind me or else I'd be the one who ended up dead.

I parked in the depths of the garage and sat listening to the echoes of my movements. The garage felt emptier than usual, though there seemed to be the usual number of cars. I was pretty sure the black one deep in the shadows belonged to Jonathan, though it was hard to tell. It seemed like all the wolves in the Den had black cars.

If it was, then this wouldn't be yet another wasted trip. If I showed up and Jonathan wasn't there, I'd be done. I wasn't going to drive all this way, just to have to deal with someone else, someone I didn't trust nearly as much as I did the Denmaster.

Even though I was anxious to get to the Den, say what I had to say, and turn my attention back to the Left Hand, I couldn't bring myself to hurry. I kept my head down as I walked, listening to the sounds around me. I put one slow foot in front of the other, moving inevitably toward a moment that would more than likely change my life.

I don't think I'd ever done anything this hard before. I was going to be putting myself out there. To tell Jonathan he could be with Keira without my interference meant I was admitting I cared. I'd much rather have someone stick me in the back with a red hot poker than have to talk about this sort of thing.

The thought actually made the wound in my shoulder ache. I grimaced. Maybe I wasn't so keen on the physical pain either, but damn it, this wasn't going to be any fun at all.

I stopped just before the green and looked the Den over. The walkways were cracked and crumbling, the grass green, but too long and filled with weeds. Stray pieces of trash littered the lawn, blown by the breeze coming off the small lake on the other side of the trees.

Then there was the building itself, with its old graffiti and dark windows. I knew that inside it looked totally different, that Jonathan's glamour hid what really lay beneath the veneer, yet it actually hurt to see it looking so rundown. I wanted the Cult to be able to quit hiding, to be able to take care of the lawn without fear of someone coming in to kill them.

It was a dream I knew I'd never realize. If it weren't the Left Hand, it would be one of the numerous counts and countesses. And if not them, I wouldn't put it past some of the more intrepid Pure-bloods to cause the Cult serious problems. Hell, I wasn't even sure if the other Luna Cult factions around the country wouldn't come along to burn the place down, simply because Jonathan had turned this Cult into something special.

With a sigh, I started forward. There was no sense putting this off any longer. I could dream of peace all I wanted, but it wasn't going to happen until every vampire and werewolf on the planet was exterminated.

And that was something I knew I'd never live to see.

I reached the doors to the Den and stopped. Thanks to the cameras around the campus, everyone inside probably already knew I was coming. Someone was more than likely waiting by the door even now. They never came out to greet me. They'd stand there by the stairs, waiting to give me whatever news awaited me.

I pushed through the doors, into the blinding light . . .

Straight into a room filled with bodies.

I froze just inside the room, unsure I believed what I was seeing.

There were about a dozen of them, all dressed in Cult robes. They lay around the room, glazed eyes staring toward the ceiling.

"No," I whispered, drawing both my gun and sword. This couldn't be happening, not now.

I held completely still. The door swung silently closed behind me. It was the only sound outside my rapid breathing and pounding heart.

I scanned the upper floors, looking for any signs of movement, of life. A hand hung from the top step. The body was out of sight, but I knew the owner was as dead as everyone else.

I knelt by the nearest Cultist and pressed by fingers to his wrist. He was still warm, but there was no pulse. This hadn't happened long ago.

The urge to call out Jonathan's name was so strong, I almost did it. He could be dead inside, his body cooling even now.

Keira.

Somehow, I knew it had to be her. She'd come in, gotten close to the Denmaster, and then killed him and his Cult. She could have been working with a count somewhere, perhaps one the Cult had wronged recently.

Then again, there was Nathan and his strange behavior as of late. Could he be responsible for this?

About a hundred other scenarios zinged through my mind, each more unlikely than the last. This could have been anything, really. It didn't have to have anything to do with Keira or Nathan or even the Left Hand.

I checked the body for any sort of visible wound that would tell me what had happened, but found nothing. There wasn't a tiny hole in his neck where a needle could have gone in, no stab wounds, crushed skull, or anything at all like that. It was as if they'd all simply fallen over dead at the same time.

I stood and took a step forward. My foot brushed the flared robe of the dead Cultist. Something crackled beneath it.

I knelt down, eyes still scanning above and all around just in case whoever had done this was still around, watching me. I used the tip of my sword to move the robe to the side.

There, lying beneath the cloth, was a plastic cup.

Looking around, I noticed there were more cups lying near each of the Cultists. It looked as if they'd had a party of some sort, one that ended with all of them dying.

A suicide pact?

I could hardly think. There was something missing, some bit of information that would help me put it all together.

But I couldn't stop thinking about Jonathan. Was he alive? Dead? Dying? How much longer did I have before his life finally slipped away?

My hand tightened on my weapons as I walked briskly toward the office door. My head was spinning and I was sick to my stomach. This couldn't be happening. I couldn't stand the thought of Jonathan possibly lying dead somewhere, all before I could tell him how I truly felt.

The office door was open a crack. If someone was hiding inside, they could have been watching me this entire time. They could be crouched there, ready to strike the moment I stepped through the doorway.

I raised my gun and used my foot to open the door the rest of the way. It swung open and I immediately dropped my aim as my heart fell through the floor.

Bunny slippers.

That was the first thing I saw.

No one else was in the room as far as I could tell. The hidden door was firmly closed.

I stepped inside and looked down at Pablo. He was lying face-down on the floor. Blood pooled beneath him, telling me he hadn't died like everyone else. There was too much of it for him to have broken his nose or lip when he'd fallen.

My hands shook as I turned him over. Even in death he had that glower on his face. His eyes were open, glazed, but hard. He'd fought back.

On Jonathan's desk sat a pitcher with a stack of plastic cups beside it. The pitcher was almost empty. A tray of scattered cookies lay at the edge of the table, as did a partially eaten cake. Even with most of the words gone, I could make out what it said: *Happy Birthday!*

The urge to vomit nearly doubled me over. I'd completely forgotten it was Pablo's birthday. Hadn't someone been planning to throw him a party? I couldn't remember if it was Nathan or someone else. In the end, it didn't matter. I was going to kill whoever did this.

I spun toward the door, rage taking over. Tears burned hot behind my eyes, but I refused to let them fall. I'd never taken the time to get to know Pablo and now, I never would. If there was a chance I could still save Jonathan, then goddamn it, I was going to take it.

I left the office and made my way up the stairs, toward his rooms. I went up slowly, gun trained upward. I wasn't about to let someone get the jump on me because I was careless.

There were another dozen or so bodies at the top of the stairs, near the railing. When I glanced to my right, toward a part of the Den where I'd never gone, I could see a few more through a slightly open doorway. No sounds came from that end.

I turned my gaze toward Jonathan's rooms. The gilded doors were closed, but I knew that if he was anywhere inside the Den, he'd be there.

Two bodies lay before the door. The men weren't wearing robes, telling me they were weres. Each had a cup nearby. They'd been drinking when they'd fallen. Glancing at one, I recognized him as one of the wolves who'd come with Keira.

I kept my ears open as I walked past him to the doors. I held my breath and pressed my ear against the wood.

Something rustled inside faintly. It was almost too quiet to hear. It was soon followed by what I could only describe as a muffled groan.

That was enough for me.

I took a step back and with all the might I could put into it, I kicked the door in. I stepped inside, gun up and at the ready.

Keira hung by her wrists from chains at the far end of the room, near the heavily curtained windows. Her bleeding wrists were bound, as were both of her legs. Something was taped into her mouth, keeping her from crying out. Her eyes were wide, frightened. She tried to move, but her movements were sluggish and slow, as if she'd been drugged.

She jerked around on the chains, making loud grunting sounds. Her eyes kept flashing toward the door behind me.

Just then, something hard and cold was pressed to the back of my head. It didn't take too much brain power to realize it was a gun.

"Well, hello there, Lady Death!" It was a man's voice. "Welcome to the party." He leaned closer and whispered into my ear. "You might want to drop your weapons."

30

Both my sword and gun clattered to the floor. I raised my hands to show they were empty, staring straight at Keira. She looked stricken in her chains, as if I'd been her last hope.

"Anything else?" the man asked, gun poking me in the back of the head. "I wouldn't want there to be any accidents."

"You can check yourself if you want to know, Gabriel." I took a guess at his name and was rewarded with a chuckle.

"Spunky," he said. "I like that."

The gun remained in place as he patted down my coat. He found the silver packets I rarely ever use and dumped them onto the floor. He checked me all over, but didn't find the knives hidden at my belt. There was a reason I had the sheaths worked into the design.

"Much better," he said. He kicked my gun and sword across the room, his own weapon pressed to the back of my head. "Now we can talk!"

There was a moment when I very nearly spun to try to take him down. I mean, I was fast. If this truly was Gabriel, then he had to be Pureblooded, right? An angel wouldn't use or need a gun to pacify others.

But all it would take is a twitch of his finger and my brains would be splattered across the floor. I had no idea what kind of gun he had back there, but I was pretty damn sure it would have silver bullets. I might be fast, but I couldn't dodge a bullet. This wasn't the movies.

Gabriel walked slowly around me, gun trailing lightly around my skull. Once he was at my side, he backed slowly up before strolling over to where my weapons now lay. He kept his gun on me as he scooped up the sword, deposited it onto the couch, and then picked up the gun. He admired it all while keeping an eye on me.

"Interesting," he said. "It seems like such a small gun. I figured you'd use something bigger, like a cannon." He shrugged. "Oh well. I'm new here, but I know how legends go. People talk. They make even the smallest acts seem heroic." He looked at me and chuckled. "Lady Death. How . . . inappropriate."

"Never liked the name," I said. I took a chance and lowered my hands, down near my waist.

Gabriel only laughed. "I can see why. It's so dramatic. I mean, how many people die here on a daily basis? You didn't kill them all. Your *kind* did."

I shrugged. "I don't exactly get along with my *kind.*"

"That you do not." Gabriel leaned against the couch. The gun was no longer aimed at my head, but was still trained in my general direction. He still had hold of my gun as well. I didn't doubt he'd use it on me.

"Where's Jonathan?" I asked when he didn't say anything more.

"Ah, the Denmaster," Gabriel said. "I thought you killed monsters. He and his are demons, just like you, and yet he lives. How does that happen?"

"We're not like the others."

He snorted. "Isn't that what they all say?" He spun in a circle, arms wide. I tensed to spring, but he brought my gun up and aimed it at me. "Oh, no you don't. I can feel your intent. It seeps off you like a mist. It chokes me with your stench."

I let my shoulders ease, never taking my eyes from the crazy man in front of me. There was no doubt there was something off in his head. His eyes had a gleam that went far beyond the manic look I'd seen from his followers. He didn't just tell people he was a messenger from God; he actually believed it.

"You know," he said, scratching his cheek with the barrel of my Glock. "I never understand why your kind always think they deserve special treatment. Demons don't belong here. You should go back to where you came from and leave the rest of us alone."

"I was born here," I said. "I am where I belong."

He gave me a lopsided grin. "Your body might have been born here, but the demon inside you was not." He straightened and moved to stand on the other side of the couch, where he set his gun on the cushion. From there, he picked up a leather briefcase and set it on the armrest. "As much as I like your spunk, I can't let you walk out of here."

The case clicked open. I didn't need to see inside it to know there would be syringes alongside a serrated knife.

"Is Jonathan dead?" I asked. I knew I'd have to make my move soon. I needed Gabriel to drop the gun, think he has everything under control before I could do anything.

Gabriel sighed as he picked up a syringe. "No, no," he said. "He hasn't gotten here yet. I've been waiting for him. I did all of this for him, in fact." He gestured toward the open door where I could still see the bodies. "I did it because he wouldn't simply lie down and die."

My entire body sagged. I'd been so sure Jonathan lay dead somewhere, it just about caused me to burst into tears to know he was still out there, alive. If I could stall Gabriel long enough, perhaps he'd show up and we could take the leader of the Left Hand down together.

"I knew who you were the moment you came inside," Gabriel said. "As soon as you stepped through that doorway, I knew." He jammed the syringe into Keira's leg. "You killed my family."

Keira's eyes rolled up into the back of her head. She'd already been drugged with something, so adding the mixture to it was too much for her. She went limp where she hung. Her wrists were bleeding and she just about slipped free.

"They were killing mine," I said, swallowing with some difficulty. Without her there, it left me to fight him alone. I'm not sure what she could have done chained up like that, but at least she'd been an option before. Now, it was just me.

Gabriel's eyes narrowed. "They were doing the bidding of a higher power, something you'll never understand."

"They were doing what you told them to do."

He shrugged. "It's all the same. I listen to God, who speaks to me and me alone. He tells me what needs to be done. I've scribed

His word, passed it on to my disciples so they can cleanse the world of your filth."

"We're not all bad," I said again, knowing it would do no good.

"Demons are demons. You might think you're doing the right thing by killing your own kind, but all you're really doing is showing how bloodthirsty you are. You cannot be saved."

"And you're any better?" My fists clenched. I wanted to draw a knife and bury it in his throat in the worst way.

But I needed him closer. As long as he was across the room, he had the advantage.

"I do His work," Gabriel said. "You can't fault me for that." He sighed and picked up another syringe. "I only wish we had more time to debate this further. I'm a busy man and you've killed my people, meaning I have to recruit anew." He sighed and rolled his eyes. "So much work. Sometimes it's hard to get up in the morning." His lopsided grin was back. "Not that you'd know what it is like to be up during the day."

He looked at the gun in his hand—*my* gun—and winced. "I really hate these things," he said. He kicked Keira in the leg. "Did you know this demon actually tried to shoot me? I underestimated her and figured she'd try to jump me like the idiot downstairs. She actually picked up a gun and tried to shoot me." He gestured toward the wall behind me.

I looked back and sure enough, there was a bullet hole in the doorframe. She must have missed him by inches.

"Lucky for me, she's a terrible shot."

Someone moved outside the room and for a hopeful instant, I thought it might be Jonathan or Nathan, but instead, it was someone wearing Cultist robes. She stepped into the room, glanced once at me, and then turned to look at Gabriel.

"No one else is in the building," she said.

It wasn't until she spoke that I recognized her.

"Mira . . ." I said, realization dawning. She's the one who'd set up the birthday party for Pablo. Hadn't Nathan said she was Pablo's girlfriend? Had she gotten close to him just so she could set this entire thing up?

It was no wonder, really. As a member of the Left Hand, she must have been going insane having to live with the "monsters" she'd sworn to murder.

Looking at her again, something else clicked. Mira looked like a younger version of the woman I'd followed and killed back at the Left Hand hideout. *She* was the sister. It had been her letter I'd found.

"Are you sure they're all gone?" Gabriel asked her.

"They are," she said. "I even checked downstairs."

She must have been in the basement when I'd come in. She could have closed the hidden door behind her and found a way to open it from the inside. I knew I should have searched the basement before heading upstairs. It was a mistake that might cost me.

"Mira here has been living in this hellhole for months now," Gabriel said, turning to me. "She's taken on the robes and tattoo of this demon-worshiping cult, getting information for me that has been invaluable in my goals. She's suffered much for her faith."

With that, he raised his gun and shot her right between the eyes.

"But her information was bad," he said, almost indifferently. "The Denmaster and his second were supposed to be here. This would all be over if it wasn't for that." He shrugged. "Besides, living this close to demons like you had to have tainted her. I've done her a favor in killing her before the taint could take over her mind."

I kept my mouth firmly closed. I knew that anything I said would only push him that much further. I wanted him close, not to antagonize him so much that he shot me. While the silver of the bullets wouldn't paralyze me, a bullet to the brain was still a bullet to the brain. It was unlikely I'd survive it. And if I did, the knife across the throat that would follow would surely finish me off.

"You know," Gabriel said, reaching into the briefcase, "I'm really not looking forward to rebuilding the faithful. It isn't as easy as you'd think. People are afraid, and they can't seem to get past their fear. They can't bring themselves to do what is right. I can only recruit the strongest willed, the ones who know that to make a difference, you have to shed a lot of blood, kill a lot of monsters."

He drew a serrated knife. He looked at it fondly before setting it on the back of the couch.

"I'd make you watch as I killed her," he said. "But I don't think you'd sit still for it. Besides, I believe it would be far more fun for our good friend Jonathan to watch as I bleed the both of you out."

He showed me the syringe. "This one is for you."

My gut clenched. I'd felt the bite of a Left Hand syringe before.

I knew what it would do to me, even with my immunity to silver. I'd be helpless after only a few moments.

But not as helpless as I was the last time. I'd have a few precious seconds to get the job done if he managed to stick me with that thing.

I stood with my back straight and watched him approach. He kept his gun trained on me as he strode forward. He stopped out of lunging range and gave me a warm smile.

"If you're a good girl, I'll make sure you die quickly," he said. "If you try to fight me, you'll suffer. You will watch as I kill the rest." He cocked his head to the side. "Perhaps I'll even keep you as a sort of pet. Watching everyone you know die should do interesting things to that thing inside you."

I didn't move. He studied my face, eyes lingering on mine. "This will only sting for a moment."

He moved so fast, he nearly caught me unprepared. Years of killing supes had honed his reflexes, made him faster than a normal Pureblood.

The syringe bit into my neck just as I struck out. I knocked the gun from his hand, but by this point, he didn't care. He pressed down on the plunger and liquid fire raced through my veins. The world did a loop and for a heart-stopping second, I thought I was going to pass out.

I held on to consciousness and dropped my hand to my belt. Gabriel stepped back, smiling, empty syringe held high. His eyes widened as I drew the knife from my belt.

"How?" he managed as I lunged for him. Our bodies collided and I drove him back all the way to the couch. My legs gave out and I collapsed on top of him.

"The silver . . ." Gabriel's composure cracked and I saw genuine fear in his eye. This man wasn't an angel *or* a messenger of God. He was just another lunatic, thinking he was better than everyone else, just because he wasn't tainted.

He was nothing more than a killer.

"Doesn't work on me," I gasped as I drove my knife into his throat and yanked sideways.

Blood splattered my face as I rolled away from him. Gabriel clawed at his throat, trying to stop the flow of blood, but it was no use. I'd severed the artery.

We lay on the ground, facing each other, neither able to move. The silver component to his injection wasn't working, but the other parts were. I could feel myself passing out.

Gabriel gave one last gurgle and his eyes dimmed as the last of his life spurted out onto the floor.

And then I allowed myself to give in. The world darkened, leaving me vulnerable on the floor next to the spreading pool of Gabriel's blood.

And then there was nothing.

31

There was a clicking sound.

There was pain.

I hurt everywhere. Despite the fact I was floating in a sea of darkness, I could still feel the fire burning through me. I wanted to stay there, to remain lost in the void, away from what I knew would be further agony.

As far as I knew, I was already dead.

Gabriel was, that's for sure. But just because he was dead didn't mean his lackeys were. I saw him kill the girl, Mira, but she might have been only one in a dozen. The rest could be converging on me even now.

It was a thought that nearly caused me to wake. I fought against consciousness, knowing that if I were still alive, I would have a world of problems to deal with. I still didn't know where Jonathan was, if he was alive or dead. He hadn't been there when he was supposed to be. He might have failed to show up because of other pressing needs.

Or someone else had gotten to him first.

The clanking continued for a moment longer and then there was a heavy thump. The floor beneath me vibrated.

"No." The word came out in a gush of breath. I didn't want to deal with anyone or anything right then. I wanted to sleep, wanted to remain coddled in the black.

I pulled my legs in close to my body and groaned. The fire was lessening, replaced by an emptiness that felt all-encompassing.

Hands grabbed me by the shoulders. I was rolled onto my back. I kept my eyes closed against the sudden rush of pain in my head. It felt like my skull was full of concrete that was slowly cracking. Each broken shard seared into my brain, making thinking straight downright impossible.

"Kat?"

It was a woman's voice. She was close, breathing heavily. I could smell her perspiration, her fear, her anger.

I could smell her blood.

I shuddered and forced open an eye. The silver had run through my system. The burning pain I'd felt had all been in my head.

Still, the knockout component of Gabriel's mixture had done a doozy on me. Add to that the blood thinners that made me feel like my brain was made of helium. I was in bad shape.

A blurry face peered down at me. She was still holding on to my arms. She shook me again, a little more forcefully this time.

"Are you all right?"

"No." This time, it came out just above a whisper. My throat felt raw. For a panicked moment I thought I felt my own blood seeping from a ragged wound that stretched clear across my neck.

"It's okay," the woman said. "It's over."

A name fluttered through my mind. *Keira.* Her name was Keira.

And it all came rushing back to me. I sat up too fast, causing the world to sway. I just about threw up on myself. I buried my face in my hands and took deep breaths until the nausea went away.

Where was Jonathan?

"I tried to stop them."

The misery was so thick in her voice, I looked up. Her wrists were slick with blood. Deep ruts were cut into them where she'd worked her hands free of her bindings. It had to have taken all of her strength to break free. I doubted someone like Gabriel would have used bindings a werewolf could easily escape from.

I glanced over at his body. He was still staring at me with those lifeless eyes. The blood around him was starting to thicken. The floor had greedily drunk quite a bit of it. It would take forever to get the stains out.

"How?" I asked, not really sure what I was asking.

"It was that woman." Keira shot a glance toward Mira's body. "She'd been getting close to everyone, poking her nose into everything. She set up the party."

That reminded me of Pablo and his bunny slippers. For someone I didn't like, his death was hitting me hard. A tear slipped down my cheek and fell into my lap.

"I should have known something was up." Keira took a deep, shuddering breath. She was sitting in front of me, legs sprawled out awkwardly. She looked about as unable to stand as I felt. "She kept asking if Jonathan and Nathan would be here tonight. I thought they would be, but something came up at the last minute. I . . ." She trailed off and started crying.

I sat there, stunned. Her sobs brought more tears to my eyes. I tried hard not to let them fall, but was in no condition to do much of anything. There was still work to do, yet I needed that moment of release. Someone would have to find Jonathan and tell him what had happened.

But not yet. I don't think I could have faced him right then.

I tried to get to my feet, but my legs wouldn't support me. I sat heavily back and rested my head against the couch. I closed my eyes and waited, listening to Keira's sobs, at my own ragged breathing.

Time passed.

I blacked out again.

A scream tore me from my slumber. Adrenaline pumped through my body and I leapt to my feet, telling me I'd been out long enough that most of the mixture had worked through my system. Keira was up just as fast as I was, looking as if she had fallen asleep as well. We were both wobbly, but the pure agony in that scream had us both on the edge of panic.

Keira looked at me. Vestiges of her wolf peered out.

Something crashed downstairs. It was followed by a howling scream.

I started to run.

Keira was right behind me. Her breathing sounded more like a growl. I knew if it came to a fight, there'd be no holding her wolf back.

I reached the railing and peered over. Bodies still littered the floor. The door to the Den was closed, but that meant little. If someone had come inside, it would have swung closed on its own.

I headed for the stairs, trying to look everywhere at once. I couldn't see anyone from where I was, but could hear them. It sounded like our screamer was in the office.

I realized about halfway down the steps I didn't have any weapons on me but a single knife. I drew it and considered heading back up for my gun. I wasn't sure who was here. If it was more of the Left Hand, I might need it.

Jonathan strode out of the office, stopping me before I could turn.

His face was a mask of rage. His wolf was coming out, his eyes a feral yellow, face sprouting fur. His fingers were clawed, his head a ravaged mess where his glamour no longer hid the damage I'd done to him so many years ago.

I hurried down the rest of the stairs and stopped in front of him. Our eyes locked.

"Jon—" I started, but it was as if he didn't recognize me.

He came at me, shifting as he charged.

Keira screamed at him to stop, but he wasn't listening. I took off at a run, heading for the front door. If I could get outside, then I could escape him, give him time to calm down. There was no reasoning with a werewolf in that state. While I could stab him with my knife so that the silver would paralyze him, I knew I couldn't do it. I couldn't cause him any more pain.

He hit me in the side, moving faster than I could manage in my partially drugged state. We slammed hard against the wall three yards away. My head rattled and I very nearly passed out again. Teeth snapped inches from my ear. His claws dug into my arms.

I tried to stab him, knowing it was my only chance, but he saw the movement and twisted my arm. The knife cluttered to the floor as my fingers went nerveless.

He reared back, ready to bite my face off, when Keira crashed into us. The bulk of her weight hit Jonathan in the side, ripping his grip from me. If it wasn't for the thick leather of my coat, he might have taken my arms with him. They tumbled to the floor in a flurry of fur and gnashing teeth.

I stepped back, dazed. Keira had shifted and for the first time, I knew there was no way she could have been the wolf who'd attacked me when I'd tracked Nathan. Her fur was brown, but was streaked with blonde. She was much larger as a wolf than the other had been.

Jonathan threw her from him. She slid across the floor and crashed against the far wall. She barked out a gasp of pain and scrambled to her feet.

"Stop!" I shouted, causing Jonathan to spin toward me. He leapt before I could take another breath.

I tried to dodge him, but my coat flared out behind me. He snagged it with a claw and yanked me off my feet. My head hit the floor with a crack. Much more of that and my brain would be permanently scrambled.

He flung himself on top of me, teeth bared. His head darted forward, toward my neck. I was too weak to fight him.

Thankfully, Keira had recovered. She landed on his back, distracting him before he could close his powerful jaws. Her arms wrapped around his throat and she jerked him backward. They fell from me, allowing me to scramble backward. She held him tight, legs wrapped around his waist, arms around his throat. She was squeezing with all her strength, trying to choke him out.

I staggered to my feet and very nearly went down again. I'd felt sick before, but now the churning in my stomach was constant. If Jonathan got loose again, I wouldn't be able to stop him from killing me. It was all I could do to keep conscious.

"Jonathan," I said, using the wall for support. "Listen to me."

He thrashed against Keira. They rolled up against one of the bodies and that only seemed to enrage him more. He tried to get up, her clinging to his back, but she held tight, using her weight to keep him from rising.

"Jonathan!" I shouted it this time. All the frustrations, misery, and rage I could muster came out in that shout. The tears I'd managed to stem surged back to the surface and spilled down my cheeks. "Please, stop."

His struggles slowed. I wasn't sure if it was because of my words and tears or if it was because Keira had nearly succeeded in choking him out.

And then I saw it. I saw the man behind the beast. He was in there.

And he was hurting.

"We didn't do this," I said, and then repeated it for emphasis. "We didn't do this."

He went limp. The yellow bled out of his eyes and he started to shift back.

Keira wasn't about to let him go. The thrill of the fight was still thrumming through her. As Jonathan's body contorted and changed from wolf to man, she seemed to grow that much more excited. In that moment, I knew she might kill him.

"Keira," I said, no longer able to shout. "Let him go."

There was a moment when I thought she might let the bloodlust win out and rip out his throat. She looked at me and there was no recognition there, only pure animal instinct.

But then, something got through to her. Her wolfish eyes traveled from me, to Jonathan and she softened. Her arms released and she scrambled back toward the office, whimpering. She vanished inside.

Jonathan lay naked upon the floor. He was crying.

I knelt beside him, shaking with my own tears. "It was the Left Hand," I whispered. He needed to hear it, needed to know that he wasn't responsible for this. "But I got him, Jonathan. He's dead."

He growled and looked as if he might shift again. I rested a hand against his back and gently stroked his sweaty body. He looked up at me and calmed, though the pain in his eyes was impossible to fathom. It hurt me to see it.

"They were waiting for you," I said, not sure what to do, what to say.

Keira walked back into the room and I stood. She'd shifted back and was stark naked. Her clothes lay in tatters on the floor where she'd first shifted.

Jonathan refused to move. He was curled up as if he didn't have the strength or will to do anything. Everything he'd worked for was lying dead around him. All of these people, everyone who'd come to him was gone.

And I knew he was blaming himself.

"He needs you," I said to Keira, stepping back. "Take care of him." I started for the door.

"No," she said, causing me to stop. "It's not me he needs right now."

I turned to find her staring at me meaningfully. She nodded toward him and headed for the stairs, picking up the remnants of her clothing as she went.

A moment later, Jonathan and I were alone.

I walked slowly over to him and lowered myself down next to his trembling body. His tears were still flowing and his stare was blank, as if he was no longer seeing anything.

I touched his cheek and ran my thumb beneath his eye. He shuddered and glanced up at me. Our eyes locked, and this time, there was no rage. He scooted close to me so that our bodies touched. He reached out a hand and I took it in my own, giving him what remaining strength I had.

We stayed there for the rest of the night, amid the bodies of those he'd sworn to protect.

And somehow, I was content.

32

I didn't know why I was there.

Only a few days had passed since the destruction of the Left Hand and the Luna Cult. I still hurt from my wounds, both external and internal. The pain of the latter was going to stick with me for a long time.

I stood beside Keira beneath the moonlight and the stars, watching Nathan and Jonathan. I could hear Jonathan's soft murmur, but couldn't make out the words. He stood a little behind Nathan, who was kneeling, hand on a tombstone, whispering his good-byes.

Jonathan had asked me to come, but hadn't explained why. I came along, figuring we were going to pay our respects to the Luna Cult dead. It wasn't too much of a stretch to believe they'd have a mass ceremony since most of the Luna Cult had stepped out of their lives, leaving loved ones and careers, to give their full attention to the creatures they worshipped.

Turns out, we weren't there for the Cultists at all.

"It was his wife," Keira said as we stood watching the two weres. "Nathan found out she was sick and kept an eye on her. When she went into the hospital, he decided he needed to talk to her one last time. Jon went with him to show support."

I stood there, numb.

Nathan had a wife?

It all suddenly made sense. He hadn't been stalking that old woman, but rather, had been watching his dying wife, wanting to be there when she finally succumbed to the illness that plagued her. Did that mean the younger woman I'd seen with her was Nathan's daughter?

I was too afraid to ask. It was bad enough to have lost the Cult, but to lose someone he'd been married to . . . it had to be nearly breaking him. In time, I might try to find out for sure. Until then, I'd have to wonder.

"Did you know her?" I asked, keeping my voice low, though I knew Nathan and Jonathan could hear us.

Keira shook her head. "When Nathan was turned, he left her, figuring it was the only way he could protect her. He was afraid he'd lose control one day. He thought it better to leave her so she could move on and live a normal life." She gave a bitter laugh. "Whatever that means these days."

A faint part of me was angry that Keira knew about Nathan's pain long before I did. But then again, she had to live with him. It was harder to keep things from those you saw every day. I was an outsider, no matter how close I'd gotten to the Cult.

Nathan stood and wiped quickly at his eyes. The funeral had been earlier that day, but he hadn't gone. I was assuming he was afraid someone would recognize him—his daughter perhaps, if that's who she was. It was either that or he simply couldn't handle it. There'd been a lot of death lately.

I felt horrible for him. I'd been such a bitch toward Nathan, thinking he was doing something against Jonathan's orders. I'd even accused him of working with the Left Hand. He must think of me as a complete and utter moron.

But yet, there I was. I don't think Jonathan would have invited me if he didn't think Nathan would approve.

Still, I felt sorely out of place. This was Nathan's moment. I never knew his wife. Until that day, I didn't even know she existed. The longer I stood there, watching him whisper his last good-byes to a woman he hadn't spoken to in probably fifty years, the more out of place I felt.

Jonathan patted Nathan on the shoulder and turned to face Keira and me. He was doing a good job keeping his emotions hidden, but

I could see the pain behind his eyes. He walked toward us and bowed his head.

"We're leaving soon," he said. He pressed a hand into mine. "Thank you for coming. It means a lot to the both of us."

"Yeah." I tried to give him a reassuring smile, but it fell flat.

Jonathan returned it with about as much success. "I'm going to wait in the car. Make sure he's okay, all right?"

I nodded as Jonathan let go of my hand. His fingers lingered for a moment before he turned and walked to the car, head down, shoulders slumped.

"Is he going to be okay?" I asked Keira as soon as I was sure he couldn't hear me.

"I don't know," she said. "He barely talks to anyone anymore. I think he's trying to deal with things in his own way." She paused. "I'm sure he'll call you soon enough."

I sighed. Even when he'd called Jeremy to have me show up, he hadn't asked to talk to me directly. I was beginning to wonder if he blamed me for the deaths of his Cultists. I mean, I was the one who was supposed to have stopped the Left Hand, and yet I'd allowed them to destroy Jonathan's livelihood.

"Thank you," I said, turning to Keira. I needed to get something off my chest. "I never got a chance to tell you before . . ."

"Don't do that," she said, waving me off. "Don't thank me for anything. You're the one who saved me. If you hadn't shown up, I'd be dead right now, as would Jonathan more than likely. You're the one we need to thank."

The thought didn't sit well with me. I might have killed Gabriel in the end, but I didn't really save anyone. If I'd been better, I'd have gotten him long before he managed to kill nearly everyone in the Cult.

Nathan stood there a moment longer before turning and walking over to us. His jaw was clenched and his eyes were red, but at least the tears had stopped flowing.

"I need a moment with Kat," he said, stopping in front of us.

Keira didn't say a word. She just turned and walked to the car to wait with Jonathan.

"I'm sorry," I said before he could speak. "I didn't mean to . . ."

I trailed off. What could I possibly say that would make anything better?

"I'm not big on apologies," he said. He sniffed and looked around as if he was afraid someone might have seen him let his guard down. It was late enough that we were the only ones at the graveyard.

"Well, I'm sorry anyway."

He nodded. His eyes met mine and he seemed to search for something in them. Finally, he sighed and gave a bitter laugh.

"There's something about you that reminds me of her," he said, indicating his wife's grave. "I think it's your stubbornness. She could be so goddamn hardheaded sometimes, it made me want to scream." He lowered his head, stoicism cracking. "I shouldn't have left her alone all of these years. Just because she was stubborn, didn't mean she didn't care."

"You did what you thought was best." I felt like a fool trying to comfort him. We'd never been friends, not really. I wasn't sure we'd ever be.

He sighed. "Yeah. And now she's gone." He looked me in the eye and lowered his voice. "If it would have been you, would you have turned her? Could you have brought someone you loved over to the other side with you so you could spend your lives together?"

And that's when I knew. Nathan kept himself apart all of this time because of things he thought he should have done. He loved his wife and had chosen to leave her rather than turn her into a monster.

I thought of Thomas, of the pain he went through when he'd been tainted. I thought of my own torments, how I hated what I'd become.

And yet, the answer wasn't easy. Could I really let someone I loved die without doing everything I could to save them? I thought of Jonathan in the car.

I thought of Ethan back home.

"I don't know," I said. "I really don't know."

He nodded as if that was the answer he'd expected.

And then he walked away.

I remained standing there looking at the gravestone as the car started up. There was a moment when I think they were waiting for some sign from me that I was okay before they drove away. I didn't know where they were going and that scared me. The Den was now an empty library. The glamour was gone. They wouldn't return there.

I stared hard at the grave and wondered, given the choice between dying and being able to live on as a monster—which would I really choose?

The answer wasn't easy.

Please turn the page for an exciting sneak peek at E.S. Moore's next Kat Redding novel SOULS OF THE DAMNED available in June 2014!

1

The door stood slightly ajar. No sound came from within, but that meant little out here. Werewolves could be quiet creatures when they wanted to be. The one I was hunting had spent a lifetime hidden from the sight of others.

Plastic wrappers littered the stairs. Crushed cans lay off the walk leading to the large, dark building. While the place had never looked pristine, it had always been taken care of. The trash and abandoned look of the Luna Cult Den was enough to cause a sliver of pain to shoot through my heart.

Before, the rundown look of the old library had been a put-on. Jonathan Alucard, the Denmaster of the local Luna Cult, had used a magical glamour to hide the true nature of the building. Now, the graffiti and scarred and pitted brick were real. With each passing day, it only got worse.

My teeth ground together as I listened at the door. I could smell old blood somewhere inside. There wasn't the telltale scent of rot that would give away the presence of bodies, yet there was enough blood to tell me someone had died sometime in the last few weeks. Either the corpse had been moved or it had been consumed. Neither was a good scenario.

I really should have left the place alone. When I'd heard the rumor that a couple of werewolves had moved in, I had to investigate to be sure it wasn't the old Denmaster. The Luna Cult was fractured. Only a few members had survived the destruction and those few had banded together to become more of a street gang than anything. Jonathan would have nothing to do with them.

The last time I'd seen Jonathan and his surviving wolves, Keira and Nathan, we were in the graveyard where Nathan said good-bye to his dead wife. Since then, there'd been no calls, no letters. There hadn't even been the faintest hint of rumor as to where the weres had gone. Even Jeremy claimed not to know where his Denmaster was.

And that's why I was here. If there was even the slightest chance Jonathan had returned to the Den, I was going to find him.

The door creaked as I pushed it open. My gun and sword were in hand, just in case the werewolves inside weren't ones I knew and trusted. The smell of alcohol mingled with the scent of blood. The air itself felt disused, abandoned.

My hand tightened on the grip of my sword as I stepped inside. No light blinded me as it once used to. More trash littered the floor. Beer cans, needles, and other unmentionables lay scattered seemingly everywhere. It was almost unbelievable how much trash could accumulate in such a short span of time. The office door to the far left of the stairs was open. No one appeared at the top of the staircase.

The urge to call out for Jonathan was strong, but I kept quiet. If there were indeed werewolves in residence, there was no telling who they might be. If they were rogues, I could be in for a serious fight.

I started for the office door when my eyes fell on a faded plastic cup. Flashes of memory assaulted me. Bodies scattered like debris. Pablo's bunny slippers. A birthday cake that spelled the end of a Cult I'd come to trust.

I closed my eyes tight to the memories, pushing them away. I couldn't let what had happened here distract me. The bodies were long gone. There was no sense in mourning them now.

A scrape from somewhere upstairs helped dispel the painful images. My aim immediately swiveled upward, but I couldn't see anyone in the gloom. Oddly, my vampiric vision didn't pierce through the shadows as easily as it used to. Perhaps Jonathan really was up there, using his glamour to shield himself in darkness.

The thought was enough to get me moving. Ignoring the office, I headed for the stairs. My heart was pounding: not because I was scared, but because I was worried what I might do if Jonathan really was up there. The man had avoided me for so long I was afraid I'd shoot him out of sheer frustration.

The stairs were littered with more trash. I stepped carefully around it, so as not to give myself away. I doubted a werewolf could have missed the sound of the door opening, but hey, not everyone is as observant as they should be. It was about time I got lucky.

The sliding sound came again as I reached the top of the stairs. My eyes were instantly drawn to the closed door down the hall. Carvings of werewolves in various states of shifting dominated the door. A circular window up top was decorated to look like the full moon. It looked somehow sad now that the Cult no longer called this place home.

A moan came from behind the doors, followed by more scraping. I approached the door warily, not sure if the sounds were a ploy or if someone was actually doing something on the other side. I really didn't want to think about what I'd do if I found Keira and Jonathan wrapped around each other.

The anger came out of nowhere. I'd done such a good job of controlling it lately, it caught me by surprise. The thought of Keira and Jonathan together was enough to send reason flying out the window. I strode toward the door, discarding stealth in favor of rage. If they wanted to screw around behind my back, that was fine. It wasn't like Jonathan and I were an item, but damn it, he should have told me.

I burst through the gilded doors, gun raised, anger causing red spots to flash in my vision. The door at the far end of the room, the one that led to Jonathan's old bedroom, was open. I caught a glimpse of a bare leg jerking out of view as I stormed toward the opening.

"I . . ." I trailed off as the scene came into full view. A girl lay on the bed, head tilted to the side, blood running down her neck. She looked at me with a faint smile. Her eyes were half-lidded and unfocused, telling me she was either near death or stoned out of her mind. Another girl was backed up against the bed, vainly trying to use her torn blouse to hide her naked body. She was sitting on a piece of cardboard.

Standing at the far end of the room were two men. Both of their eyes glowed yellow, yet they'd managed to keep from shifting. Both looked to be no older than eighteen, but that meant little with werewolves. Neither of them was Jonathan.

"Who the fuck are you?" the wolf on the left growled. He glanced toward the girl on the bed and slid ever so slightly her way.

"Don't even think about it." I aimed straight for his head. If he so much as twitched toward the girl again, his brains were getting scrambled.

The wolf raised his hands. He, like everyone in the room not named Kat, was completely nude. Sweat glistened on his body and a trail of blood dribbled down his chin. It wasn't hard to figure out what he'd been doing.

"Thought you were going to have a little snack after your screw?" I spat the words, so angry that I very nearly shot them out of pure disgust. The girl on the floor started to cry. She did not appear to notice what was going on around her.

"No," the were said. "We were just having some fun." He licked the blood from his lips. "No one was going to get hurt. They wanted this."

I seriously doubted that. More likely, the two weres had gone to a college frat party and picked up the girls after supplying them with enough drugs and alcohol to keep them from protesting. This wouldn't be the first time I'd broken up a would-be slaughter.

Yet I didn't pull the trigger. I glanced at the girl on the floor. She didn't appear to be bleeding anywhere, nor did I see the telltale signs of violence that would show me she'd been forced into anything. Still, if they'd drugged her to get her here, it wasn't any better than if they'd held her down against her will.

"Did they hurt you?" I asked, mostly to hear her speak. If she sounded as drugged as her friend looked, the wolves were dead.

The girl shook her head. "No," she whispered. She looked up at me, displaying bright blue eyes that appeared clear of influence, though they were red from her recent crying bout.

"What about your friend?" I indicated the bed.

"This is what she wanted."

If this had been a year ago, I probably would have already shot the two weres on principle. The girls were teenagers. They didn't know what they were doing. All of this probably seemed like a game to them, a fun night out with a little danger involved. This sort of thing usually ended with bodies in a Dumpster.

My aim firmed, but a nagging voice in the back of my head told me not to shoot. Jonathan wouldn't have wanted me to. He would want the chance to tame the wolves. He would keep them from feeding on girls like this, would do his best to make sure they never hurt anyone again.

But Jonathan isn't here.

Reason warred with rage. I wasn't sure if I was angry at the kids or if I was pissed at Jonathan for not being here. In the end, my confusion made my mind up for me.

"Go," I said, fighting back the anger. I stepped away from the door. "Never come back."

The two weres glanced at each other and as one, began to edge around the room toward the door. I followed their movements with my gun, finger on the trigger, ready to fire the moment one of them made a move I didn't like. Werewolves are fast. Not being ready could easily get me killed.

The wolves ignored their clothes and slipped out the door naked as the day they were born. Chances were good they'd shift as soon as they got outside and would be halfway across the ruined campus before I could give chase.

As soon as they were out the door, they turned and ran. I gave them a good thirty seconds to make themselves scarce before lowering my gun and turning toward the girls.

"That was fucking stupid," I told the girl on the floor. "They could have killed you."

"They wouldn't have." Her voice trembled as she spoke.

"You can't know that," I said. "I don't care if you've been fucking him for months. A werewolf can lose control at any time. You'd be dead before you realized what was happening." Or at least, she would if she was lucky. I'd known more than one wolf who liked to play with his food before eating it.

Tears poured down the girl's cheeks. She was still cowering against the bed, trying to conceal her nudity.

"Get dressed," I said as kindly as I could. I didn't want to terrify the poor girl to death, though she needed something of a scare so she wouldn't do something so mind-numbingly stupid again. "And get your friend dressed. I'll make sure it's safe to leave."

I didn't wait for a reply. I turned and walked out, leaving her to gather what dignity she had left. I probably should have stayed, but, damn it, I was frustrated enough to make a mistake if I stuck around. A part of me had been positive I'd find Jonathan there, but instead, I find a couple of teen girls making the biggest mistake of their young lives.

At least they'd live to regret it. That was more than I could say about many people who tempt fate.

The wolves were long gone by the time I left the library. A faint howl in the distance could have been one of them, or just another were out on patrol. There was no way I could know for sure.

Still, I scouted the area to be certain they were gone. The girls took longer than I liked, but eventually emerged, leaning on one another. They looked terrified and I hoped that would keep them from ever coming back.

Once they were safely away, I headed to the old Den parking garage. The walk was long and as each minute passed, I grew angrier. By the time I headed down into the depths of the garage, I was as pissed as I'd been back in the Den.

"Fuck!" I shouted, kicking a stone across the concrete. It bounded into the darkness and fell silent.

Tears burned my eyes. I wiped them away angrily. I shouldn't be crying over someone who apparently wanted nothing to do with me, but I couldn't help it. I'd made a lot of progress in accepting others into my life and then suddenly, they up and vanish on me. It wasn't something I could easily accept.

I mounted my bike and tore out of the garage. A big part of me wanted to hunt down the two weres, but I resisted. It wouldn't make me feel better. In fact, it would probably only make me feel guilty.

The first drops of rain pelted me as I sped home, just to accentuate how shitty a night I was having. Could things get any worse?

I was soaking wet and pissed off by the time I got home. I stalked through the kitchen into the dining room, where I threw my weapons down on the table so hard they slid across the surface and fell to the floor on the other side. I looked up to see both Ethan and Jeremy staring at me.

"What?" I said, running my fingers through my wet hair. I was about to say something snarky when I noticed how pale Ethan looked.

Jeremy took a hesitant step forward. "Kat . . ."

"What's happened?" My mind raced. Something was clearly

wrong. And since Ethan and Jeremy were standing right here, that left only a few possibilities.

My throat went dry. Everything took on an unreal sheen, as if I were looking at the world through a haze of heat. I felt like throwing up.

"I'm not sure," Jeremy said, carefully. "She hasn't woken up."

Keira. Something had happened to Keira. My heart clenched. I strode forward, stopping inches from Jeremy.

"Where is she?" I asked through clenched teeth. If Jonathan died without me . . .

"Kat." Jeremy licked his lips. "You don't understand."

"Where is she?" I shouted. I reached out like I was going to grab him by the shirt, but stopped myself. Beating up on the messenger wouldn't accomplish anything.

"In your room." Ethan spoke in a whisper.

I didn't wait around for them to tell me more. I was positive Keira was lying in my bed, dying from some horrible wound. I needed to see her, needed to find out if she could tell me anything about where Jonathan was, if he was alive or dead.

Jeremy and Ethan followed me up the stairs. I practically ran up them. Jeremy was talking, but I couldn't make out a word. I had only eyes for the door at the end of the hall.

"Kat . . ." Jeremy said, pleading for me to stop one last time. "It's not what you think."

I burst through the door and strode to the bed. The covers were piled up on someone. Blonde hair spread across the pillow.

I hesitated halfway to the bed. Keira didn't have blonde hair. If it wasn't her, then who was in my bed?

I moved forward, but was unable to see a face. The covers were pulled up high enough to cover everything but the hair.

With a tentative hand, I reached out and pulled back the covers.

No, it wasn't Keira sleeping in my bed.

It was Sienna.

CPSIA information can be obtained at www.ICGtesting.com
Printed in the USA
BVOW08s1500080316

439522BV00001B/12/P

9 781601 832450